Whiteout!

Whiteout!

Duncan Kyle

St. Martin's Press   New York

For a Brand
who pulled
a chestnut
from the fire

Copyright © 1976 by Duncan Kyle
All rights reserved. For information, write:
St. Martin's Press, Inc., 175 Fifth Ave.,
New York, N.Y. 10010.
Manufactured in the United States of America
Library of Congress Catalog Card Number: 76-10557

Library of Congress Cataloging in Publication Data

Kyle, Duncan.
  Whiteout!

  I. Title.
PZ4.K989Wh3 [PR6061.Y4] 823'.9'14 76-10557

Chapter 1

It was cold, but at Thule they know how to handle cold, as they also know how to put the fear of God into newcomers. When the doors of the Galaxy freighter opened and the Arctic wind drove out in seconds the accumulated warmth of hours, they allowed that extra minute or so of delay before I could leave the plane. My teeth were already giving one or two preliminary and percussive chatters by the time I'd reached the foot of the aircraft stair, descending into a whipping crosswind that flicked ice particles stingingly against my face. By the stark airfield lights bulldozers were scraping at the runway.

At the foot of the stair, a sergeant stood with his back to the wind. His green parka hood was up, with the fur rim drawn tight so that he looked at me through an aperture no more than four inches wide.

'Mr Bowes, sir?'

'Yes.' I was facing him and one opens one's mouth to speak. I closed it quickly as the wind picked at a tooth filling.

'Weasel's right here, sir,' the sergeant said. Twenty yards away a small tracked vehicle painted in day-glow orange sat with its diesel snarling and steam scudding from its exhaust. I ran across and slid inside gratefully, slamming the door. The cold slid in with me, but the roaring heater battled and won and soon it was like an oven inside. I opened my coat and took off my gloves.

'Sir.' The driver, also parka-clad, turned to look at me. 'Sir, don't take off those gloves.'

I was more than willing to learn. First I put the gloves on, then I asked why.

He grinned. 'People forget, is all. No gloves, you get out, you grab the door handle, you leave half your hand right there on the metal.'

'Bad as that?'

'It's okay. Watch regulations, y'know, and it's okay. Just don't get careless. You from England, sir?'

5

'Yes.'

'Know Bentwaters base in Suffolk?'

'You were stationed there?'

'Sure was. Two years. That was great, I tell you. Two years in Suffolk, then wham, you're here.'

'Been here long?'

'Six months. Furlough next week.'

The door opened. The sergeant climbed in rapidly, but the cold was faster. In the time it took him to open the door and close it, the temperature must have dropped thirty degrees. I shivered. The heater roared on.

'Move it,' the sergeant ordered, and the Weasel clattered forward. Side and rear windows were opaque with snow crust, but through the windscreen I could see the dark bulk of a big hangar. As we came close, the driver hooted three times, a door rolled up and we passed into the bright interior.

'Office is right over there, Mr Bowes. We'll get your bag.'

I thanked him, climbed out and walked across the concrete floor towards the glass-windowed cabins in the corner. What happened next would depend on the weather. My TK4 Hovercraft, now sitting snugly in the belly of the Galaxy, would have to be taken a hundred or more miles up on to the Greenland icecap. If the weather was anything less than severe, the idea was that I should drive it at least part of the way. In good conditions, and with luck, it would be no more than a three-hour trip and could be made with relative confidence, because the TK4 had already completed some snow and ice trials in Canada effectively and impressively. It was sturdy and reliable and could possibly prove very useful to the American engineers conducting their complex Polar research and development programme up here. If they bought the TK4, they'd buy three of them, which was an important order for the smallish company I work for. But they weren't sure yet; they wanted more trials, this time at altitude and *in situ*. It's one thing to watch the machine skating across smooth snowfields and another to try to operate it in eighty degrees of frost and hurricane winds; for a lot of the winter those are prevailing conditions seven thousand feet up on the icecap.

I opened the door and went in, and a man sitting in an easy

6

chair reading *Time* magazine, glanced up, then rose. He was wearing khaki indoors and there were two silver bars on his collar. He held out his hand. 'You're Mr Bowes?'

'I am.'

'Captain Fraser. How'd you like some hot coffee?'

'I'd like it.'

'Coming right up.' He opened a big vacuum flask and poured, then handed me the steaming cup. 'No problems?'

I sipped. 'Not yet. It's early days, though, isn't it?'

'Sure is. Getting up here's the easy stage. They'll tow the Galaxy right in here in just a minute, then you can unload.'

I nodded. 'What's the programme?'

He grinned. I was to learn that a grin was a curious commonplace up here; an unconscious and almost universal weapon in the battle to preserve psychological balance in a hostile environment. The words came through the grin. 'We had two rough weeks. Rougher still on the cap and it looks like it's, ah . . . continuing uncooperative.'

'Forecast's bad, then?'

'Forecasts!' he said dismissively. 'Yeah, well, we wait and hope.' Then, visibly, he checked himself, and when he went on his tone was altogether more formal, as though there were a refuge in military crispness. 'This climate breaks all the rules, Mr Bowes. Forecasts aren't reliable. Okay here at Thule, maybe, but up there on the cap prognostications won't hold.'

'So?'

'They've been four days out of radio communication. Before that ten days. One radio schedule in two weeks and no planes in or out. Your chances of piloting up there aren't too good right now. Provisionally we figured to send your hovercraft up on the Swing – '

I interrupted. 'Swing?'

'Jargon. The snow train. You know about it?'

'I've heard something.'

'Basically it consists of big tractors hauling box cars. The box cars have runners instead of wheels. It just keeps going, day and night, till it gets up there. Kind of a train on sleds. We'll load the hovercraft on a wanigan.'

I grinned this time. 'Wanigan?'

'Box car. You'll get used to the Newspeak. The trip up there on the Swing can take from four days to maybe four weeks, but it sure gets there.'

'And me?'

'Ride the Swing, too, huh?'

'For four weeks? What's the alternative?'

'Wait for a weather slot and fly.'

I said, 'I think I'll do that.'

When the Galaxy was in the hangar, I brought the TK4 down the ramps under its own power.

Then it was back into the Weasel.

Camp Hundred, the research and development base on the ice-cap, had its own supply camp twenty miles away from the giant US Air Force field at Thule, and it was there I was heading. By now it was snowing again, not heavily but not gently, either. In the Weasel's bright headlights, the snowflakes blew across horizontally and the driver had to sit forward in his seat and concentrate hard as the road wound between high snowbanks. Inside the Weasel the temperature was uncomfortably high, fed by that noisy fan that discouraged conversation and almost drowned, too, the sound of radio traffic that emerged continuously from the little set above the driver's head. He'd explained the system to me earlier: the Weasel was safe and reliable, *but . . .* but if it broke down, he hollered for help and help came. There was a little stove to provide heat if the engine didn't. It sounded easy and simple; everything had been thought out; there was a *system* and the system worked. But sitting there in the roaring dark it was all too easy to think about breakdowns in twenty miles of icy emptiness, long miles of snow driven by freezing winds that would turn the warm security of the Weasel into a deep freeze cabinet in a matter of minutes.

But I was excited, in a small boy kind of way, with a tune running unwanted through my head the way tunes sometimes do: *From Greenland's icy mountains to India's coral strand . . .*

After about an hour, the diesel's roar diminished suddenly and the view ahead changed. We were turning to a halt, and a big wooden hut, painted orange like the Weasel, showed through the

8

snowblow. The driver said over his shoulder, 'Don't knock, sir. Walk right in. I'll get your bag.'

I found myself pausing to glance at my glove before touching the door handle, and reflecting that one lesson had been learned.

Camp Belvoir is named after the Corps of Engineers' headquarters in faraway, peaceful Virginia, and there they kitted me out: long woollen underwear like my grandfather's, khaki battledress over it, a thick parka lined with wolverine fur, windproof trousers, a khaki, fleece-lined cap with ear flaps, silk gloves with woollen felt overmitts, and big heavy boots of thick white felt.

I looked at the boots, puzzled. 'Surely these aren't waterproof?'

The stores sergeant cocked an eye at me. 'You reckon on rain?'

'The snow will saturate them, surely?'

'Trick is,' he said, 'keep 'em real dry, like Sunday in Missouri. Listen, you're outside, cold don't get through that felt. Your feet are warm, and the heat can't get out. Felt keeps heat and cold apart. Snow's cold, so it don't melt; feet's warm, so they don't freeze. Right? Just you be sure of one thing: you come indoors, you kick every last snowflake offa that felt, and put them boots by to warm and dry.'

I nodded. 'I see.'

'Sure you do. I'm still gonna tell you. You come in and don't kick the snow off; the snow melts, right? Just a little, but it's plenty. The boots ain't wet, they're just kinda damp. Then you go outside and the goddam damp freezes and the cold goes straight through, right? Freeze your goddam feet off in ten minutes. Before you know it you're walking on two stumps, okay?'

'I'll remember.'

He grinned. 'Now you'll remember.'

Major Cohen, commander of Belvoir, said, 'That's not enough. Pile up your tray.'

I wasn't particularly hungry and said so.

'Pile it up,' he said. 'You need the calories.' There were two big steaks on his own tray, two vast jacket potatoes, assorted vegetables, rolls and butter, about half a pint of ice-cream and a big glass of milk.

I glanced back along the line. Service was cafeteria style in the mess hall at Camp Belvoir and all the plastic trays were loaded with food. I took another potato, a small one, and Cohen placed a glass of milk on my tray.

'You eat well,' I said.

'Five thousand calories a day,' Cohen said. 'And we need it. Just being here burns food. Up on the cap they eat close to seven thousand.'

'And get fat?'

'Hell, no. You know what Uncle Whiskers thinks about fat soldiers. They *need* the food. Up there three thousand calories would be a slimming diet. Think they'd haul it up there if they didn't have to?'

He led the way to a corner table and sat down. 'You met the Bear yet?'

'The Bear?'

'You haven't, huh? Well, he'll be along.' He cut into a steak. I followed his example. It was very good steak and I said so.

'Once upon a time,' Cohen said, 'I was attached to your people, the British. Not long, but long enough.'

'The army?'

'Sure. Maybe I should have tried for the Wrens, but I wasn't as cute, then.' He grinned. 'Korea, it was. I was only a kid, you understand. But this I remember: they ate their bully beef off the regimental silver. Now us, we're barbarians, right? We eat off plastic trays, but we eat steak.'

I said, 'Who or what is the Bear?'

'The Polar Bear.'

'Go on.'

'Major Barnet M. Smales, US Army Corps of Engineers, Commander of Camp Hundred. The Polar Bear.'

'He's *here*? At Belvoir?' I was surprised.

'Sure he's here. Been here two weeks and three days. Flew down for some welfare supplies and couldn't get back.'

'I'll look forward – '

He interrupted me. 'Wish he'd get his goddam ass the hell back up there while I've still got some kind of an installation around here.' He was staring at his food, talking loudly. Footsteps scuffed behind me and I half turned as Cohen added, 'He's nothing but a goddam highwayman. If it's loose, he steals it.'

The man with the white beard stared at Cohen, and at me for that matter, with what looked like malevolence. He joined us at the table and sipped at a steaming mug of coffee. 'You told this guy I was a goddam polar bear?' he asked Cohen.

'Yeah.'

'He's right. Shake a paw.' Smales extended a hand towards me and I shook it. 'Now lemme see, you're . . .'

'Bowes,' I said. 'Harry Bowes, from Thomson-Keegan.'

He nodded. 'What a dump, huh? Even the chow's lousy. Wait'll you get to Hundred. Can't you even feed your guests, Cohen?'

Cohen said, 'Seventeen days we fed the Bear. We're running clear out of seals.'

'Out of ping-pong balls too,' Smales said. 'Two dozen girls, you'd expect a problem, but two dozen ping-pong balls!'

Cohen sighed theatrically. 'It's kleptomania,' he said to me, touching his index finger to his temple. 'Know what he did last night?'

'Tell me.'

'He walks into the sergeants' club. They're shooting pool in there. Middle of a game, right? So he lifts the twelve ball right off the table. Now why was that?'

'Because,' Smales said, 'we're a twelve ball short at Hundred.'

'So one of the sergeants, he says, "Sir," he says, and you'll see here at Belvoir we observe the proprieties, "Sir," he says, "without that twelve ball, the whole pack's useless, right?" So what does the Bear say? I'll tell you what he says. He says, "Okay, I'll take the rest." So now he's got two packs and he's still one goddam twelve ball short.'

'Strategic reserves,' Smales said.

'He didn't even let them finish the game. Why didn't you let them finish, Barney?'

Smales said, 'I might have forgotten.'

11

Cohen spread his hands in appeal to me. 'You see. Don't stay more than two weeks in this guy's hands. What he's got, it's contagious. They come down here like plagues of locusts. Can't keep their hands off nothing. He stole my skis last time here.'

'Borrowed his skis,' Smales corrected amiably.

'Like Stalin borrowed Czechoslovakia.'

It went on like that and I listened as they batted insults back and forth like the ping-pong balls Smales kept demanding. It dawned on me after a while that it wasn't just banter; Smales was intent upon removing to Camp Hundred any trifling thing that could conceivably make life easier.

After a while I asked how long it might be before we reached Camp Hundred. Major Smales pointed out that Cohen's guests couldn't wait to leave his lousy hotel, then he said he didn't know. Something in his eyes suddenly told me he wasn't far from anger and I wondered why. Smales finished his coffee, rose and left us, and I said to Cohen, 'Something's wrong?'

He frowned. 'Barney's worried about morale.'

'You mean the place can't live without him?'

Cohen shook his head. 'It's not his absence that matters. It's what's up there.'

'And what's that?'

'Six dead men. No, make it seven.'

Chapter 2

I drove back to Thule Air Base next morning in a sober mood. Cohen had told me the details. Having told me, he'd said, 'Look, forget it,' but I couldn't forget; I'd thought about it most of the night, sleeping intermittently and badly. No wonder Smales was concerned about morale. Until two weeks before, Camp Hundred had had a perfect safety record, apart from the odd bumps and bruises; there hadn't even been a bad case of frostbite in the three years the camp had been in existence. Now there had been two separate tragedies. The first, and worst, had been a helicopter crash, and nobody knew how it had happened. It seemed that four men, one of them an army padre, had been taken out of the underground camp to a helicopter and had climbed aboard. The vehicle that had carried them had about-turned and gone back. It had stopped at the tunnel entrance to watch the lift-off and then gone below. Next morning a bulldozer had gone to clear the overnight snow from the entrance and the driver had spotted the wreckage. Pilot, radio operator, padre and the three soldiers were dead. What made it worse was that two of the men had apparently survived the crash; they'd been badly injured, but alive and must have tried to crawl back to Hundred. They had frozen to death. Now there were six bodies lying in a snow tunnel up in the icecap. What was almost worse was that they'd been there two weeks: a ghastly daily reminder to every man in the place that death was very close at hand. If it had been possible to fly them out quickly, the tragedy would gradually have receded, but the weather had prevented any flying to or from Hundred.

'Couldn't you,' I'd asked Cohen, 'have brought them out on the Swing?'

He'd shaken his head: 'Camp Hundred's big and the bodies are sealed off in a tunnel. It's an uncomfortable situation, but it's stable. They look at the closed door and think what's behind it, sure they do. But think of that Swing. Only thirty guys, and one

13

of the wanigans is a hearse. No, brother, you couldn't risk the damage to morale.'

It was a shuddery thought that the aircraft that flew up to Camp Hundred carrying Smales and me would be an empty hearse, on its way to collect the bodies.

No less unnerving was the second tragedy, which had happened the day after the helo crash. A man had got lost in a snowstorm and vanished. He'd apparently been on his way back to the camp from a surface hut only three hundred yards away, when a sudden snowstorm had come down. 'Christ knows why!' Cohen had said angrily. 'There was a guidance line for the guy to move along. You get caught in a bad phase, you clip your belt to the guide line and keep going. That's regulations. I've done it; everybody's done it. But . . .'

But . . . There was always a but. *But* meant the weather, or the ice, the wind, or the cold, any of the eternal omnipresent hazards, the dangers that never relented when man was busy surviving in an environment of total hostility. There was so much joking, but only on the surface; below, never forgotten, was the knowledge that only technology and determination, only complete obedience to a carefully charted system of precautions, made life possible at all. For two weeks now Camp Hundred had been cut off, even from radio communication; for two weeks the bodies had been lying there; for two weeks the feelings of claustrophobia and loneliness must have been growing. Daylight was down to less than five hours out of twenty-four and shortening fast. The sense of adventure I had felt the night before had begun to evaporate already.

But next morning the run down to the big Thule base was quick and easy. In the hangar, I checked the TK4 and made sure all the spares were loaded. Then I climbed aboard and started the engines. No problems; she'd stood the trip well. I stopped the engines and went across to Fraser's office. Fraser, for the moment, wasn't there. I helped myself to coffee and sat looking at his copy of *Time* for a while, then the door opened and Fraser and another man came in.

'Hi,' Fraser said. 'Got me another visitor here. Mr Bowes, meet George Kelleher.' I stood up and shook hands. Kelleher was a big, loosely-built man with a slightly mournful expression. 'Mr Bowes,' Fraser went on, 'drives the hovercraft over there. Mr Kelleher's a nuclear engineer.'

Kelleher said, 'You taking that machine to Hundred?'

'That's the idea.'

He looked doubtful. 'Those things stable in lateral winds?'

'Up to a point.'

Fraser said, 'We've got a tractor and a wanigan standing by. And the mobile crane.'

'If I can,' I said, 'I'd like to run it up to Camp Belvoir myself. If the forecast is – '

'I warned you about forecasts,' Fraser said.

'All the same.'

'Yeah. Well, it's your neck, pal. I just checked it out and you should be okay. Prognostication Phase One for the next three hours, if you want to believe it. That's wind speeds up to thirty-four miles an hour. Shouldn't be that strong, but . . .'

'Direction?'

'Off the cap. Near enough due east.'

'Headwinds, then,' I said. 'Perfect.'

Fraser turned to Kelleher. 'Seems you've got a choice. There's the Weasel, or you can ride with Mr Bowes.'

Kelleher pointed to the TK4. 'What's it smell of?'

'Paint, mainly,' I said. 'A little oil.'

'You sure?'

'More or less.'

'I'll come with you. These BO machines they got up here make me sick to my stomach. These guys do a six-month stretch up here. They got everything. They got Scotch and they got candy bars, movies, you name it. But they never heard of soap.'

I nosed the TK4 out carefully, following the Weasel round the perimeter to the cut-off track for Camp Belvoir. It was full daylight now, and just for a moment a little beam of sunlight pierced the grey overcast. On the runway a flight of Phantoms suddenly hurled themselves forward then vertically up; black smoke-rings blasted from their after-burners to hang for a second or two until the vortex of following turbulence wiped them away.

15

The Weasel led me gently away from the base, on to the road to Belvoir, then accelerated up to about thirty-five miles an hour. I let him go for a while before I increased revolutions on the TK4's little twin turbo props. This kind of run, in these conditions, wasn't much different from the Canada trials. But I was very conscious that this wasn't Canada, that the Greenland weather is just about the most capricious and punishing in the world and that, from now on, I would have to operate at ever-greater altitudes and in ever-worsening conditions. When Kelleher had asked me about stability in lateral winds, he'd put his finger on the whole point of the TK4. A hovercraft skims over a surface with hardly any friction. That's their great advantage, but it's also their weakness. Without friction, naturally there's no grip, so a sudden sideways blow can bang you badly off course. If you're running over big areas of water or snow, that may not matter much; it's a bit different if you're suddenly going to be smashed into a wall of rock or over a precipice.

The problem can never be wholly solved. But Thomson-Keegan, my outfit, had built various ideas into the TK4 to increase stability, and it was our belief – borne out, so far, by experience – that in Arctic conditions for which they were designed, our modifications worked. There were three principal ones. The first was a small pair of steering skis. They were retractable because they wouldn't be in permanent use, but when they were lowered, there was another twenty per cent of steering control. What you lost was efficiency; you got less propulsion out of a given power output, and you could no longer ride over large bumps. But on reasonably smooth snowfields, they worked well.

The second modification was a steel plate, also retractable, at the tail of the TK4. It worked like a sailboat's keel, slicing about a foot into the snow surface. It had a similar effect to that of the skis, in effect holding the machine to its course longer, and giving more time for any necessary corrective manœuvring. The third Thomson-Keegan gimmick was in the engine mountings, which could be swivelled to redirect the propeller wash and enable the pilot to counter wind thrust. None of the mods was particularly original; the point was that they'd been made to work without throwing the whole machine off balance. The US Army was interested, but that's all. My job was to turn interest into a conviction that the TK4 would be a valuable Arctic tool. In other words, I was a salesman, too, on this trip.

So, on the trail away from Thule, I was very cautious with the rudders as we slid smoothly along in the wake of the Weasel. I felt at the wind, tested skis and tail plate, and generally motored as cautiously as a maiden aunt worried about the sip of sherry she'd had.

The track, mercifully, was easy to follow, pretty straight and with flags on bamboo poles atop the snowbanks. But a hover-craft is never really at home on any kind of road; there's too long a gap between decision and effect, and when you want to slow or turn, you'd better be certain there's plenty of room.

All the same, the wind was steady and without gusts, and after a while I relaxed a bit and moved her along faster, keeping the Weasel just in sight.

'Smooth, I'll say that,' Kelleher said beside me. There was a little sigh which may have been relief.

'Don't worry, I'll get you there.'

He laughed. 'Not too sure I want to go.'

'Spent much time at Hundred?'

'Enough. I was there when we put the reactor in. My outfit built it and it's still my baby. Any little problems, me for the deep freeze.'

I asked, a little self-consciously, 'What's it like up there?'

He hesitated. 'Hundred's got a kinda feel you can't put in a sentence. I try to tell my wife. Naturally she reckons it's some kind of pleasure centre. You know. Las Vegas on ice, booze and Eskimo broads.'

'But.'

'Oh, you'll sense it. Look at it this way . . . Ice is plastic. It moves and it distorts. The place can't last above a few years. But nobody knows how temporary is temporary. You're up there on top of seven thousand feet of ice, right? Surveys say it's solid. There's indices of compaction, stability studies, graphs, measurements, but who in hell knows what's going on down below? Hundred did a two-foot sideways skip last year. Not much, right?

But maybe it opened up something, somewhere, I dunno. You worried?'

'Interested.'

'Me, I'd be worried.' The brief seriousness was submerged and the necessary patina of humour returned. 'I'd be worried about my dough, is what I'd be worried about. They got bridge players, poker players, pool players up there, those guys'll hustle you clean out of your long johns. Got any money?'

'A little.'

'Leave it at Belvoir. Take nothing. No cheques, no cash, no credit cards, no gold watches, wedding rings, no tooth stoppings even. Travel light.'

'You paint a pretty picture.'

He grinned. 'Like I said, my wife don't believe it, either.'

Thirty-two minutes after leaving Thule, I was creeping the TK4 into Camp Belvoir. The trip had been neat and uneventful. Wind had come up a bit, but not enough, nose-on, to cause any bother, and I was lucky that the hangar doors didn't necessitate any fancy manœuvring. Within twenty minutes she was all tucked up.

I went to the headquarters hut and scrounged hot coffee from Cohen's sergeant clerk. Cohen wasn't there, but he came in a few minutes later. 'Hear you brought the great ship in!'

'She's in your hangar.'

'Yeah. Listen, we got news. Radio contact with Hundred. Wind's dropping up there, snow's stopping too. Looks like we may have a flying slot.'

'When?'

'Soon. Hours – maybe minutes. That's the way it happens, pal.'

Smales strode in, glancing at his watch. 'Looks good!' He saw me and said, 'Better get that buggy of yours loaded.'

'She's refuelled already,' I said. 'Ready for off.'

He shook his head. 'We got a slot, not a big weather break. You fly up with me. The Swing'll bring the hovercraft. If you want to supervise loading, do it now.'

'Right.'

Cohen pressed a button on the telephone on his desk. 'Get me

18

Sergeant Scully.' He waited, looking up at me. 'Scully? Listen, I want a tractor, a flat-top wanigan and a mobile crane over at the hangar right away. Yeah, a forty-five-foot wanigan. Get that hovercraft loaded, it's going up on the Swing.' He hung up and said to me, 'Scully'll have the machinery there in five minutes.'

And in five minutes it was all there, big powerful equipment roaring in the cold air. Both tractor and mobile crane had fifty-six-inch tracks and a lot of muscle was controlled by a good deal of skill. I unwrapped the TK4 and drove her out into the open and on to the lifting pallet, and I'll admit my heart was in my mouth as the crane driver went to work. One slip or misjudgment could do a lot of damage, but the corporal operating the crane levers never let that pallet move more than a couple of degrees out of the horizontal, and he popped the TK4 on to the wanigan with no more apparent effort than you or I would need to put a cigarette packet on a table.

We were still chain-strapping her down when my shoulder was tapped. I turned and Cohen's sergeant clerk put his face close to mine, bellowing to make himself heard over the roar of the diesels.

'Better move, sir. The major says you leave in five minutes.'

I hesitated. I wanted to see the wrappings put back safely. The last padded chain was already being snapped into position. Scully joined us, shouting, but I didn't hear the words.

'What?' I yelled.

'Leave it to me' he shouted. 'When he says five he don't mean six!'

I looked at him doubtfully and he laughed. 'Be okay,' he shouted. 'It's a promise. Give you a dollar a scratch, right?'

Scully's efficiency had just been well demonstrated and I hadn't much option.

'Thanks,' I yelled, and headed at a run for my room. A couple of minutes later I was in the Weasel again with Kelleher and Smales, and we were tearing back down the Thule track and Smales was looking at me with amusement. I said, 'Well, when you move, you certainly move.'

'That we do, old chap,' he said with a wildly exaggerated English accent. 'That we do.'

'So what now?'

He said, 'We fly from Thule, if the slot's still open.'

'Why Thule? If time's so precious – '

His face was suddenly grim. 'Fixed wing. You heard about the helo crash?'

I nodded.

'We decided no helos go into Hundred, not till we get an investigation going. We go by Caribou and there's no strip at Belvoir, only a helo pad.' His tone lightened. 'You'll feel at home in the Caribou.'

I said, 'Not particularly. It's built by De Havilland, Canada. Nothing to do with us.'

He glanced down. 'Hey!'

'Yes?'

'You didn't kick the snow off the felts.'

I felt myself flush as I bent to brush the snow crystals away. When I'd finished, I looked at the gleam of moisture on my fingers. 'Will it matter?'

'Not this time,' Smales said. 'You can toast them in the heater in the Caribou. Be dry when you reach Hundred.' He looked at me levelly. 'Just remember,' he said, 'they're *your* goddam feet!'

The Weasel clattered on to the swept concrete of the enormous runway at Thule. Over in front of the Corps of Engineers' Polar Research and Development hangar, the silver, twin-engined Caribou with the ice-orange wings and tail, was warming up, its tail loading ramp drooping. The Weasel went directly over to it and we got out and climbed the ramp. It was cold as hell in the bare cabin, where one of the crew stood waiting.

'Is that slot still open?' Smales demanded.

'So far, Major.'

Smales looked at his watch. 'Daylight sure won't hold.'

'We've done it before.'

'I know, I know. Okay, let's get the hell out of here.'

'I'll tell him to move his ass,' the crewman said. 'He's only a captain.'

Smales grinned. 'Tell him I said so. I outrank him if you don't.'

'Strap yourself in, sir.'

The seats ran the length of the Caribou's fuselage, leaving a broad space in the middle for cargo. There wasn't any cargo, however, except two wooden boxes which must have contained Smales's loot from two weeks of scrounging at Belvoir.

Whether the captain had been told or not, he moved. The airframe shuddered a little as the ramp cranked upwards, and almost before it was secured, the plane was moving. The Caribou's a high-wing monoplane with plenty of power and plenty of lift, and I don't suppose it used more than about a tenth of the endless runway before the wheels lifted and we droned off.

Smales nudged me. 'Don't wait for the seat-belt sign. There isn't one. Heater grill's over there.'

I nodded, unstrapped myself and crossed the cabin to dry off the boots. In truth, they weren't very damp and the heater was powerful, almost too powerful. My feet were becoming uncomfortably hot when Smales said, 'Not too much. Sweat wets the inside.' So I returned to my seat, feeling rather helpless. In a set-up like the one they've got up there, you hand yourself over to the machine and move when they want you to move. You don't know anything; you're just anxious to remain safe and avoid being sworn at. An unwanted humility is draped over you like a wet sheet. Smales said, 'Be a great sunset.'

I turned to look out of the window. Beneath us the icecap was climbing sharply up from the coastal strip. Around us were low mountains, coloured and shaded, black, gold and red in the dying light. The endless snow beneath us was variegated like the left-hand bands of the spectrum.

Smales said, 'It doesn't last.'

'He's a real romantic guy,' Kelleher said.

'I painted it once,' Smales protested, smiling.

'If he painted it,' Kelleher said, 'he painted it army green or ice-orange. If he paints in oil, it's diesel. To this guy canvas is for windbreaks and charcoal's for fires.'

Twenty minutes after take-off, the light had gone and the landscape had become silver and black, with a dull gleam to it.

Smales walked forward to the cockpit and came back nodding. 'Weather's more or less.'

'More or less?' Kelleher said.

'Snowflakes flying; the wind's up to ten.' Smales glanced at his watch. 'Eighteen minutes, that's all. Just make it hold.'

I said, 'Are you talking to me?'

Smales flicked his glance upwards. 'The man up there. If he made it, he can make it hold.'

'It'll change that suddenly?'

He said harshly, 'It's changing now.' There was tension in every line of him. 'Minute and a half in a Phantom, that's all, but not in a goddam Caribou.'

Kelleher said, 'Yeah,' and lit a cigarette. Two minutes later Smales was walking towards the cockpit again and Kelleher grinned at me. 'My wife's like that,' he said. 'All watches and questions.'

Smales didn't come back this time, and I wondered what must be happening up ahead. I noticed Kelleher, too, kept looking at his watch, and it started me off. Fifteen minutes had gone before Smales returned, scowling. He said, 'Snow's thickening and it's twenty knots across. Increasing.' He sat down and fastened his lap strap.

I said, 'What kind of landing strip is there at Camp Hundred?'

'Snow. Six hundred yards.'

We waited, as the Caribou's nose dipped and the pilot made a turn correction. Nobody spoke as the plane began to glide smoothly down. Glancing out of the window, I saw the flaps move. One wing lifted to the crosswind and was forced down by another rapid correction. Then the power wound down, prior to touchdown. I glanced at Smales. His eyes were closed; he was willing the plane down. There were only seconds to go when the airframe shook to sudden emergency application of maximum power and the Caribou's nose rose abruptly and kept rising. Smales's eyes flicked open angrily and the cabin door opened and the crewman came back, stopped in front of Smales and said simply, 'Runway lights failed, sir.' He was ashen.

'The hell they did!' Smales was already going up forward.

My stomach was knotting itself. We must have been under a hundred feet, throttled well back and dropping, when the lights failed. Luck, or skill, or a combination of both, had kept us from a fatal stall, but the margin must have been minute.

Kelleher, his skin greasy with cold sweat, was staring at the cabin floor. 'What happens now?' I asked.

He raised his eyes and looked at me. 'Thule,' he said. 'Just pray it's Thule.'

'It'll have to be, surely, without lights.'

'You'd think so,' Kelleher said. His voice was odd, rusting a little with straight fear.

'But?'

'But Barney's up there.'

The Caribou had levelled off and was circling, starboard wingtip lifting at intervals to maintain the pattern.

Six minutes had gone since we nearly crashed, and still the Caribou circled. I loosened my seat-strap and turned to look out of the window. There seemed to be nothing down there but the endless, icy waste. Then I saw a light. Correction: two lights – and close together like headlights. There were two more behind. I blinked. They *were* headlights!

Kelleher said, 'Like I said, that's Barney. What he's doing is he's moving everything with lights up on top. We go down by tractor lights.'

Below us, as I watched, the lights seemed to grow dimmer. Then Smales came back, grim-faced, and strapped himself in without a word. Kelleher didn't say anything either, and the silence was not the kind I felt like breaking. I stared forward, waiting for the nose to tip down.

It was over in less than two minutes. The pilot should have come in slowly, an inch over stall speed, hanging in the sky until the skis touched, but he daren't do that; he had to have power to counter the gusting crosswind that kept bucking the Caribou sideways. I could imagine the gritted teeth and the 'Okay, let's go!' up there in the cockpit. We came fairly bucketing in, hit once and bounced hard, hit again one ski only and the starboard wingtip lifted, then another bounce and we were down and running. I suddenly found myself staring straight down a head-light beam that temporarily blinded me, and by the time I'd rubbed some sight back into my eyes, we were slowed right down.

A hand slapped my arm. 'Move!' Barney Smales said. The

rear ramp was already lowering and the freezing air had flooded in. I rose and followed him to the ramp, down the stairs and into the waiting Polecat. Kelleher followed, slamming the door. He slumped in his seat for a long moment, then summoned a grin. He said, 'Uncle Sam wants ten years of my life *and* the taxes.'

We waited perhaps two minutes before Smales joined us. He looked angry and Kelleher asked why.

'She's freezing down. Can't wait. Okay, let's go.' As the Polecat moved off I saw the Caribou through the windscreen, already taxiing.

I said, 'Not that fast?'

Smales said, 'She stood a minute and she was sticking. Three and the ski runners would be fast. There's never time. Never any damn time!'

'So she's empty?' Kelleher asked.

'Damn right.'

I understood then. The bodies. The Caribou had to go without taking the bodies and they'd stay at Camp Hundred, radiating depression, until the next weather slot opened.

The little Polecat scampered over the snow, moved on to a sudden downslope, and a second or two later had entered a long, brightly-lit tunnel whose snow walls were festooned with pipes and cables.

Smales tapped the driver's shoulder. 'My trench.'

When the Polecat stopped, Smales jumped out, and we followed him through an archway into another and smaller tunnel in which stood a big wooden hut decorated with the crest of the Corps of Engineers' Polar Research and Development group with the word Commander stencilled in orange on the door. Smales opened it and went inside, pausing to kick snow off his boots.

A black man with a master sergeant's multitudinous stripes looked up and said quietly, 'Okay, sir?'

Smales nodded. 'Sure. What's new?'

'No problems, sir.'

'You sure of that?'

'I'm sure.'

'You put that can in the wall?'

24

'Soon as I heard you were coming, sir, I put the can in.'

'Good.' Smales jerked his head. 'Follow me, gentlemen.'

We trooped after him, back into the main tunnel and then into another side trench. The hut there bore the words 'Officers' Club'. Instead of going directly in, Smales walked towards the tunnel wall. From a hole in the wall, a length of thin orange line hung down. He pulled on the line until a stainless steel bottle came out. Holding it reverently in mittened hands, he walked towards the hut. Kelleher, smiling, opened the door with a flourish and Smales marched in first. We entered a pleasant, comfortable bar and Smales put the bottle carefully on the counter, then went behind it and took three glasses from a shelf and, opening the cap of the bottle, poured an almost watery fluid into the glasses. Then the mittens came off as he handed us the glasses.

He raised his own. 'The welcome you just had, gentlemen, was not in Camp Hundred's best traditions. We aim to start improving that right now. *A votre santé!*' With the French toast he gave a little Germanic bow and poured half the contents of the glass down his throat.

I wondered what it was, sipped it, and identified a dry Martini. I said, 'My God, it's cold!'

'Among other things,' Smales said, 'we have perfected the art of Martooni here.' He poured the second half after the first. 'There are people in this club who call it Martini University. Swallow it. You need one well down to appreciate the velvet texture of the second.' He bustled round producing olives and onions, peanuts and pretzels. 'When I retire from this man's army, I'm gonna open a bar and make a million. Make a better Martooni and sure as hell the world will beat a track to your door. Beats the hell out of the mousetrap. Now, gentlemen. Tonight we dine with class. State your requirements. Cookie's got a whole two hours.'

The man's gaiety was remarkable and infectious. He'd walked in here, fresh from an experience that still had my scalp crawling, and had turned on the good cheer, had literally switched it on. But there was nothing spurious about it. He was back in his kingdom and happy about it, and his natural ebullience placed the experience squarely behind him and would doubtless keep it there. He was an intricate man.

But *I* couldn't forget. It was all too recent and the mental scar tissue would stay with me. When I could, when a suitable moment occurred, I was going to ask what exactly had happened, but the moment refused to occur naturally; Kelleher was telling Irish jokes and Smales was telling Jewish jokes Cohen had told him down at Camp Belvoir. Finally I asked him about it as we stood side by side under the showers an hour or so later.

He said, 'Arctic foxes.'

By that time I was mildly befuddled with his treacherous Martinis and thought he was joking. I laughed politely and he said, 'They're not funny.'

'All right.'

He said, 'It happens this way. The foxes follow the Swings up along the trail, living off garbage. The Swing crews bury it, but the foxes dig it up and follow the source of supply. Here we bury our garbage deep, so those old foxes, they're goddam hungry.'

'Hungry enough to eat electric cable?'

'Not the cable, no. But they chew off the insulating material. We got the lights strung both sides of the runway, but one good bite in the right place and you got a dead fox and a lot of darkness!'

'Can't you get rid of them?'

He said, 'It's a sin of omission. Sure, we could put down poison bait, but Jesus, did you ever see an Arctic fox? They're beautiful, believe me. If I could shoot 'em clean, then sure. But poison, no sir.'

'No matter how dangerous?'

He put on a heavy Southern accent. 'Ah see yo'all is a logician, sir.' Then switched it off. 'The answer's no to poison.'

That was the moment the lights went out.

Chapter 3

Barney Smales said, 'Stand still.'

'I wasn't thinking of moving.'

There were slopping noises as he moved round in the darkness and first one shower was turned off, then the other. 'Better hold on to my hand. You'll trip over something and break your limey neck.' He led me quietly across the wooden floor of the big hut and round a partition to where towels and clothes hung.

'It must be nice,' I said, 'to be able to see in the dark. What's caused all this?'

'Generator.'

'Is it serious?' I found the towel and began to rub myself dry.

Smales said, 'It's one out of three. Plenty of back-up. But if the stand-by generator fails to come in, why, then we could be in a little trouble. Just move your limey ass, huh?'

I stopped towelling, and began feeling for my clothes, and asked, 'How long before it matters?'

'Four minutes. Five maybe. No more. After that the water pipes start freezing. They freeze, they bust wide open and then, brother, we got to rebuild the whole damn structure.'

The lights came on again. Smales was fully dressed and fastening his boots. I was still trying to button my shirt. He said, 'Okay now. Take your time. Reckon you can find your way to the club?'

I nodded.

'I want this little explanation about generator breakdown.'

Fully-dressed, snow-booted and parka-ed, I closed the door of the shower hut, stepped out into the chill of the tunnel, and glanced at the pipes that hung up there on the snow wall. The hazard was obvious. The pipes were bound with insulating material, but they hung an inch away from snow so compacted that it was almost ice. There were heaters built in at intervals along the pipes. With the system working, you turned on a tap and hot water came out; after four minutes without power, the men at Hundred would find themselves melting snow in old buckets for drinking water. I shivered briefly in the icy air, stopped looking at the pipes, and hurried off to the club trench. To reach it, I had to go into the big, central tunnel, the one they called Main Street, and there I looked again at the long lines of pipes and electrical conduits suspended from the walls. Camp Hundred ate up a lot of power.

With Smales away at the generators and Kelleher already busy at the reactor, there was nobody I knew in the club. I stood for a moment in the doorway, looking at the little scene of Polar domesticity. Over in a corner, four men sat at a card table, three concentrating hard, one leaning back, hands in pockets, watching his partner. The place was quiet and even the four or five men at the bar were turned towards the card players. Then one of them turned, saw me and came over. 'You're Mr Bowes, from England?'

'Yes.'

'Glad to have you here. I'm George Herschel, engineering.' He was a major, fiftyish, red hair greying, broad and cheerful.

We shook hands and I nodded towards the card players. 'Something important?'

Herschel grinned. 'See the guy in the corner? Well, he's got a kind of weakness for little slams. People listen to the bidding with half an ear and then when he has a slam going, we kinda make a bet or two.'

I smiled. 'Will he make it?'

'He better. They been redoubled. Drink?'

'Thank you.'

'Take your pick.' I looked along the lines of whisky bottles, then began counting. There were more than thirty brands: Scotch, Bourbon, Irish, Canadian.

'Tomatin,' I said, 'since it's there.'

He poured for me. 'Barney. He likes a bar to offer a choice. Ice?'

I shook my head. 'Just water.'

He passed the water jug and said, 'Now, let's see. Just what was happening in England around the middle of the seventeenth century? Don't wonder why. Just answer.'

28

I thought for a moment. 'Mayflower? The Pilgrim Fathers?'

He nodded. 'The water you're drinking fell as snow right around that time. Water well's down to over four hundred feet. We melt the snow for water.'

I poured water and raised my glass. 'To the Pilgrim Fathers?'

'Right.' We drank. 'Now come meet some of the guys.'

The little slam went down to mixed jeers and applause, money changed hands and after that I was made to feel very welcome, and also was sharply cross-questioned. I had, after all, been in the real world only a short time ago and they wanted reassurance that it was still there.

'I do seem to recall,' the slam-loser said, 'that they used to have something called girls out there. That right?'

'They used to be there,' I said. 'They've become extinct while you've been away.'

The conversation wasn't exactly elevated, but it was fairly typical. The society was recognizable, and its patterns, or most of them, were familiar. Here was the atmosphere of all the places where men are thrown together, unassorted, in a group, and have to learn to live with it. There was the endless flow of bad jokes and badinage, the careful but occasional and elaborate courtesy, the wall pin-ups and the bar. Claustrophobia in comfort, but claustrophobia.

The doctor saw me looking round and said, 'Not a sane man in the place. Nor a window.' His name was Kirton and he was a tall, dark, heavy-set New Yorker.

'Not even you?'

'Me least of all.'

'What are you suffering from?'

'Me? Loneliness.'

'No patients?'

'You kidding? I'm a gynaecologist, in theory anyway. Play chess?'

'Sorry.'

He said mournfully, 'I'm in the wrong army. There was one chess player up here. Just one, then he went back. All they send up here is bridge players. Now if I was in the Red Army . . .'

Herschel said, 'Be grateful, Doc. You'll be back home in three months. They do three years.'

'But there's chess. The years go quickly. What's tonight's movie?'

Herschel said, 'I dunno. *Grapes of Wrath*, maybe *Gone with the Wind*.'

Kirton winced. 'I keep begging them. If you're in the old movie business, I tell them, let's have *Birth of a Nation* or something. Keep me in touch with my specialty. You like music?'

'Yes.'

'Drop by tomorrow. I got an operating room, the acoustics are great. Good coffee too and beautiful blondes.'

'The blondes are on the walls,' Herschel said.

The door opened and closed. I glanced round. Barney Smales was hanging up his parka by the door and silence fell. For a moment I thought it was in deference to his rank, but when Kirton said, 'So who threw the switch, Barney?' all he got was little looks of irritation. The silence sprang from tension; they were waiting for Smales's news, anxious about it.

He said, 'Fuel, they reckon. Fitters are stripping it right down.'

Somebody behind me asked, 'How long?'

Smales shrugged. 'All night maybe. Feed pipes may be clogged. Who knows? Hey, Doc, give those fitters something so they stay awake, huh?'

'Sure,' Kirton said. He turned to me and winked. 'An opportunity, they said in the army literature, to practise real medicine in on-the-spot conditions. They really said that. Benzedrine for diesel fitters!'

Smales said, 'Meanwhile, in honour of our British guest, we're having a change of movie tonight.' He looked at me with bright-eyed amusement. 'We're gonna run *Scott of the Antarctic*. And for those of you who are always complaining about too many dames, I'll tell you. After half-way through reel one, it's all men with beards. Great, great, great entertainment!' He came over and clapped me on the shoulder. 'Just want to make you popular.'

At dinner, I found myself seated next to a young lieutenant named Foster, clean-cut, well-pressed and shiny. Also morose, or perhaps my choice of word is poor; but certainly I thought him morose at the time. Later I learned he was depressed with good reason: the man who'd been lost on the surface a couple of weeks earlier had been a young cousin of his. At any rate, he didn't much want to talk and I was beginning by now to feel tired. Seven thousand feet up on the icecap, weariness settles easily. Later, like the rest of them, I endured the Antarctic manfully, contrasting the appalling suffering of Scott's party with the thirty brands of whisky in the club. Everybody else, everybody, that is, who stayed awake, must have done the same. When the lights came up, Barney Smales was on his feet quickly, looking at faces, smiling a little to himself. Even his choice of films had psychological purpose.

Then I went to bed. I switched off the light and lay in the darkness, eyes open, thinking about this weird place and the people I'd been put among. They were proud of Camp Hundred, yet it sat on them like lead weights. They tried so hard to create a tolerable environment where nature was deeply unwilling to tolerate life. They had beaten back nature, but not very far, and it lay outside, up above, all around, snarling and whistling and waiting. Above me was the ceiling, above that the tunnel roof, and above *that* forty-knot winds and forty-minus temperatures and a million or so square miles of snow. I snuggled lower in the warm bed and thought soberly that the TK4's trials would be trials indeed, and not just for the machine.

Next morning the room was stuffy and sweaty. Too warm, too airless and four blank walls with only the outline of the door frame for relief. I dressed, walked to the shower hut, undressed, showered and shaved, dressed, went to the mess hall, took off two layers of clothing and saw Kelleher champing stolidly at a plateful of steak and eggs. Picking up a moulded plastic tray, I moved along the cafeteria line, making my selections. Corn flakes, milk that was cold and delicious and apparently fresh but which I later learned was reconstituted, ham and eggs and tomatoes, fresh bread rolls that were still warm from the oven, fruit juice, coffee. Then I joined Kelleher and said the logistics were impressive.

He nodded, unimpressed, and said he thought the tomatoes were showing their age. I said it was miraculous they were there at all, since they'd had to travel umpteen thousand miles in

31

conditions ill-tuned to the well-being of tomatoes.

Kelleher said, 'Well, I'll tell you, bud. This is not a day you'll find me whistling in admiration of the miracles of technology.'

'Trouble with the reactor?'

'That's what that thing is? You could have fooled me. It looks like a goddam junk yard.'

I waited. He flicked a sour glance at me. 'You'd think, maybe, that a guy wouldn't carry money in a top pocket when he's working in clean environments. So what happens is this. We renew the uranium rods, we get the water in all nice and clean. No spillages, no bumps, no problems. We're all ready to start warming, right? Go critical in a few hours, right? So I take a last look around first before we throw the switches, and what do I see?'

I said I couldn't imagine.

'Two quarters and a goddam nickel, that's what I see. Right there in the kettle. What do those guys think they're gonna do in there, dive for pennies?'

'So what happens now?'

He forked egg into his mouth and washed it down with coffee. 'Sleep, that's what. Then we take the goddam thing apart again, then we work all night again, and then tomorrow maybe, if some idiot don't drop his knife and fork in there, we start thinking about going critical again.'

I said, 'Tough luck.'

Kelleher put down his fork. 'No,' he said. 'I can take tough luck. Buddy, I know all about the psychology problems they got. Sure they get tired. Concentration gets thin. Sure. But this is carelessness and, what's worse, it's dangerous carelessness. You get outside metallic contamination when that baby's critical and you really got problems.'

Kirton joined us then, nursing a cup of coffee. Kelleher said, 'What you'll do, Doc, is you'll get pale and thin and die. Where's your two thousand calories?'

Kirton said, 'I'm not like you. I lie around all day getting fat. Sometimes I think I might as well take the ice-cream and the bread and apply them direct to my waistline here. That's where they finish up anyway and it would sure take a load off my digestive system. How's the steam engine?'

Kelleher made a rude noise.

'Oh yeah! And number one diesel?'

'Who knows!' Kelleher looked round the mess hall, then pointed with his fork. 'Either they just finished, or they're still working on it. See over there? Those guys with the oil there are diesel fitters.'

I looked across. Three men sat at a table in near silence, eating, and looking unhappy. I said, 'I don't think they've finished.'

'Half systems go,' Kirton said.

'Half?' I was conscious all the time of being the new boy, the one full of naïve questions, the one who sat quietly and listened.

Kelleher said, 'One reactor, three diesel generators. Belt, suspenders and two hands to hold the pants up, right? So now the belt's broken and the suspenders have gone. Two diesel generators left and we're holding our own pants up.'

I blinked at him. It was so easy to duck reality, sitting there in the cheerful mess hall eating good hot food, but too often reality tapped you on the shoulder and looked deep in your eyes.

Kirton said, 'So eat the steak and get to work.'

They'd both gone and I was smoking a contemplative cigarette when Smales came in, loaded up a tray and joined me. It was the German accent this time. 'So, Engländer,' he said. 'You enffy us zis efficiency, nicht wahr?'

I grinned at him. 'I hope you're like us. Muddling through in the end.' The grin syndrome had got to me already, I thought. 'But it does seem like quite a little chapter of accidents.'

'It does,' he agreed affably. 'And we have 'em I admit it, now and then. Good eggs.'

'One minute you sound like Erich von Stroheim, the next like P. G. Wodehouse,' I said. 'Meantime, I'd like to know about the hovercraft.'

'M'sieu, m'sieu,' he soothed. 'Ze Swing she leave today. Two days, zree, she is here.'

'I prefer Bardot. What about the diesel?'

'Don't *you* go neurotic on me! You play ping-pong?'

'It's been known.'

'Okay, so we'll have some healthy activity. Right after breakfast. You reckon that floating fan of yours will work up there?'

'It's pretty good.'

'It'll need to be.'

I said, 'Before I start, it'd be nice to know where people stand. Don't you like the idea?'

'I just like things proved, well proved, before I start loading lives aboard.'

'It's pretty well proved.'

He looked at me, eyes suddenly hard. 'So are diesels.'

'Things are bad, then?'

'Fuel's contaminated. Some kind of build-up in the combustion chambers and feed lines.'

I was about to ask what the contamination was, when a soldier appeared at the table, breathing hard, face red with exertion. He saluted. 'Major Smales, sir.'

'What is it?'

'Sir, it's the bulldozer, the one that sweeps the doorstep.'

'Well?'

'They found tracks, sir. In the overnight snow. Big tracks. Looks like there may be – ' he hesitated, then found the nerve to continue – 'there could be a polar bear in the camp, sir.' He watched Smales with nervous eyes.

'A polar bear?' Barney repeated softly, looking at his plate.

'They're big tracks, sir.'

Barney swivelled sweet eyes up to look at him. 'You got some kind of a bet on this?'

The soldier swallowed. 'No, sir.'

'Because if money's riding on this,' Barney said, 'you'll be shovelling snow till your ass falls off.'

'Yes, sir. But it's true, Major. Those tracks, they come right in the tunnel entrance.'

Barney nodded dismissively, pushed his plate away and said, 'Polar bears, yet!' in a stage Yiddish accent. Then he walked over to a wall installation and lifted off a microphone. A moment later his voice was booming out of a loudspeaker. 'Okay, now listen. This is the Commander. I got a report there's a polar bear down here.'

Subdued laughter erupted at several tables and Smales looked round balefully. 'A real bear, this one, with a white fur coat. All right. Nobody leaves the hut he's in. Any man not in a hut gets inside fast and stays there pending new orders. If the bear's here, he's hungry. He's walked a hundred miles and you'll taste real good to him. I want a Polecat from the vehicle bay outside the mess hall on the double. Await further instructions.' He hung up the mike, returned to the table and shrugged on his parka.

I asked, 'What exactly do you do now?'

'You want to come, come.'

We waited at the mess hall door until the Polecat's engine snarled up outside, then opened the door and took rapid steps across to safety behind metal doors. Smales said, 'Bear can't be here, he'd make for the mess hall.'

'Has this happened before?'

He shook his head. 'They saw tracks once, in Chance's time, the last commander. But nobody ever saw a bear. Meanwhile, we aren't exactly equipped for polar bears.' He told the driver to take us to the command hut. 'But if he's here, he's trouble. If he's standing between us and the door of my office, there's no way.'

I said, 'Damn it, this is the army. You *could* shoot him.'

Smales shook his head. 'We're not a fighting army. We're on Danish territory here; there are agreements, terms of use. We've only one stick that spits fire and it's on my office wall. If we can't get it, somebody's got to do battle with fire axes. But not me.'

The driver turned. 'Trench entrance will be too narrow for the cat, sir.'

'Turn her round,' Smales ordered, 'so the lights shine down the trench. Main beams. Blind the bastard if he's in there.'

'Okay, sir.' The driver busied himself with the track levers, manoeuvring the little vehicle into position across Main Street. 'Can't see anything, sir.'

'Right.' Smales put his hand on the door handle. 'If he's in here, at least we got him blocked.'

The driver said, 'Want me to go, sir?'

'So you can read what's on my desk?' Smales said. 'Not in a million years.'

He slipped suddenly out of the cab and sprinted across the fifteen yards that separated us from the command hut, stood for a long few moments fumbling with the key, then slid inside, slamming the door. The driver and I both let our breath go at the same moment.

Smales' reappeared quickly and again sprinted for the Polecat. Safely back inside, he patted the rifle, an old-fashioned .303 wooden-stocked army weapon and said, 'This is what the Danish Government allows us. It was captured from Sitting Bull. I'm the only guy here old enough to remember how to use it. Now, let's look at that doorstep.'

At the tunnel entrance one of the big, fifty-six-inch-track bulldozers stood snorting and thumping. As we got out, a corporal climbed down from the cab and pointed. Six deep prints, already partly filled, showed in the fresh snow that had blown in during the night beneath the shelter of the roof. Beyond the overhang, where there was more snow, no tracks were to be seen. The tunnel floor, where the snow had long ago been churned into dirty ice crystals, carried no tracks.

'Think it's a bear, sir?' the corporal asked Smales.

'How the hell do I know. I'm not an Eskimo tracker! But whatever made those tracks had big feet. So we've sure got to act like Mr Bear's inside here.'

He turned and looked back along the deserted length of Main Street.

'Perhaps,' I said, 'the bear came in here, went all the way along, and out the other end.'

Smales turned to the corporal. 'You swept the step up there yet?'

'No, sir.'

'Okay. What we'll do, we'll start at the far end. If there are tracks going out, that's all jim-dandy. If not, we work our way right back here, checking trenches as we go.'

'What do you want me to do, sir?'

'Get back in the 'dozer,' Smales said, 'and stay right here. If we flush him out and he comes this way, you put a scare in him with the dozer, a real scare. But don't try to kill him, polar bears are getting kinda rare.'

We climbed back into the Polecat and roared rapidly along Main Street to inspect the other ramp. No tracks showed in the smooth white slope of new snow. Smales and I looked at one another. Tracks leading into Camp Hundred, no tracks leading out; if a polar bear had made the tracks, he was in among us.

The search began. There were seventeen trenches to examine, most of them constructed in the same fashion. They had been cut originally with Peters snow-ploughs, the Swiss machines which throw snow out of a kind of chimney and pile it to one side. Each time the plough had made a pass, it had cut deeper and piled the snow higher. When the trenches were thirty feet deep, they had simply been roofed over with curved corrugated steel and snow heaped on top. Where each trench connected with Main Street, a wall of snow bricks had been built to narrow the entrance. Some of the walls had doors in them, others were merely arched openings, depending on the use made of the trench. Storage tunnels, by and large, could be locked. The ones holding living quarters, laboratory huts and recreation facilities remained open. Most trenches had one additional refinement, an escape stair at the far end so that in case of fire or some other disaster, the men could climb out through a hatch on to the icecap outside. If you could call that escape.

Where trench doors were locked, Smales didn't bother opening them. Where the entrances stood open, he'd repeat the process he had followed at the Command tunnel and wait until the Polecat's lights were glaring inside before peering cautiously round the corner of the snow wall. Then he'd go in. A minute later, maybe two minutes later, he'd reappear, shake his head, and wave the Polecat on to the next trench. The minutes he spent in the trenches were long minutes, even to me, secure, warm and safe inside the Polecat. What they must have seemed like to him, I can't imagine, but as an exhibition of cold courage, what Barney Smales was doing was impressive. Oh, he had the gun, right enough, but polar bears are white, and so were the tunnel walls, and there were shadows and bright reflections and piles of things the bear could have been behind, and the animal would have the faster reflexes.

He worked his way doggedly along the length of Main Street, finding nothing. Each time he came out of a trench he'd shake his head and I'd sigh with relief and the driver would move the

Polecat along. One tunnel he didn't even approach. It housed the six bodies and was locked. Finally we were back where we started, by the bulldozer. There was only one tunnel left now, a few yards in from the bottom of the ramp, with the words 'Reserve Fuel Store' in stencilled paint on the wooden door. I saw Smales glance at it, then glance again and finally walk over and push the door. It swung open and he looked inside, then came out and waved his arm. I climbed out of the Polecat and joined him.

'What do you make of that?' he said.

I looked, then went inside, stepping over the coaming. This was one of the shorter trenches, no more than thirty yards long and on two levels. The floor of the rear half of the tunnel had been cut a couple of feet deeper to accommodate two of those big neoprene-plastic fuel tanks that look a little like very big black rubber dinghies. But these two no longer looked like that, indeed were barely visible in the huge pool of diesel oil that had leaked out of them and now lay in a dark lake that rose half-way up the two-foot sides. Where the neoprene of the collapsed flexible tanks was visible above the oil, I could see slashes in the plastic. I pointed and Smales said, 'Yeah, I saw.'

'Would a bear do that?'

'A zoologist I'm not. But nobody else would, that's for sure.' He was silent for a moment, then said, 'There's forty thousand gallons right there.'

I'd been looking at the slashes and thinking about the claws that could have made them and the strength of the beast. Now I looked at Smales and said, 'This oil can't be used?'

He nodded. 'Damn right.'

'So you're short of oil?'

'Let's just say,' Smales said, 'that the way things stand right now, the oil we got is six whits more precious than rubies . . .'

Chapter 4

For Smales there were now urgent things to be done, the most important being a set of calculations on fuel supplies and consumption rates. He dismissed the Polecat, and told the bulldozer driver to continue sweeping the doorstep and marched off towards the command trench. I, on the other hand, had nothing at all to do. Remembering Dr Kirton's invitation, I strolled towards the hospital trench. I'd just gone inside when Barney's voice came over the loudspeaker to say that all personnel could now move about freely, and should resume their duties. The bear had done some damage, but was not in Camp Hundred. All the same, caution was to be exercised, and if there was any further damage, it must be reported immediately.

Kirton raised his eyebrows. 'You hear what Pappa Bear did?'

'Yes. He ripped open two of the fuel tanks.'

Kirton whistled. 'We got problems. Oh well, they're not mine and they're not yours. Not yet. Coffee?'

'Thanks.'

'Cream or straight? Bach or Mozart?'

I said, 'I'll take the coffee straight and leave the music to you.'

Kirton was big, bulky and gave an initial impression of clumsiness; it was belied by the precision of his movements. Just pouring coffee and putting on a record, he showed surgical sureness and dexterity. My records tend to have scratchy accidents. I thought enviously that all his would stay perfect.

'We'll soothe ourselves,' he said. 'See if you know this.'

As it happened, I did. I'd known a girl once who was nuts about that piece. I said, 'Albinoni. The adagio for violin and organ.' I settled back in my chair, but I wasn't really listening. Events were totting themselves up in my mind. There was the bear, and the fuel tanks. Yesterday: the coins in the reactor and the contaminated fuel that had stopped one diesel generator. Also yesterday, there was the failure of the landing-strip lights. Quite a list. I sipped my coffee and looked at Kirton, who sat with his eyes closed, looking rapt. But he must have been thinking, too, because as the Albinoni ended he said, 'You sure brought a jinx up here.'

'Blame me if you like. We call our jinxes gremlins.'

'So you sure brought a gremlin.'

I said, 'No, the sod was here. While you were having all the accidents, I was happy, ignorant and far away. Tell me, *is* this place unlucky?'

He shook his head. 'No, it's not. Or it wasn't. Funny thing, they always reckoned this was a real good-luck operation. They built it without losing a man. Not even a serious injury. Then a few years with a safety record damn near perfect. It's all in the last two weeks.'

I said, 'Tell me I'm mad if you like, but could any of this be deliberate?'

He looked a bit surprised, and then smiled. 'You mean sabotage?'

'Well, could it?'

'Not a chance. Sabotage anything up here and you sabotage yourself. If the machines stop working in a long bad weather phase, people are gonna die. The guy would have to be psychotic.'

'You said last night everybody's a little mad.'

'A little maybe. But nobody's that crazy.' He grinned. 'Except, er . . . now look, Mr Bowes, you seen your shrink lately?'

I said, 'I haven't got a shrink.'

'No? Well, how about if I read my shrink books and then you come and tell me all about your father? Listen, what you got is the first, faint stirrings of what's known to science as the Hundred Heebies. It's all too complex here for our poor puny minds. Now finish your coffee and the doctor will take you for a nice walk.'

'Where do you want to walk to?'

'I want to see what the bear did.'

We dressed and walked down Main Street to the fuel trench and Kirton looked at the ripped neoprene and said, 'He's got muscle, that old bear!'

I nodded. I was thinking that the animal's behaviour had been pretty strange, even by the doubtless eccentric standards of hungry bears. Camp Hundred was full of food. Looked at from a hungry bear's point of view, there were a lot of comestibles walking round on two legs, never mind all the orthodox grub in the food stores. So why had he left all the food alone and just slashed the tanks? 'He certainly seems,' I said, 'to have been cross about something. And not very hungry, either, unless he enjoys drinking diesel oil.'

'Yeah.' Kirton gave me a glance, then said, 'I wonder . . .' He turned, crossed to the door and swung it closed. 'Look at this. He got food all right.'

The floor behind the door was littered with ripped-up tinfoil and torn plastic. I asked what it was.

'Emergency rations,' Kirton said. 'There's a pack in all the trenches with doors, just in case somebody gets locked in. Hangs on the back of the door.'

'Clever old bear, then,' I said. 'I suppose the food's wrapped in the plastic?'

'No problem with claws like his. You and I break our nails trying to open plastic packages, but he sure wouldn't have any trouble.'

'No. But he'd have trouble finding the food in the first place, unless he could smell it.'

He said, 'You're doing that thing again, you know. He'll have a big, sensitive, black nose, that old bear, and there'll be some residual smell on the outside of the pack.' Kirton bent and picked up a chunk of some kind of compressed cake from the floor. It still had shreds of foil sticking to it and he looked at it reflectively. 'Gnawed by a polar bear, how about that?'

I said, 'He's certainly a light eater. He walks a hundred miles, has some fruit cake and a couple of bars of chocolate, and goes away.'

Kirton rubbed at his moustache as he looked at me. 'Tell you what I'll do. I'll take some of this junk and do some microscope work. If the bear dined here, there's gonna be saliva on these things, and saliva means bacteria. Maybe I could do a paper on it, how about that? Saliva analysis of – damn it, what's its Latin name?'

'I don't know. Ursus something.'

'Yeah, well, Saliva Analysis of Ursus something by Joseph

41

Kirton MD, etc. That's *one* nobody's done before.'

Perhaps he was right. He knew a lot more about the Arctic than I did, he knew the people here, above all he knew the feel of the place. So if Kirton found my suspicions merely amusing, perhaps I'd better forget about them. A lifetime's experience confirmed that accidents came in batches; there'd been gremlins a-plenty round the TK4 Mark One, all of them apparently inexplicable until the reason was finally discovered and we found that this gunge or that scrobbler hadn't been allowed for.

He moved off, holding the ripped remnants of the emergency food pack in cupped hands. I glanced at my watch. It was after eleven. Outside the wind whistled and snow seemed to be blowing in several directions at once between the ice walls at the sides of the ramp. Feeling vaguely useless I was about to amble after him when a voice said 'Sir' and I turned to face a man with stripes on his parka who introduced himself as Sergeant Vernon and said Major Smales had instructed him to give Mr Bowes the ten-dollar tour of Camp Hundred, if Mr Bowes would like that. I said Mr Bowes would like it very much and he said it was his pleasure, sir, and we could start with the water well, which I'd probably find interesting. The well was in a trench almost at the centre of Hundred, away from the command hut, next to the mess hall, and not far from Kirton's hospital trench. At first sight, it wasn't impressive, just a four-foot-high circle of corrugated steel with a metal framework above it and a couple of pipes running from it up to the wall. I looked over the edge of the barrier and saw a dark hole. Then Sergeant Vernon flicked on a switch and the hole suddenly turned brilliantly white and beneath me appeared an astonishingly beautiful sight. The hole was only about four feet in diameter but it was very deep, and obviously widened a good deal underneath the narrow entrance.

'What makes Hundred unique in Cold Regions Research installations,' Veron said, 'is that we can turn on heat and water in real quantity. So we have comfort. Heat, as you know, comes from the reactor, and with plenty of it, we can have all the water we need. This is the system that supplies it.'

'By melting snow, of course?'

'That's right. When Hundred opened, this well was started.

42

What happened was this: they used a jet of steam to bore a hole in the snow right here where we stand, and pumped the resulting water away. So there was this narrow circular hole running down. The melted snow was tested for pollution – radioactivity mainly – and then, when we were past the 1945 snow layer, Hiroshima and so on, they began to widen it.'

'The atom bombs contaminated snow here?'

'Oh yeah. They sure did. But below the 1945 layer, it's clean. Now, imagine the nozzle of a hose pipe, okay? Well, that's what we got down there, only it's steam that's coming out. The steam melts snow, water gathers in the bottom, and a pump sucks it up. The nozzle rotates slowly, under the pressure of the steam – same principle as a lawn sprinkler, you know those things? – and that means you're cutting into the snow in a circle. You with me?'

'Ingenious,' I said.

'And simple. By regulating the steam pressure, you regulate how far into the snow you're cutting. Don't want to cut too far, for obvious reasons. So then, gradually, the nozzle has been lowered, to melt snow farther down, and what we have right under us here is a structure shaped like . . . well, like a giant onion maybe. Narrow neck, widening out gradually.'

I looked at the two pipes, one plastic, one flexible steel, that dropped down, from where we stood, into a black circle in the base of the huge ice chamber below. 'I don't see the nozzle, or the pump.'

Vernon smiled. 'This is only the top onion. One little problem we got with this well is that we can't cut the bulbs too wide, otherwise we might start undermining ourselves. So, to be safe, when the top one got down a hundred and fifty feet, we went through the whole process again, cutting a neck, then opening out another onion. So now we have a structure like three onions, one on top of the other, and the steam hose is turning four hundred and some feet down. Down there in the bottom of the third bulb there'll be around a hundred thousand gallons of water and the system's automatic. As the water's drawn up, the steam comes on and melts some more.'

'Very clever,' I said, meaning it.

He shrugged. 'Maybe a bit too clever. We don't want to sink too many wells at Hundred, because ice is plastic and who knows what might happen if it starts to fill its own empty spaces. So we stick with this one. But maintenance gets to be kind of tricky.'

'What kind of maintenance does it need?'

'Maybe I used the wrong word. Should have said inspection. We have to check that everything's okay; be sure the steam jet *is* cutting a circle and hasn't twisted so it's eating at the snow in one direction only.'

I blinked. 'You mean someobdy really has to go *down* there?'

'Sure.'

'Tricky is an understatement, then. What you mean is dangerous.' I looked down the hole again. 'Are those things icicles?' From under the lip of the entry hole, monster spears of ice hung deep into the chamber like dragon's teeth.

'They're another little problem. Some of the steam floats up, and it either condenses or it melts snow on the way, and icicles form and keep growing.'

'And if one of those fell on somebody?'

'We got to be careful, sure. In the second and third chambers they're even bigger, but we can't knock them down or they'd smash the equipment.'

'So who goes down?'

Vernon said, 'A volunteer.'

'I can see why. Have you done it?'

'Yeah, I have. Twice, as a matter of fact. I kind of liked it in a spooky sort of way. It's interesting. Down there you can see the layers of snow. Every year a new layer and the deeper you go, the more the layer's been compacted by pressure. You can read history down there. If you look real hard, you can see there's a thin black line in bulb two. That's when the volcano Krakatoa erupted.'

'But that was in Java! Did ash really get as far as this?'

He smiled. 'So the experts say. Must have been a hell of a bang, right? Anyway, they reckon that around five hundred feet we'll be down to snow that fell in 1492 and the major says he's gonna bottle it and market Columbus water. Don't know if we'll make it, though. I reckon – personally, you understand – that it's gotten too deep. They'll have to start another well.'

He switched off the wall lights, and I looked at him with a certain admiration. Nothing, I thought, would persuade me into the bosun's chair that hung from the well-head framework. 'Well, thanks,' I said. 'Where now?'

I was taken to the reactor trench where, understandably, they were rather too busy to want to entertain guests. Kelleher was already back at work, frowning and preoccupied, visibly tired with only two hours quick sleep behind him and delicate and highly responsible work to do. He looked up briefly and said, 'Come tomorrow and we'll show you the whole deal.' Next we went to the huge tractor shed, cut deep into the snow, where half-a-dozen giant tractors and bulldozers stood, as well as assorted Weasels and Polecats and, incongruous among them, two tiny orange Ski-doos, fast little snow-scooters. There were laboratories, mainly full of electrical and electronic equipment, the sleeping quarters, all like my own, stuffy and sweaty and windowless. There was a separate club for the sergeants, another for the enlisted men, and each had its rows of bottles, its tables for ping-pong and pool. The kitchens were probably as good as any of Mr Hilton's. Vernon explained it all cheerfully, still as impressed by it all as I was. It was even more impressive, as he pointed out, when you realized that every item, from the reactor itself to the knives and forks, had been hauled on sleds across a hundred miles of the icecap.

When we'd finished, he invited me into the sergeants' club for a drink and I went with him, knowing what to expect. Nor was I wrong. Sergeants, in any army, are the people who have their affairs properly organized. An officers' mess has a social pyramid and its members range from youth to late middle age, so the social mix isn't naturally comfortable and some strain always shows. Sergeants, on the other hand, give or take a little seniority, are of similar age range, all mature men, and there are no problems about who calls who what. More important, they're the men who make an army work. So, while the officers' club was comfortable and faintly scruffy, the sergeants' club gleamed. While the officers poured their own drinks, the sergeants had a white-jacketed barman, who'd clearly been drilled and drilled again and who, when he left the army, would undoubtedly get a job in some first-class hotel, because he was skilful and had style, and was kept steady to the mark by knowledgeable eyes. I was welcomed formally by the black master sergeant, who wore a collar and tie and well-pressed khaki, and who said it was his privilege to give me my first drink, sir, and what was its name.

I smiled to myself and asked how the sergeants had solved the problem of stuffy bedrooms, and Master Sergeant Allen said it wasn't entirely solved but would I care to see? He showed me his own room. The *pièce de résistance* was a mock window complete with curtains, and behind the glass was a huge blown-up photograph of treetops and blue sky. They had, he said, nearly a hundred such photographs, and the view was changed regularly. 'Why,' I asked, 'don't the officers have pictures, too?'

He smiled politely. 'Maybe they didn't think about it.'

He also explained that they had discovered how much colour helped and had arranged to have kapok sleeping bags covered in bright material, to look like quilts. Then there was the matter of starched sheets, and a faint smell of pines and the humidifiers hanging on the central heating radiator. It was all, he said, mainly psychological.

We went back to the bar then, and the steward made Martinis, with everything coming from a big freezer behind the bar: glasses, bottles, ice, shaker. The sergeants were impressive people. I asked Vernon how long he'd been at Hundred. He said it was his third tour of duty.

'Third?' I said. 'I thought people couldn't wait to get away.'

'No, sir, it's not like that. I enjoy my duty here. I wanted to come back.'

'And will you again?'

He frowned. 'I better explain, sir. A little over two weeks back, we lost a man. Only a kid really, but I reckon it was my fault. No, sir, I won't be coming back this time. I'm quitting the army.'

The master sergeant said, 'Nobody blames him, excepting him. Major Smales told him that, I told him, everybody told him.'

'These things happen,' I said uncomfortably. I liked Vernon. He seemed a solid citizen, dependable and strong. 'What will you do when you leave the army?'

46

'Home to Wichita,' he said. 'Look around. Find some job. I'll be okay. But let's talk about something else, huh? Tell us about that air-cushion vehicle of yours.'

I did, and with some relief. The two of them were deeply aware of the need for faster transport over the icecap, knew the problems and gave me as much information as I gave them.

After I left the sergeants' club I went over to the radio room to see if there was any news of the Swing's progress. There wasn't; the last contact had been at midnight and the radio operator suspected the snow train had run into a white-out, which would make contact unlikely and almost certainly stop the train.

'I thought nothing stopped it.'

'Just white-outs, sir. Bad one, you get just no visibility at all. Air's full of minute ice particles and it looks like milk. No sky, no horizon, no ground. You just have to wait till it goes away.'

'How long does that take?'

'Minutes, hours, days, who knows? Then you get a wind and – pfft, it's over.'

I went in to lunch. Neither Kelleher nor Barney Smales was present, but the silent young officer I'd sat beside the previous day was there.

'May I join you?'

'Surely. Guess I owe you some kind of apology.'

'No,' I said.

He made an effort to be friendly, but his heart wasn't in it. He apologized again and said he couldn't seem to throw off the gloom.

'Can't the doctor help?'

'Happy pills? Gets a whole lot worse when they wear off, so I stopped them. Sounds crazy, I know, but what I really want is a good long walk.'

'Difficult.'

'Impossible. But I guess it's kind of an *idée fixe*. Something in my head says if I can take the walk, it will be okay. But I can't, so round I go in circles.' He smiled faintly, embarrassed at the revelation.

I said, 'It's claustrophobia, really.'

'Yeah, I know.'

47

'Everybody's got it, more or less.'

'I know that, too. It's just . . . you know what happened?'

I shook my head.

'They were out at the seismology hut, that's around three hundred yards out on the cap. There was a sudden bad phase and they were trapped three days in there. When it cleared a little they started back and hit a white-out. Three hundred goddam yards and they hit a white-out! Daylight, clear air, but it just fell on them. Didn't last but a few hours, either, but somehow Charlie got loose from the guide-line. Sergeant Vernon, he's a real good man, he stayed there an hour, damn near froze to death; he shouted and he damn well waited, but Charlie was gone! Just vanished right into the cap.'

I said, 'Vernon feels badly. You know he's leaving the army?'

'Yeah, I know.'

When we'd finished eating, I said, 'Since you can't go for a walk, how about exercise of a different kind? Ping-pong.'

He started to say no thanks, changed his mind and said, 'Why not?' and we played for more than an hour, working up a sweat in the heated recreation hut. At first he seemed to have difficulty in keeping his mind on the game, but after a while the old American hatred of being beaten at any game began to assert itself, and he played a good deal better, the lines disappearing from his brow as healthy perspiration gathered on it. Ping-pong seems a pretty feeble palliative, but at least when we'd finished he wasn't any worse and may have been a fraction better.

Afterwards I had a shower, then lay for a while on my bed, reading. I was bored, frustrated by inactivity and conscious of not belonging. Once my TK4 arrived, I'd have a purpose and things to do; meanwhile I was something of a nuisance, a spare body hanging around asking tourist-type questions and wasting time. And if inactivity could bore me so quickly, what must it be like for some of the others, Doc Kirton, for instance, who had to endure it for a whole six-month tour? I decided I'd go and alleviate his boredom and my own, and perhaps find out what kind of bacteria polar bears carried around, so I put on all the layers of clothing and walked round to the hospital. Kirton's outer office was empty, but there was a red light glowing on the door of the operating theatre. He must have heard me come in, though, because he called, 'Who is it?'

I told him and he called back, 'I got something to show you, but I'm busy right now. See you later.'

So I left. It might have saved a lot of trouble if I'd just sat in his office and waited.

Instead I went to the library and got a couple of books, then returned to my room to read. In fact I dozed off, awakening just in time for dinner, and after dinner there were a couple of quick drinks and then the evening's film, the Burton/Taylor *Cleopatra*, which seemed to go on for ever. Just before I finally went to sleep that night, I remember thinking that for the first time since my arrival, nothing unpleasant had happened that day. The damaged generator was apparently in working order again, the reactor was due to go critical tomorrow. It was a reassuring thought to sleep on.

Unfortunately, it wasn't true.

On the way to a late breakfast next morning, I called in at the radio room, hoping for news of the Swing, but there was none; they were still out of radio contact. The operator smiled at my anxiety. 'Don't worry about it; the Swing always makes it. Weather's good, they're quick. Weather's bad, they're slow. But they sure as hell get here.'

I nodded, thanked him, and left. It looked like being another fragmented, tedious day and I really wasn't looking forward to it. The stuffiness in my room had given me a rough mouth and a dull headache and I decided that after I'd eaten, I'd go and get a couple of aspirins from Kirton. Everybody else must have breakfasted earlier. The result was that I ate alone and consequently quickly. I stayed at the table long enough to smoke a cigarette, then put on all the wrappings again and left for the hospital. Kirton wasn't there and I debated rummaging around for aspirin in his cupboards, but decided against it in case what I took turned out to be cascara, or something. So I went to the Officers' Club and drank coffee and read *Time* magazine while the headache got worse. An hour later, Kirton still hadn't shown up at the Officers' Club and, when I returned to the hospital, he wasn't there either. Hoping the cool air that blew along Main Street would clear my head, I took a stroll towards the command trench. But I never got there. At the far end of Main Street, where the tunnel led up on to the cap, a group of men were standing beside the bulldozer. I walked towards them and, as I came closer, saw they were looking at something on the ground. I couldn't see what it was, because there were too many people; I just kept walking until I reached them. About five seconds later, I was doubled over by the wall, vomiting my breakfast back, retching until I thought my boots would come up.

A single glance had been enough to tell me what had happened: a man had been ground to pulp under the fifty-six-inch steel track of the bulldozer, and all that was left was a ghastly smear of blood, flesh and ripped clothing.

I felt a hand on my shoulder and Barney Smales's voice said, 'Get the hell out of here, Mr Bowes.' He spoke gently, but he meant it.

I retched dryly once more, then straightened, and asked, 'Who?'

Smales said, 'It's kinda hard to tell. We think it's Doc Kirton. Now go!'

Chapter 5

I went, not looking back. One look had been more than enough. In the officers' club I found a bottle of brandy and poured a large slug down my throat. Inevitably, it merely made me sick again. Apart from that it did nothing and my mind continued to present me with its snapshot of the scene, of Kirton, plastered in bloody fragments over the ice floor and the bulldozer's track. I shivered and tried the brandy again and this time, thankfully, it stayed down. Then I went to find the master sergeant and said, 'Give me some work. Manual work.'

He looked at me sympathetically. 'You saw, huh?'

'I saw.'

'Shovelling snow is good,' he said, and actually ran with me to the other end of Main Street, where he gave me a spade and pointed to the ramp and said, 'You can't dig it all away, but you can try.'

I worked like a dog until I was exhausted, until sweat streamed down my body, attacking the snow with deliberate fury to try to drive the other scene from my mind, until my body and mind were protesting not at memory but at strain. At last, still feeling foul but with some degree of self-control restored, I replaced the shovel on its wall bracket and staggered back along Main Street to the command trench and went in to see Barney Smales.

He scowled at me and said, 'I told you to get the hell out!'

'And sit twiddling my thumbs thinking about it!'

'Nothing else you can do. Nothing any of us can do.'

'You can tell me how it happened!'

He said wearily, 'How can I? I don't know myself. 'Dozer went right over him. More than once. Driver didn't see him, so it looks like he was covered in snow.'

I stared at him. 'You mean he was already dead?'

Barney Smales sighed and his lips tightened.

'Don't you think it's rather important to know?'

His eyes snapped angrily. 'And don't you think, Mr Bowes,

51

that you're being just a little bit insubordinate! You a morbid pathologist as well as a fan flyer?'

'Of course not. But if he was dead – '

He interrupted furiously. 'Don't say it!'

'I'll say it,' I said. 'It could be murder.'

'Sure it could. And it could have been a heart attack or a cerebral haemorrhage, too. You're so damn smart, you tell me how I can find out!' He broke off and sniffed. 'You've been drinking,' he said accusingly.

I said, 'Brandy.'

'In the *morning*?' He'd done it well and the rôles were changed; I was firmly on the defensive now, a morning drunk making trouble.

Still, I tried once more. Or began, anyway. I said, 'Kirton was – '

But Smales wasn't having it, dismissal and disgust combining in a single gesture of his hand as he said, 'Sleep it off.'

But I didn't sleep. I lay on my bunk and thought a lot and finished up with a conclusion or two. One was that Camp Hundred, with all its hazards, was now without a doctor. But it was Kirton I thought about most. If he'd had a stroke or a heart attack, as Smales had said, then perhaps I was being foolish. But Kirton had been no more than thirty, and a relaxed, strong-looking man at that and the odds, surely, were against it. There was perhaps a possibility that he'd been killed accidentally, blundering into a moving tractor or something like that, and an even more remote possibility of suicide, which I included in my mental list only to dismiss it. If he hadn't died of natural causes, an accident, or killed himself, then somebody else had done it.

There were also the nasty little coincidences. Kirton's body had been only yards away from the entrance to the Reserve Fuel Store, where the polar bear had slashed the tanks and eaten the emergency rations. And it had been the morning doorstep sweeper who'd first discovered both the bear's tracks and Kirton's body. The same man? I decided that was one of the things I ought to find out. I'd go into the tractor sheds and talk propulsion and ask questions. But first there was something else.

The hospital was my first stop. It was unlocked and I went in, switched on the lights, and stood by the partition between the office and the theatre. What was it Kirton had shouted? That he had something to show me, or tell me; something like that. And that he'd see me later, because he was busy. Had he had a patient in there? If so who? An appointments book lay on the desk and I flipped it open. There weren't many entries anywhere, and only one for the previous day, at 3.30 p.m. It said, Pfc Hansen, nasal polyp.' Well, I'd try to check on Pfc Hansen, too. But I was more concerned about the microscopic examination Kirton had promised to do on the food wrapping. His microscope was in a wooden box which stood on a side workbench, but there was no slide on the clips though there were plenty in a special rack beside it. However, they were only numbered, not labelled, so I'd neither any way of identifying the right one, nor the knowledge to understand it if I did.

I did find something, though, before I left the hospital. The torn lumps of tinfoil and plastic wrapping from the emergency rations lay discarded in a waste basket by his desk. But there was nothing else: no pad with notes on it, no torn-up scraps of paper in the waste basket. So Kirton had looked and found nothing to interest him? It could only be that. Nothing worthy of remark, nothing to make notes about. The whole thing negative. But then I thought: *Nothing?* No bacteria? Yet the morning before, when he'd said he'd use his microscope, he'd said also that if the bear *had* eaten the stuff, there'd be saliva and *therefore* bacteria. I collected the wrappings, found an envelope, put them inside and tucked them in my pocket. They were certainly no use to *me*, but if I left them, they'd be thrown out. I left, aware that I was jumping to conclusions and that some of them were pretty wild.

Then I collected the two fat volumes of the TK4 maintenance manual, took them along to the tractor shed and introduced myself to the top sergeant there, a bulky cigar-smoker called Reilly. He looked at me and the manuals, took the cigar from his mouth, spat out a flake of tobacco and said, 'This all we get?'

'The principle is that it's all you need,' I said.

'Jesus!' he said. 'No project engineer. Not even a coupla lectures?'

I explained about the TK4 and its great simplicity. It was designed on the basis that any bunch of competent mechanics with reasonable workshop facilities could do all that was necessary by way of repairs, servicing and maintenance.

Reilly said, 'Yeah?' on a rising note, full of disbelief.

I smiled. 'If you buy the TK4 – '

'I'm not buying, son.'

'If the army buys, then?' He nodded. 'If that happens, naturally we'll send a whole crew over to see her through the first operations. But the idea of the trials is to see how well it can be operated without all that. We tried it in Canada and it worked pretty well.'

Reilly grinned behind the cigar. 'This ain't Canada, son.'

I said, 'But that's the idea.'

He hefted the manuals, about six pounds of assorted paper, and said, 'And this here's a little bedtime reading?'

'I'm afraid so.'

Reilly looked at me out of small blue eyes. 'Answer me a question, willya? If this TK4 of yours goes over a guy, what's it do?'

I said soberly, 'He'd be a bit battered by the air. The rubber skirts might scrape some skin off. It wouldn't kill him, if that's what you mean.'

'That's what I mean. I just been clearing the doc offa them tracks.'

He was already turning away. 'Don't worry, son, I'll read the books.'

I said quickly, 'Who found Doc Kirton?'

He turned back. 'I did. So?'

'You were driving?'

'Right.'

'And the bear tracks. Who found those?'

He took a step towards me, almost aggressively.

'Why you wanna know?'

'I wondered, that's all.'

He said, 'Kid name of Hansen.'

'He's got a nasal polyp,' I said.

'Had. The doc fixed it yesterday. Just before . . .' he stopped.

I said, 'Yes, I know,' and walked away, but I could feel his eyes on my back. Because I was an interloper? Or for some other reason?

As I went in to lunch, Barney Smales was leaving the mess hall. He stopped and looked at me thoughtfully, then said, 'When you've eaten, come and talk to me, huh?'

'No time like the present.'

He said, 'Not now. The food's necessary. Eat first.'

I wasn't hungry, but I ate a little, then went to the command hut. Smales took me into his office and closed the door. He was frowning, but his tone was friendly enough as he said, 'Are you normally this suspicious?'

I said, 'I'm renowned for my sunny outlook.'

'You are? I'd take convincing. Listen to me a minute, Bowes. When you run a place like this, there's plenty of problems. They come up all the time. Old problems, new problems, recurrent problems. You come in category two. You're a new problem and I want to know what's eating you.'

I said, 'It simply seems to me that too many dangerous things have been happening for it all to be coincidence.'

'And you think maybe there's murder, sabotage, the whole works?'

'I began to wonder.'

He sat back in his chair, toying with a ruler from his desk, then said, surprisingly, 'I can see how you might think it.'

'I'm relieved to hear it.'

'But *I* don't think it.'

'I gathered that.'

'So what I want to do is go over it with you, right? Tell you what I think and why I think it. What's the first one, the runway lights?'

'If you take them in sequence, yes.'

'Okay. Well, this morning I went out there in a Weasel with Herschel and two electricians and we had a look at the cables. Wanna know what we found?'

'Of course.'

55

'They'd been chewed. Not in just one place, either. There were more than forty places. Damn foxes just keep on chewing. Sooner or later, there's a short circuit and bang go the lights. We renew those cables, we have to, around every six months. That satisfy?'

I said, 'Not entirely, no. The short circuit happened at the exact moment a plane was coming in. A plane with you in it. And Kelleher.'

'Yeah. Okay. But it was the first plane in two weeks, right? Two weeks since the lights were used.'

I wasn't satisfied. 'But the lights did go on. It was when the plane was coming in that they failed.'

'That's right. That's why I inspected the cables myself. Because I'm not as green and trusting as you think I am. But you get all the teeth marks and you get a dead fox – '

'Did you?'

'Oh, sure. There he was, right beside the cable. You see, Mr Bowes?'

'I do now.'

'Okay, next problem's the diesel generator, right?'

'Certainly.'

'And you say to yourself, how in hell did the fuel get contaminated? Well, I can't tell you.'

'But. There *is* a but?'

He laughed. 'Sure there is. It happens up here. Fuel comes in to Thule by tanker. It's pumped ashore into storage tanks. Then when they bring it up here, it's pumped out again into neoprene. Then it's brought up here and stored, also in neoprene. But rubber pipes are used in pumping, and rubber can go solid and crack in bad cold. Pieces flake off the inside of the pipe and get in the fuel. It's happened with Swing-haul tractors, too. Just one of the hazards.'

'It's not as convincing as the dead fox.'

'I can see I got to work on you, Sherlock. Let's put it this way. It's happened a few times at Thule, *and* at Belvoir, *and* on the Trail up here. *And* here. We know this one. It's one of the standing hazards.'

I shrugged and moved on. 'The coins in the reactor?'

'Carelessness. That's what Kelleher says and I believe it. Tell you why I believe it, too. Not because we had that problem before. We haven't. But because carelessness and lack of con-centration are standard here. You're not the man you were three or four days ago and neither am I. You're affected by the altitude, by claustrophobia; you resent the necessity to put heavy clothing on to go to the can.'

I shook my head. 'There's a good reason. I can understand it well enough.'

'Okay,' he said. 'But you resent it. You wish you didn't have to do it. It's a goddam drag. There's a million things. We eat a lot but we get no proper exercise. There's no sun, no space, damn little privacy. We don't take enough fluid and dehydration's a constant hazard, so don't forget to drink your milk. People don't sleep well here. There's no visible difference between night and day down here – or up on the cap, for that matter, through the winter darkness. We've had all the tests done. Doctors, shrinks, efficiency people. Know what they found?'

'Well, obviously that people aren't as efficient,'

'That's right. They're just about half as efficient. Half! And that's everybody. Officers, enlisted men, visiting scientists and engineers. Everybody, including you, Bowes, is at roughly fifty per cent of normal. Give you two instances. There was a guy up here last winter working on ice movement, a specialist in glaciers. He was also a hot shot bridge player. Not just good, he's a real top player, gets his name in the *New York Times*. He's sitting in the club one night playing a contract and he suddenly turns nine colours of green and red.'

Smales waited for me to ask why, and I obliged.

'Because he'd forgotten what trumps were, or if it was a no trump hand, and even whether he was trying to make a contract or defending. There's the dummy hand sitting there opposite, and he didn't even know *that*. His mind had gone blank. What is it, Bowes, is it carelessness? Now the other guy, he was an officer here. Civil engineer. Had been here six weeks and he'd lost the ability to add up, right? Two and two he could do, but fifty-eight and thirty-seven he had to get a pencil. Those coins in the reactor kettle, they're a nuisance, sure. And worse. If I knew

57

who'd done it, I'd kick his ass from here to Fort Belvoir, Virginia. But I have to accept that things like that are gonna happen.'

'And the helicopter crash? And the man lost on the surface? And Doc Kirton?'

He sighed and ran his hand wearily across his forehead. Then he said, 'Okay. I got no explanations. *But*. There's been five years of operations up here. That was the first air crash. The first. It was bound to happen sooner or later. It makes me sick to my stomach, but statistically it was coming. Same with the guy lost on top. We got nearly three hundred men here. Five hundred sometimes. They live and work in the worst weather conditions in the world. It's a miracle it hasn't happened before. Can you accept that?'

'I suppose so.' I couldn't accept it quite as readily as he apparently did, but there was obvious truth in what he said and I'd no wish to be needlessly offensive, especially as this was olive-branch time. 'And Kirton?'

'Doc Kirton's death,' he said, 'is a mystery to me too. I don't know how he died, or why. Nor have I any way of finding out. For that you need an autopsy and we'll damn well have an autopsy as soon as I can get a pathologist flown in here, or Kirton's body flown out. Then, maybe, we'll know. Meantime, I refuse to speculate. Okay?'

'No,' I said. 'It's not okay. Not until you've had the pathologist's report. If Kirton's death was natural, or some kind of accident, then of course you're right. If it wasn't, *if* he was killed, then – '

He said dangerously, 'You trying to tell me my duty?'

'It was you,' I said carefully, 'who said we're all working at fifty per cent.'

Smales grinned suddenly. 'Okay, okay,' he said. 'Maybe you got something. I get defensive about this place. I know it.'

I said, 'Did anybody dislike Kirton?'

'Who knows? I doubt it. Kirton was a good guy. Look, I'm not an idiot, I'm not naïve, I'm not smug, or I hope not. But when you raise the matter of my duties, you're on a tricky spot, because *I'm* not even sure what they are. Oh, there's administration, the rest of the paper work. Discipline, sure. Normal commander's routine. But beyond that there's the area of morale, of keeping

58

this joint working, and that's a knife edge. Standard military discipline won't work up here. You've seen all the beards?'

I nodded.

'Beards aren't allowed in the US Army. But a lot of the men get sore faces, real sore, if they shave every day. Other guys feel dirty if they don't. So I give the option. I give every little lift I can. If some eighteen-year-old kid wants to grow a beard, gets to feeling a little proud of it, that's fine by me. It helps him keep going. But it's all fragile. Nobody knows how the doc died, right? Maybe, here and there, people are doing some speculating. But what if I took your line? What if *I* say, "Look, this could be murder, fellas, but there's no way of knowing and no way of finding out." Then they all start looking over their shoulders and the place starts to fall apart. But if you want to know what I believe, I think it could only be some kind of accident. Why? Well, I'll tell you. Doc Kirton was a self-contained sort of guy. He stayed in his hospital and did his job, when there was work to do. Otherwise he played music, a little chess, and kept to himself. He wasn't the kind to make enemies. He was a good doctor and a good guy. Period. I haven't satisfied you, have I?' He smiled.

I smiled back. 'Not entirely.'

'Well, I'll tell you. This morning I thought you were paranoid, then I thought you were drunk. Now I don't think either of those things. But I *do* think you're wrong, and I can't afford to have suspicion flying round this camp.'

'So shut up?'

He looked at me. 'Not even that. You want to listen while people talk, you do that. You're not busy, you're wandering around, that's natural. I could stop you, but I won't. And I'm interested in every little thing that happens in this place, so you hear something, you tell me. Okay? Now come with me.'

We put on parkas and over-trousers and went out, along Main Street and into the kitchens. Smales went over to one of the cooks and said, 'I want a pork chop.'

The cook said, 'Major Smales, sir, you got the wrong guy. I'm the kosher cook.'

Smales laughed, apologized and tried another man, then

59

returned with the chop in his hand, held in a pair of cooking tongs. 'Right, come on. Get the mitts on, the parka hood up and tied tight.'

We went along the trench to the escape hatch, and up the metal spiral staircase, and Smales pushed back the hatchcover bolts, then wound the handle that raised it. As the lid opened, wind and snow howled in. He looked down at me and shouted, 'Wind's forty miles an hour. Temperature's fifteen below. Keep your back to the wind.' Then he climbed out on to the icecap, and I followed, and we stood side by side, backs to the Arctic wind, feeling the hard snow crystals pattering continuously on the cloth of the parkas.

Smales raised the tongs, keeping his hand carefully in the shelter of his shoulder, the pork chop poked upwards into the wind. He bellowed, 'Start counting seconds. One, two, three . . .'

We shouted in unison. By the time we'd reached thirty, I could feel the cold beginning to reach my heels, even inside the felt boots. By fifty, my feet were beginning to be cold. At sixty, Smales waved me back to the hatch cover and climbed in after me, then wound the cover down again. The noise of wind and snow receded, then disappeared, and he handed me the pork chop. It was frozen solid.

He said, 'That's what we live with. Don't forget it. It explains a lot.'

And he left me standing there, at the base of the stair, looking at an inch-thick pork chop that had become hard as a plank in sixty seconds. We hadn't moved more than six feet from the hatch-cover up there, and it had been an impressive glimpse of the implacably hostile environment in which Camp Hundred managed to exist. More than any words could have done, those sixty seconds underscored the nature of the job Barney Smales had to do.

After that I drifted round to the radio room. There'd been contact with the Swing during the morning and good news: it was under way again, but, having been held up by the white-out and two big crevasses that opened on the trail, it was still only thirty miles on, with seventy still to go. Several days would probably be needed yet before my TK4 arrived at Camp Hundred.

It may have been auto-suggestion, following the talk with Barney, or it may have been reaction to the morning's horror, but I certainly felt fifty per cent below normal. I was headachy, listless and generally out-of-sorts. It was one of those don't-feel-like times. I didn't feel like lying down and reading; didn't feel like going for some coffee; didn't feel anything much except uselessness and dissatisfaction; the Hundred Heebies, Doc Kirton had called it, and I decided I'd better snap out. I made myself march with reasonable briskness along to the reactor trench. Kelleher had said, 'Come back tomorrow' and it was tomorrow. I went in and could see at once from the faces that something was wrong.

One of the technicians came over and handed me a radiation badge and I pinned it on automatically. There's a little piece of film inside which records radiation exposure and when it's developed they can tell if you've had too much. It's a bit late by then, of course, but the practice is universal.

'I suspect,' I said to Kelleher, 'that I've come at the wrong time again.'

He said, 'Oh, boy!'

'Anything I'd understand?'

'Sure,' he said. 'Anybody can understand it. What I can't damn well understand is *why*!'

'Still can't go critical?'

'It stops us good. There's a major requirement we have here. We've got to have clean water in the kettle. I mean *clean* water. In the usual installation, what we do is we use distilled water. Here it's not necessary, because the well water is totally pure. Nothing purer than melted snow three centuries old, believe me; it's been tested and it's been used a long time right here.'

'And it's not pure now?'

He shook his head wearily. 'I nearly didn't run a test, do you know that? Damn near. But the book says test and we tested. Water's contaminated.'

'By what?'

'I don't know, It's very small, but it's there. Shows on the scope. We're gonna have to drain, clean and refill. *After* we find out where it's getting in. Some damn thing, some damn place, is leaking into the pipes. Either that, or . . .' Kelleher didn't finish the sentence, but the implication was clear.

Either that. Or the well itself was contaminated.

Chapter 6

I was about to ask whether Smales knew, but there was no need. The door opened and Smales stalked in, grim-faced. He grabbed a radiation badge and pinned it on as he walked over to us and confronted Kelleher. 'Are you sure?'

'I'm sure, Barney.'

'You tried again?'

'Three times we tried it. Three samples. Whatever it is, it's small, but it's there.'

Smales said, 'Either the pipes or the well.'

'It's got to be.'

'Okay, we'll take stopcock samples right back to the well head, see if we can find where it gets in.'

Kelleher said, 'It could be the well, Barney.'

'I know it. But no man goes down there unless we absolutely have to do it. Can your guys take the samples?'

'Better if they do.'

'Right, let's go.' Smales turned to me and said, 'Talking about suspicions, how come you're always around bad news?'

'Coincidence, I hope.'

'I hope so, too. Okay, let's move our asses.'

Uninvited, I went with Kelleher, and he made no objection. He carried a plastic pack with him, and when we reached the stopcock nearest to the reactor shed he turned it on so that water was flowing out fast, then broke open the pack and extracted a length of plastic tubing and a bottle. He pushed the end of the tube carefully into the mouth of the drain tap, waited until water flowed through the tube, then used it to fill the bottle. When that was done, he took a glass stopper from its plastic wrapping, sealed the bottle with it and wrapped it again in a plastic bag.

'Whole thing's clean sterile,' he said. 'No dust, nothing.' He put his hand in his parka pocket, fished out a pen, and marked the bottle label with a number. Then we went back to the reactor shed and he ran it through the electronic testing machinery. He said, 'There you are.' The scope flickered.

One by one the technicians returned, each with one or two bottles. Every bottle was tested, and every time the scope indicated impurities. Smales stood watching, tight-lipped. Finally, Kelleher sighed and turned to him. 'Sorry, Barney. It's the well. It has to be the well. Something dropped down there.'

Smales said, 'That damn well trench is off limits!'

'I was taken in there,' I said.

'That was with my permission and under supervision. I'm damn sure Sergeant Vernon didn't let you drop something down there!'

'I didn't try.'

Smales said, 'Okay.' He crossed to a wall mike, switched it on and began to speak. We could hear his voice over the Tannoy: 'This is the Commander. I'm sorry to say we need a volunteer again, to go down the well. Any man who's willing, go to Main Street, to the entrance to the well trench, five minutes from now.'

Kelleher said, 'One day you're not gonna have a volunteer, Barney. It's a lot to ask and it's getting worse. Then what'll you do? Order some guy down.'

'No, I won't,' Smales said. 'I'll order no man down that hole. If it happens, I'll go myself.'

Four men stood waiting at the trench entrance, and Smales gave them a little nod of appreciation. I knew two of them, Sergeant Reilly from the tractor shed and Sergeant Vernon. The other two I'd not seen before. They were both privates, one only about eighteen. Smales looked from one man to the other. 'How d'you want to do it? Do I pick somebody, or do we draw straws?'

Reilly said, 'Me, I'd like to see it, sir.'

'Me, too, sir,' the youngster said quickly.

Vernon said quietly, 'I've been down there twice, Major. I know the way.'

Smales turned to the boy. 'How old are you, Kovacs?'

'Eighteen, sir.'

'Get back to your work.'

'But, sir – ?'

'No reflection on you, son. But go back.'

The boy saluted and left, half-disappointed, half-relieved.

'You too, Jones,' Smales said. 'This is non-com or officer work.'

'Yes, sir.'

That left Reilly and Vernon, and Smales said, 'Reilly, how many men could take over from you in the motor shed?'

'One, sir. Maybe two.'

'Not enough. You're too fat, anyway. You wouldn't get through the holes. Looks like you're it, Vernon. Sorry.'

Vernon nodded, his facial muscles tight.

'You don't want to back out?'

'Only half of me, sir.'

Smales said, 'When you go, the army's going to miss you, Vernon. Okay, let's get going.'

Captain Herschel came hurrying in, apologizing for being late. He'd been in the bath.

Vernon tied his cap's earflaps under his chin, then lifted the bosun's chair down from the steel framework and strapped himself in. 'Ready, sir.' Herschel handed him a lamp and a water test pack.

'Right,' Smales said. 'Take it, Herschel.'

Captain Herschel moved a switch and the rope tightened, raising Vernon from the ground. He fended himself away from the corrugated steel barrier with his feet and then, when he was high enough, sat still in the swaying chair.

Smales and Herschel reached up to steady him, waiting until the chair stopped swinging. Then Herschel said, 'Real still now, Sergeant. You comfortable?'

'I'm okay, sir.'

The electric motor whined again and slowly the chair descended into the well-head, until only Vernon's head showed. 'At twenty feet we'll check the walkie-talkie,' Herschel said. 'Good luck.'

Vernon's head disappeared from sight and the steel cable paid out slowly from its reel. I noticed that it was marked at intervals of a yard, and began to count slowly to myself. The motor stopped again and Herschel spoke into a little radio handset, 'All okay?'

Vernon's voice came back. 'Lower away, sir,' and the cable

began to move again.

Smales stepped to the edge and looked over and Herschel said warningly, 'You'll watch that cable, Barney!'

'Like a snake.' It was obvious why. Vernon's safety depended upon the cable remaining vertical. If it began to swing, even a little, the swing would be wildly magnified down below, where Vernon would be at the end of the pendulum, and the giant icicles were less than three feet from him. 'He's doing okay,' Smales said. 'Keep going.' He beckoned me over, repeated the warning about the rope, then said, 'Look down there.'

Already Vernon was far down in the shining whiteness. I'd counted twenty-five yards of cable, seventy-five feet, just over half-way down the first chamber.

Smales said, 'Down below there's another hole just like it, and below that, another yet. In case you miss the point, that's kind of a brave man down there.'

Vernon's voice crackled up through the walkie-talkie. 'Christ, I want to cough!'

'Suppress it,' Herschel snapped. 'Keep it under till you're in the neck of Chamber Two, then steady yourself.'

'That's what – ' Vernon's voice paused, and I could imagine the straining muscles seeking to control the cough reflex.

'You okay?'

'Okay, sir.' Vernon was nearly at the neck.

'Want me to stop it?' Herschel asked.

'No, sir. I got it. I'm okay now.' A few seconds later he disappeared into the black neck of the second chamber. Faintly I could see the gleam of his hand lamp. I looked up, watching the cable unroll.

Herschel said, 'Two ten feet. What's it like down there?'

'They're bigger than ever, sir. Jesus! Must be sixty feet long, some of these things.'

'You clear of them?'

'In just a second . . . clear now, sir.' His sigh of relief came through.

I could see nothing now; nothing except that steel cable running ruler-straight into the dead centre of that hole in the ice a hundred and fifty feet below.

66

'Coming up to three hundred,' Herschel said.

'I'm near the neck.'

'Want a rest there, Vernon? How's the cough?'

'Okay now. Keep lowering.'

'Three ten, three fifteen. You should be through any time now.'

'I'm through, sir.'

'See anything?'

'No, not yet.'

Smales said, 'Tell him not to go down to water level if he can help it.'

Herschel passed the instruction and Vernon's voice crackled back. 'Sure won't. But there's nothing to see, except a couple of icicles must have crashed down here. There's big hunks of ice floating.'

'Nothing else?'

'Not a thing. It all looks clear, too. Equipment's okay, so the icicles can't have hit it. Can't see how they missed, though.'

'Three fifty,' Herschel said. 'I'm calling a halt.'

'Can't see nothing down here, sir.'

'That lamp powerful enough?'

'Lower me just a little more, sir. Twenty feet. No more than twenty-five.'

'Okay, It's your neck.'

I glanced at Barney Smales as he frowned into the depths, his jaw muscles standing out tautly. He said, 'Ask Vernon if he can see the bottom.'

The question was put.

'I'm looking over it now, sir. Slow scan with the lamp.'

We all waited, then Vernon's voice came again. 'Nothing in there. Water's clear and nothing shows.'

'Can you fill the bottle?'

'I'm trying, sir, right now. Damn thing won't go under. When I lower it, it floats. Hold on, I'll try again.'

The rope quivered as he moved, far below, in his seat, and Herschel said, 'You be careful there, Vernon.'

'Still floats, sir. Got to get lower, try and scoop it up from the seat. But lower slowly, sir.'

'I sure will.' Herschel switched on the motor again and allowed the rope to unwind a few inches at a time. 'How's it going?'

'Yard more, sir.'

The rope unrolled, then stopped.

'And again.'

Herschel controlled it with tremendous care. 'How's that?'

There was a grunt of strain from the handset. 'Maybe a foot more.'

'One foot. Okay?'

'Damn thing has too much . . . buoyancy,' Vernon said jerkily. 'Hold on, I'm trying – ' The taut line jerked suddenly and Herschel said, 'You okay?'

'Yup, okay, sir.' The strain was audible. Then Vernon said, 'Guess I'll have to get my feet wet.'

Smales snapped: 'No!'

'Commander says no, Vernon,' Herschel said. 'It's too risky. You'll freeze your feet. Try another time with the bottle.'

Again the rope quivered. Then Vernon reported. 'Got a few drops, I think. Yeah, just a little.'

Smales turned to Kelleher, who had stood grave and silent throughout. 'That enough?'

'Should be,' Kelleher said. 'Have to be, won't it?'

Smales nodded to Herschel.

'We're bringing you out of there, Vernon. Real still now!'

'No, sir. Let me try again.'

Smales shook his head.

'Commander says no. You got that?'

'Yes, sir.'

'Hold tight.' The motor whined and the line began to reel in over its spool.

Smales turned to me. 'Okay. Step back.' He remained where he was, leaning over, staring down into the depths of the hole. Kelleher came and stood beside me. He said, 'Coming up out of there's worse than going down. More tendency to swing the chair. I wouldn't be in that seat for a million. And all for a few drops of water!'

Vernon's voice came suddenly. 'Can you hold it, sir?'

'Something wrong?' Herschel demanded.

'Just cramped.'

'Where are you?'

'Under the neck of Chamber Three. Be okay in a second, sir.'

'Okay.'

Everybody waited. About a minute passed and the rope kept vibrating. Then Vernon said, 'Okay, sir.'

Herschel let the rope move again. It didn't stop this time until about two minutes later Vernon's head appeared suddenly over the top of the corrugated barrier. He was pale and obviously shaken and the precious bottle was clutched in his mittened hand. As Herschel stopped the motor, Kelleher stepped forward to take the bottle from him and hold it up to the light. There was about a quarter of an inch of water in the bottom.

Smales and I pulled the chair over, and as Vernon unstrapped himself, he said, 'Gee, I'm sorry, sir. I just couldn't make it sink. If I'd had something to force it down . . .'

Kelleher said, 'This'll just have to do it. You did a fine job there, Vernon.'

'You'll get a commendation from me,' Smales said. 'No use to you now, but you'll get it.'

Vernon thanked him, picked up his parka and put it on and Smales said, 'That's it. We're gonna have to sink another hole. Can't go on this way. How bad down there?'

Vernon turned to face him. He looked very drawn. 'It's kinda scary, sir. I have to say that.'

'I believe you. Thanks, Vernon. Go get drunk.'

Vernon managed a grin. 'I don't think so, sir.'

Smales said, 'It's an order, Sergeant.' Then he turned to me. 'What's the best Scotch we got in the officers' club?'

'Tomatin,' I said. 'Though it's a personal opinion.'

'Well, do me a favour, Bowes. Get a bottle of Tomatin and take it to Vernon's quarters. Then pour it down his goddam throat!'

I obeyed the first two instructions, but not the third. Vernon took the glass and sipped it, shuddered once, and said, 'If it's all the same to you, sir, what I'll do is sleep.'

It turned out that the water was pure.

I'd passed a lot of hours just waiting about, since my arrival at

69

Camp Hundred, and I was passing another, reading in the library hut, when Lieutenant Foster came in. It was an hour or so before dinner. He smiled and said, 'Hi!'

I said, 'How are you feeling?'

'Okay, I suppose.' He sat down and started turning the pages of *Newsweek*, but he wasn't reading. I said, 'Tell me about your cousin,' thinking it might help if he talked.

'I thought I told you. They were coming back from the – '

'No,' I said. 'I meant what sort of a man was he?'

'Charlie? Oh, he was okay.' Foster paused and fumbled for a packet of cigarettes. His hand shook a little as he lit one. 'Had kind of a bad patch, but he was over it, I guess. Making good. And then . . .'

'Would you like to tell me?'

'You some kind of a head doctor?'

'No.' I smiled. 'Don't if you don't want to. But *Newsweek*'s doing you no good. If you'd prefer a game of ping-pong or a drink at the club?'

'First one, then the other.'

'Right.'

We played for half an hour or so, neither of us particularly well, then put on our wrappings and went to the club. As we went inside, Barney Smales was taking the top off his Martini jug. Herschel was there too.

Smales poured four glasses, added olives to three and a silver onion to his own, and handed them round. He said, 'Well, at least these are pure. We'll drink to purity, gentlemen.' He was clearly angry but holding it back, overlaying it with an excessive bonhomie.

I said, 'The water?'

His eyes swivelled at me. 'The water,' he said, 'is contaminated in the reactor, contaminated in the pipes and clean in the well.'

'So it's somewhere in the pump,' I said, 'or the pipe between the bottom of the well and the top.'

'That's how I figure it, too.' His tone had an edge of sarcasm.

'And now you replace it?'

'That's right. Four hundred feet of neoprene pipe. Only we haven't *got* four hundred feet of neoprene pipe.'

Herschel said, 'Or any other kind.'

'Haul it up and wash it,' I said.

'With contaminated water?'

'Clean water,' I said. 'Melt some snow.'

Smales said, 'I thought of it. We could only trickle it through. Couldn't get a big enough pressure head. What it needs is steam-cleaning, but you can't shoot high-pressure steam through neoprene.' The heel of his hand was drumming on the bar top in frustration. 'I'd just like to know what the hell we got in that tube. This kind of thing, most places, it's a dead rat, or something like that. But we got no rats here. In any case, it's not blocked, water's getting through.'

They were still discussing it when I left them. The obvious answer, it seemed to me, was to start a new well and quickly, but there seemed to be an almost superstitious attachment to the old one. I'd actually heard Smales and Herschel agree on the need for a new well, but they seemed to avoid even mentioning it now, continuing to prowl round the problem of cleaning the pipes. Nor could I understand why Camp Hundred, lavishly equipped, should be short of a few hundred feet of piping, especially when several hundred men depended for their work, their comfort, and ultimately even for life itself, on a steady and large supply of fresh water. They were double and treble-banked on everything from generators to food. So why on earth was there only one water pipe? I decided to see if I could find some sort of answer, but knew it wouldn't be easy. One and all were getting a bit tired of my questions, however much they might *say* they weren't. But as it happened, I didn't get the chance to start asking until a good deal later, because not long afterwards a soldier knocked on my door, presented Major Smales's compliments, and the major would be glad if I could come to the command office right away. No, sir, he didn't know why.

But Smales wasted no time in telling me. He'd decided to send a Polecat on a hundred-mile dash to Camp Belvoir to pick up replacement neoprene and thought it might be a good idea if I went along.

I said, 'Why me?'

'Because you're out of your head with boredom, one; but the

other reason, the good reason, is that you'll get some sense of terrain and operating conditions.'

'All right,' I agreed. 'Leaving when?'

He said, 'Twenty minutes. Herschel, you and a driver.'

I must have shown my surprise. He grinned. 'Yes, at night, Mr Bowes. Wintertime we operate at night, because it's night all the damn day. You get a good run, you'll be there in four hours.'

I nodded. 'Just one Polecat?'

'That's right,' he said cheerfully. He was rather enjoying himself, I thought, as he went on, 'Swing's somewhere between Mile Thirty and Mile Forty, and coming this way. Anything goes wrong there's a safety wanigan every three miles along the Trail and you can wait out till the Swing gets there. It's safe enough. You'll be okay. Anyway, be a change for you. You get there, sleep, and come right back. Pyjamas if you use them, toothbrush, razor. That's all you need. Okay?'

I said, 'It's that urgent?'

'I want that reactor back on line,' Smales said. 'And I want it fast.'

At the door I paused and asked the question: why no spare pipe?

Smales laughed. 'I knew you were going to ask. And I'm not answering. Have a good trip.'

I went and slung a few items into an airline shoulder bag and went along to the tractor shed. The Polecat was there, warmed and waiting, and the driver sat inside. Herschel hadn't arrived yet, but Foster had. I said, 'You going too?' Smales had said only Herschel, the driver and me.

'Boss man thought the trip was a good idea,' he said. 'He's a good guy, the old Bear.'

Then Herschel arrived, and we all climbed aboard. Reilly swung over the lever that slid back the hangar-like doors of the tractor shed and the Polecat growled willingly as it was put into gear, and we went out into the snowblow.

Herschel and the driver sat on the front bench, with Foster and me on the seat behind. Herschel turned after a moment. 'It's a low phase two out there,' he explained for my benefit. 'Means winds around thirty-five to forty. Temperature's two below zero.

That combination gives a windchill factor of thirty-eight below, which ain't too bad if you think what's outside the window of any aircraft you ever flew in.'

'It sounds bad enough,' I said.

'Oh sure. A killer. Cold plus wind, it multiplies up.' He turned to face forward again and stared out through the windscreen, where orange flags on high bamboo poles whipped in the wind, one every five yards, the bright colour almost glowing in the Polecat's powerful headlamps. Then, to the driver, he said, 'What we'll do, we'll blast this thing along until we reach the Swing, two hours down the trail. We'll stop there and they can give us chow. After that, we go like smoke for Belvoir.'

A thought struck me. 'What happens if there's a white-out?'

Herschel turned. 'Well, let's see. First we pray we don't hit one. If we do, we hope it's right near a safety wanigan and we can see enough to find it. If it's real bad, we sit tight and wait till it goes away. Though *that* can take a little time.'

'Long enough to die, by any chance?'

'Could be,' Herschel said. 'But it's heavy odds against. White-out's a still air phenomenon and we've strong winds.' He was filling his pipe, stuffing tobacco into the bowl with his thumb, and he glanced across at the driver cheerfully. 'What worries me is this guy, who holds all our lives in his sweaty hands, eh, Scotty?'

'Yes, *sir*,' Scott said with relish.

'You seen any of those icecap mirages lately, Scott?'

'Tuesday, sir, I saw these two French broads. Monday I saw Verrazano Narrows bridge.'

Herschel said, 'Tell you what. Any broads you find on this trail, you can keep. That's a promise. Did you ever get confused?'

'Not yet, sir.'

'By God, but I did,' Herschel said. 'First tour up here, I got snowblinded by the damn moonlight. Wearing dark glasses, too. I got half a mile off the Trail. God knows which crevasse I'd have been in if another guy hadn't seen it and come after me.' He turned and looked at me. 'You'll be interested. When you're driving that air cushion vehicle of yours, you're gonna have to find out if you're susceptible. There's two separate phenomena.

73

If you get snowblinded, sun *or* moon, doesn't matter which of the two does it, but if you get snowblinded, you swing off on a left-hand curve. Nobody can work out why.'

'Always to the left?'

'Always,' he said firmly. 'The other thing is icecap mirages. What happens is you start to see poles that ain't there. Lines of them, with flags on top. They always, and I mean *always*, lead off the other way. To the right. Driver heads straight off the Trail.'

The thought sent a little shudder down my back.

'Funny thing, though,' Herschel went no. 'First one, when you're snowblind, it happens to anyone, whether he's been here days or months. Even the Swing drivers, and they spend six months going backwards and forwards between Belvoir and Hundred; even these guys do the left-hand shuffle. But the other, the mirage, that one wears off when you have been driving a while. Milt Garrison, the Swing commander, reckons one full trip and the danger's over. What he does, he's got a new driver, he keeps him in the middle, between two other tractors with experienced guys.'

'And nobody knows why?'

'Nope.' He puffed contentedly on his pipe.

I glanced over the driver's shoulder at the speed. The Polecat was sliding easily over the snow at close to thirty miles an hour. It occurred to me that if I suddenly discovered I was snowblind or suffering mirages, my speed in the TK4 could easily be double that. I tapped Scott on the shoulder. 'Do me a favour?'

'If I can, sir.'

'Ride with me in the TK4. Keep me on the straight and narrow. And don't see any French girls.'

He laughed. 'Sure thing, sir!'

We must have done about twenty miles when Herschel opened his bag and brought out a big flask. 'Who wants coffee?'

Everybody wanted coffee. The highly-efficient heater in the speeding Polecat dried the mouth. Herschel half-filled cups, one at a time. He also had a bottle of scotch, and slopped a little into three of the cups. 'No scotch for you, son.'

Scott said, 'Considering my name, I reckon that's injustice.'

Herschel grinned. 'It's a hard world. That true, Mr Bowes?'

'Harry,' I said.

'Okay, Harry.'

'It's true.'

We found out how true just after the fiftieth of the mile markers – steel drums painted ice-orange and placed on raised snowbanks beside the trail – had gone by. Suddenly, and without warning, the engine began to run raggedly and then stopped, and the Polecat, still in gear, ground to a halt.

Chapter 7

Scott, the driver, had tried the starter a dozen times. Each time the engine spun over, but it never fired, never gave a single cough, and already the wind outside was sucking away the interior warmth; in just a minute or two the temperature had dropped noticeably. Suddenly Herschel said angrily: 'Fuel. Damn tank's empty!'

Sure enough the fuel tank gauge needle was pointing right over to the left.

'You check that, Scott?' Herschel was no longer the jolly officer, nor Scott the privileged private. Rank had surfaced.

'When we got aboard, sir. Tank showed full then, sir.'

'You sure?'

'Sir, that needle was right on full.'

'Who filled her up? You?'

'No, sir. She was all done. Sergeant Reilly's boys gassed her up.'

'Sergeant Reilly's boys are gonna shovel snow till their asses drop off,' Herschel said grimly. 'Where are we? Mile Fifty?'

'Close to Fifty, sir.'

'Let's move.' Herschel turned. 'There's a wanigan at Forty-Eight, another at Fifty-One. Which way's the wind?'

Scott switched on the dashboard display. 'South of East, sir. Thirty-eight mph.'

'We'll go forward to Forty-Eight. It's a longer walk, but the wind's at our backs.' Herschel turned. 'You guys wearing the whole outfit?'

Foster said, 'Yes, sir.'

'And you?'

'Yes,' I said.

'We'll check that out before we leave the 'cat. Answer me, item by item.' He ran through the list: snow boots, socks, long johns, woollen trousers, windproof trousers, vests, shirts, woollen jackets, parkas, hats, hoods, silk-lined gloves, over-mittens. As he spoke each word, he checked his own clothing, too.

'Okay, let's get the hell out. This damn Polecat's turning into a deep freeze. When we get out, we stay close to the marker poles and we walk two together. I'll walk ahead with Scott, you and Foster side by side behind us, right?'

We nodded and he said: 'One more thing. Pull the drawstrings of the parka hood tight.' I pulled. 'No, tighter than that. So tight it comes nearly to a point. You only need a one-inch aperture there, so you can see through it. Main thing is it keeps the warmth of your respiration right in there with your face.'

I pulled the strings, gradually drawing the hood closer. The other three, more practised, had already finished and sat encased, with a khaki-green cone pointing forward where their faces should have been.

Herschel's voice, when he spoke again, was muffled. 'No halts except for injury. I'll pull the stretcher. Out you go.'

The door opened, the wind howled in, and we clambered down into the freezing darkness and stood for a moment while Herschel and Scott pulled the steel sled-stretcher from the clips on the Polecat's side. When that was done, Scott switched off the lights and slammed the door. Now the other three were no more than dark shapes against the snow.

We set off, the dry snow loose underfoot, and walking was awkward. There was some compression, but the snow didn't bind and it was more like walking on sand. Through the inch aperture, I kept my eyes on the sled as Herschel dragged it along behind him, at once a sensible precaution and a grim warning. Every ten paces or so, Foster tapped me on the shoulder. The first time it happened, I turned towards him enquiringly, but he was continuing to walk, facing forward, his head not turned my way. I understood then. This was a way of maintaining contact with visibility sharply reduced, yet another of the endless list of careful precautions observed by the men who lived and worked high on the Greenland icecap. So it was ten paces, tap, ten paces, tap. And two miles to go, thirty inches to the pace, how many paces? How many taps? I did the mental arithmetic for the sake of something to do. Something over four thousand paces; something over four hundred taps. One, two, three, four . . . eight, nine, tap. One, two, three . . .

In front of us Herschel and Scott marched determinedly on. Nearly thirty years difference in age separated them, but Herschel was the stronger, moving easily, even with the stretcher trailing behind. Occasionally Scott had to hurry to regain his place beside him. Around us the wind snapped, whipping at sleeves and trousers, but also pushing us along. Two miles with the wind was going to be far easier than one against.

We'd gone some distance, more than three-quarters of a mile, I guessed, when I began to feel the cold. The exertion helped, no doubt, our bodies generating warmth that the high insulation properties of several layers of the special Arctic clothing kept in. It was my feet that felt it first. Ten minutes ago, perhaps a little longer, I'd been sitting warm in the speeding Polecat, thinking how snug I was. I now realized the word should have been smug. My feet had been warm. Good and warm. Very warm. *Sweating*! Which could mean damp in the boots! I began to feel slightly panicky. A night or two ago, I'd seen the ravages of frostbite gruesomely recreated in *Scott of the Antarctic*. I remembered, too, reading about Maurice Herzog, the French climber who dropped his gloves near the summit of Annapurna and watched them fall away down the mountain and knew in that moment, with total certainty, that he would lose all his fingers. Which he did . . . seven, eight, nine, tap; what about the others? Their feet must have been sweating in the Polecat, too. Were *they* also feeling the cold? My heels no longer seemed to feel much as they came down, and I began to try to stamp harder, but it wasn't like walking on a hard surface; the snow absorbed the impact and still I felt nothing; it was merely increasing the strain on my thigh muscles, so I stopped.

Ahead of me, Scott stumbled and fell, but scrambled up quickly and ran a few steps to catch up with Herschel again. I told myself fiercely not to be stupid. Twenty-five to thirty minutes of hard walking in proper clothing, with the blood circulating briskly, was hardly likely to end in frostbite. I was being neurotic. All the same, the feeling seemed to be going out of my heels. And what was worse, I seemed to be having difficulty keeping up. Herschel and Scott were a bit further ahead, weren't they? Tap, ten paces, tap. Was it just my heels, where the wind was striking? Or were my toes losing sensation, too? I tried to wiggle my toes. They seemed all right. But my legs were beginning to ache from the effort of walking on the sand-like surface. I wished it *were* sand, and that I was walking along a beach in warm sunshine! Herschel and Scott *were* drawing ahead! Tap, tap, on my shoulder. I turned my head to look at Foster and he waved his arm, signalling me to go faster.

We came to the wanigan quite suddenly. I doubt if I'd have seen it, but Scott and Herschel must have been able to judge the distance, or else the marker barrels gave them information, because they suddenly turned to the right, and as I followed, the flat orange rectangle of the safety wanigan loomed out of the dark. Drifted snow lay against it to a height of about eight feet, so that only the top couple of feet was visible. Herschel went quickly over to it and dug with his hands in the snow until he unearthed a shovel. Rank counted. He handed the shovel and the hard work to Scott, who obediently began to shift snow. It took only a couple of minutes, but enough for a chill feeling to begin, before most of the wanigan door showed, and we went in, slamming it behind us, and shutting out the noise. Inside, it was startlingly still and quiet. And Herschel said, 'My goddam feet must have been sweating in the Polecat! Soon as we get some light around here, we'll have a nice, stinking, feet-rubbing fiesta.'

And we did. The air was full of the smell of feet as we sat on the floor in pairs, with the stove going warmly, rubbing. The same thing had happened to all four of us: there were eight pale heels, each of which began to tingle, then to burn as circulation crept back. There was no damage, nothing permanent, but like Smales's pork chop, it was another demonstration of power and vulnerability. It was also, I thought grimly, further proof of what Smales had said about minds working at only fifty per cent efficiency. Every man in the Polecat, all four of us, had known all about boot hazards, but the heater had been turned high and we'd revelled in it!

But now it was back to comfort. The safety wanigan was, to all intents and purposes, a large and well-fitted caravan and contained everything necessary to sustain the lives of four people for four weeks, including a wall-rack full of big bottles of liquefied gas. With the stove burning, I got a quick guided tour. As it happened, the wanigan we were in was a new type, recently off the experimental list, and of a novel construction. Its walls were made of expanded polystyrene foam, sandwiched between layers of glass fibre. Foster was engaged on this very project, seeking better designs, but the principles of the thing were breathtaking. The glass fibre/polystyrene walls had tremendous thermal insulation properties, and a single kilowatt of heat was enough to maintain a temperature in the seventies, even if the hut were empty. With four men inside, heat was scarcely needed at all.

Foster said, 'See the implications?'

I shook my head. 'I see the value up here, yes.'

'Bigger than that,' he said. 'This thing's constructed of uniform panels. Floor, walls, roof, all uniform. They just bolt together. More panels, you make bigger huts, okay. But there's something you maybe haven't thought about. Polystrene beads are small. Not when they're expanded, but for transit. Glass fibre's light and can be compressed. And a little resin goes a hell of a long way. Now: you fill a big plane with barrels of beads and resin and bales of fibre. You put in the moulds and the styrene blower – that's the machine that expands the beads – and you can make these panels anywhere. What'll shake you is how many.'

'Go on.'

'We can get enough materials in one Galaxy freighter right now,' Foster said, 'to build a camp for three thousand men.'

'Three *thousand*?'

'Right on. What's that? Big village or a small town. Tell you who's interested, the United Nations, that's who. Think of the potential of this in a disaster area, floods, typhoons, earthquakes. One plane comes in and they start fabricating panels and in a few days you got three thousand people housed!'

I nodded, fascinated.

'And well housed.' Foster, talking about this project, was a changed man, full of enthusiasm. 'You go outside and kick the wall, the sound can't hardly be heard inside. Twenty people in a thirty-two-foot hut, sleeping ten each side, and you need no heating at all, even up here.'

Herschel interrupted good-humouredly, 'You gonna place your order now, sucker, or hold out till this hustler's taken you to a nightclub?'

'I think I'd buy,' I said.

He nodded. 'Me, too. I'm gonna try to build a house of this stuff home in Maryland if the regulations'll let me. Be cheaper than bricks and lumber. But before we build the house – ' He went to a radio set in the corner, switched on and called Camp Hundred. There was a lot of crackling static, but they answered. 'Wanigan Fifteen to Hundred. Polecat inoperative, repeat Polecat inoperative. We are sheltering Wanigan Fifteen. Inform Commander.'

'Roger Wanigan Fifteen. Stand by.'

Smales came on a couple of minutes later. There was no jargon from him. He said, 'Herschel, it's Barney. What in hell went wrong?'

'We ran out of gas.'

'Out of – Jesus Christ!'

Herschel said, 'We'll wait for the Swing, Barney. Ride on up with Milt Garrison.'

'Yeah, but he's got no neoprene on board. This Swing's all food and fuel and we're in a little trouble here.'

I felt myself stiffen.

Herschel asked, 'What trouble?'

'We lost another generator.'

It was an hour before I thought of it – that fifty-per-cent mind, I suppose. But it ought to have hit me earlier; it ought to have hit a three-year-old. I said to Herschel, 'Can you contact the Swing?'

'Sure. Be doing that real soon. Swing can't be more than ten miles off. We'll have to tell them we're here. They won't see the Polecat until they're two miles on. Remember, we walked here.'

'Look,' I said, 'we still have one way of getting to Camp Belvoir.'

He shook his head. 'Swing can't spare – ' He stopped then, looking at me, then grinning. 'That ACV of yours is on the Swing, right?' But the grin faded almost as soon as it had appeared. 'No,' he said, 'can't risk that. It's not proven up here. Once the Swing's gone by you've fifty miles in the open.'

I said, 'She can do it. And unless we use the TK4, there's no way of getting the pipe up to Hundred. How long before the Swing reaches us?'

He gave a little shrug of annoyance. 'Can't calculate it. They're ten, maybe twelve miles away. Best speed is three miles an hour – just like the old time Conestoga wagons on the plains heading West.'

'Progress,' I said.

'Sure. But they don't hold a speed like that. Every three miles the bulldozers uncouple to pull these safety wanigans out on top of the snow, so they don't get buried. Takes a few minutes every time. Then they got to couple up again. They stop to change drivers. Maybe they run across a new crevasse. Five to six hours if we're lucky. Could be twelve or fourteen if they have a rough stretch. Could be days if it's real bad.'

'For ten or twelve miles?'

'I told you once before, Harry. There's been times it's taken six whole weeks to get a Swing up here.'

It would be quicker, I thought, for Smales to send another Polecat from Hundred. Or, for that matter, for Cohen to send one from Camp Belvoir.

Herschel said, 'No dice. No Polecats at Belvoir, only Weasels, and this time of year they're too small.'

'All right,' I said. 'But isn't there a spare tractor with the Swing?'

He nodded. 'Two loose bulldozers for crevasse filling. And they take over in a tractor breakdown, too.'

'Couldn't one of them bring the wanigan with the TK4 on it? Detach that one wanigan from the train? What speed could it make?'

He said, 'Five, maybe six miles an hour.'

'Here in two hours,' I said. 'Two more after that and we'd be at Belvoir. Turn and come back and we'd probably have made the whole trip before the Swing even reaches this point.'

'You're good and confident,' he said.

'I've reason to be. I know the machine.'

'But not the icecap.'

I said, 'You know it. Scott knows it. Foster, too. You can each hold my hand in turn.'

He gave a sudden nod, rose, went to the radio and switched frequencies. 'Safety Wanigan Fifteen to Swing.' He repeated it and waited.

'Swing to Wanigan Fifteen. Who's holed up?'

'Holed up is right,' he said. 'Major Herschel here. Get me Warrant Officer Garrison on the double.'

There was a pause, then a new voice came over the transceiver. 'Garrison, Major. Sorry you're all holed up there. Be right with you by morning.'

Herschel said, 'I want better than that, Milt. Your traction fully operational? Or have any units gone down?'

'We're okay.'

'Then you can spare a 'dozer?'

'Spare – hey, what for?' Garrison's voice had hardened.

Quite distinctly we all heard another voice, presumably the radio operator's, say, 'Is that guy nuts!'

Herschel chuckled. 'Tell him no, just a major.'

Garrison laughed, too. 'Got a real white-faced boy here, Major. Will you explain, please?'

Herschel said, 'The hovercraft wanigan. I want the 'dozer to haul it up here fast. Then we can head right on to Belvoir.'

Garrison said, 'She's only on trials, Major. And not ours. You know how to pilot that thing?'

'No, but I got the driver right here.'

'Well, okay. I'll fix it.'

'How long d'you reckon, Milt?'

'We're near on Mile Forty, but we been hitting a crevasse or two. I'll have the guys move it, that's a promise.'

Herschel thanked him and switched off.

'What about Major Smales?' I said.

Herschel's eyes crinkled. 'He ain't here.'

'Meaning?'

'Meaning he'd say no. Barney's a belt-and-suspenders man. Wouldn't go for this kind of a half-ass game. Barney doesn't trust that machine of yours anyway. He told me. What he likes is lots of steel and lots of diesel power and lots of back-up, and lots of precautions. He's right, too. So was Chance, Luke Chance, commander before him. That's why Hundred's got the safety record it has.'

'Had,' I said.

He looked at me. 'Stay off it, huh?'

'Apart from one thing.' I nodded. 'But there's something I'd like to know.'

'Go on.'

I said, 'If Barney Smales is as logistics-conscious as you say, if he's that cautious, if he insists on triple-banking even lavatory seats, then why the hell isn't there a spare pipe?'

Herschel's brows came down. 'That's classified.'

'Neoprene? Don't be – '

'Not neoprene. The information.' But I could see now that those frowning brows were having trouble staying down. They kept twitching and revealing a glint in Herschel's blue eyes.

I said, 'Come on. Let's have it.'

He was really laughing now, shoulders shaking. He said, 'Barney forgot. He forgot the requisition.'

I grinned back at him; at least there was one mystery that was no mystery.

He said, 'Can you cat-nap?'

'Sometimes.'

'Try it now. You got two hours.'

I doubted whether I could sleep, in that warm, almost un-ventilated, over-insulated wanigan, redolent with the twin smells of heat and feet. But I did, until the sudden blast of cold air from outside broke through with the news of the arrival of the tractor. I rose blearily and began to dress.

The bulldozer driver had a problem. He'd been thinking about it for two hours and he thought we all had a problem. He said, 'Sir, we got no crane. How we gonna lift that thing off the flat-bed?'

Herschel looked at me. 'Has he got something?'

'No,' I said. 'She'll be all right. But I want to check it. Wait here till I come back.'

'I'm coming,' Herschel said. 'You don't go out alone.'

So we went to have a look. There were no great problems,

certainly none that couldn't be solved with a few scrapes of the bulldozer blade. We went back inside and I told the driver exactly what I wanted. 'You can push snow towards the side and front of the wanigan?'

He nodded. 'Sure.'

'Okay. I want a ramp made. Not too steep, in fact as flat as you can get it. She can ride over a three-foot vertical obstruction when she's riding the cushion, but I don't want to chance anything when we're moving off from stationary. Got it?'

He nodded. 'Got it, sir. Only take a minute.'

While he was manœuvring the bulldozer and pushing snow towards the wanigan, I was busy with the chain-strapping that held the TK4 down, fumbling at the metal awkwardly in my heavy felt mitts. It was no use. I couldn't shift the fastenings. The ramp was completed in a few minutes, but the hovercraft remained firmly tied to the flatbed's deck-boarding. The 'dozer driver left his cab, came over and shouted into my hood, 'She frozen down?'

I bellowed back: 'Just the strappings.'

'I got bolt cutters.'

'Thanks.'

He brought them over and I simply sheared through the chains, then kicked them away and climbed up into TK4's cabin. The turbines had been specially adapted, with heaters built in for cold weather starting. I let them warm for a minute, then tried the engines. Vroom, vroom, and a nice, healthy blast of power first time. Pity, I thought, that Barney Smales hadn't been there to see it! By the light of the bulldozer's powerful headlights, I could see the other four standing on the trail, watching. I wound up the feet cautiously. Okay so far. She was riding on the cushion. Suddenly she began to slide back under wind pressure. I corrected, eased her forward on to the ramp and floated downhill to the trail, then turned her round, opened the door, waved an arm, and Herschel, Foster and Scott climbed up too. The bulldozer driver waved and walked off towards the safety wanigan.

Herschel said, 'He'll wait there till the Swing comes up.'

'He's left the engine running,' I pointed out.

'Yep. Safer that way.' I asked him about the crevasses. 'They filled three on the way up here. Two were on the trail up to the cap out of Belvoir, but the other was around Mile Twenty-Eight. Big one. Twenty feet wide and maybe a hundred deep. What's this thing do if we hit one like that?'

'Will there be a snow-bridge?'

Herschel said, 'Sometimes. You reckon you can get over a snow-bridge?'

'Moving fast, the pressure per square inch is very low,' I said. 'Remember there's no contact. If the crevasse is big and open, we'll probably have to go round. Narrow ones we could float over.' I grinned at him. 'Don't get worried.'

I gave her a touch more power and let her slide forward, the lights knifing into the empty darkness ahead. The wind was astern at nearly thirty knots, which wouldn't make for easy steering, but I was confident in the TK4.

Scott, sitting beside me, said, 'What can she do?'

'Anything but crossword puzzles,' I said. 'If you mean speed, she can go up to about fifty miles an hour, depending on the skirt clearance from the ground. Use the power to lift and you don't have as much left to push.'

He said, '*Fifty?*'

'Fifty.' But I kept her to just over forty, enough so I didn't have to worry too much about wind speed.

At the start, snow began building up on the windscreen, and I employed one of the little refinements Thomson-Keegan had built into her – a two-foot wide jet of air, blasting up the outside surface of the glass, that diverted the snow before it even landed. In case of trouble with that, there was also a 12-inch Kent Clear-vue rotating panel in the glass, and it could be heated, too.

After the Canadian tests, we'd incorporated those two skis forward, to give additional steering control in narrow manœuvring spaces, but I had no need of them now and kept them retracted. The Trail to Belvoir was a good hundred yards wide, and ran almost dead straight across the immense snowfield.

After about twelve minutes a battery of lights became visible and I got my first glimpse of the Swing coming close. I slowed and stopped. It was immense. Imagine three goods trains running side by side; that's what it was like, the only difference being that instead of engines, each train was pulled by a tractor, and the goods wagons had sled runners instead of wheels.

We didn't get out. Instead, we switched the radio to the Swing frequency and talked briefly to Garrison, saying little more than hello and goodbye.

After that we were alone in the dark again, skating fast over the Trail. Scott, in the seat beside me, kept watch ahead with a curious, almost unblinking stare, as the marker poles came one after the other out of the night, to flicker their little orange flags at us, then vanish behind. Once I asked Scott, 'Are those flags real?'

'They're real.'

'If you catch me circling right, stop me.'

He laughed. 'If I see those French broads again, *then* I'll stop you.'

Herschel told me about the Swing and its awesome statistics. It had now been running, more or less day and night, for about five years. The crews lived aboard for six months at a time, driving six hours on, six hours off. The huge Caterpillar low-ground-pressure diesel tractors could go ninety hours without refuelling and each of them hauled a weight of up to 160 tons.

I said, 'The crews must go slowly mad.'

'Nope. They like it. You know, they got a project on, those guys. Milt Garrison's behind it, but he ain't gonna get it. What he wants to do is take the whole Swing from Thule over to Nome, Alaska.'

'Over the *ocean*?'

'Sure. In winter when it's frozen.'

I said, 'But it's three thousand miles. At least that.'

'Nearly four,' Herschel said cheerfully. 'They could do it, too. But there's a whole bundle of opinion down at Corps of Engineers headquarters, says the US taxpayer won't like it. And he sure won't. But wouldn't that be something!'

'I said, 'You're one of the ones who like the Arctic.'

'That's right. Scott too, eh Scott?'

Scott said, 'Sure thing.'

'What about you, Foster?' I said.

He didn't reply for a moment. Then he said, 'I like the work. I like the projects. But it's all too damned angry.'

We had no crevasse trouble at all. The TK4 gave a beautiful performance demonstration, and about an hour and a half after leaving the safety wanigan, even allowing for reduced speed on the gradient down the side of the icecap to the flat coastal strip, we came easily into Camp Belvoir and I ran the hovercraft into its hangar, and turned smugly to Herschel. 'Okay?'

He said, 'Just one thing missing. No stewardess. No scotch.'

I said, 'Nothing's impossible.'

The TK4 had made that fifty-mile trip over the icecap, in high winds and a murderously low temperature, with no more fuss than if it had been skating along a motorway.

We all went off to have some food, and after it Herschel went off to see Cohen and to organize the loading of the neoprene piping and perhaps, if he was anything like Barney Smales, to do a little gentle pilfering, too. Scott was playing pool with one of his friends and Foster and I were nursing another cup of hot coffee and waiting for the off.

The last few hours had made a change in him, and I said so. He said, with a rueful smile, 'Just got on top of me at Hundred, I guess. I keep thinking about when I get back and have to explain what happened to Charlie. To the folks, you know. They're going to want to know why I didn't stop it.'

I said, 'You feel that, too, don't you?'

He shrugged. 'I guess so. Just a little.'

'Well, you were his cousin, not his keeper. That needs to be understood.'

Foster said, 'I was always his keeper. That's part of it.'

'Did he need one?'

'Charlie?' Foster sighed. 'Yeah, I suppose he did. He's . . . he was one of those kids who could get in a mess fast. Always.'

'I know the kind.'

'Yeah. Charlie was like that. Funny thing is, though, I thought he'd just got himself straight. Really straight. Permanently.'

'How?'

He looked at me for a moment, hesitating, then told me. He must have thought that talking to a total stranger he was never likely to see again, would do no harm.

'Well,' Foster said, 'when he was maybe sixteen he hit the drug scene. Before that all kinds of trouble. You could've predicted it. You could have said, give Charlie the chance and he'll go on drugs. And he did. Soft stuff. Hash. Then the pills. Didn't even keep it secret. The whole family knew and worried a lot. If he'd been a bad kid – oh, I don't know. But he wasn't. There was this about Charlie, everybody liked him. They liked him, but they couldn't do anything about it. He was going to hell in a bucket. Heroin next stop, because that's the kind of kid he was. And then . . .'

I waited.

'Well, then one of those things happened. We had an old aunt, great-aunt, really. Lived in North Carolina, only one in the whole pack of us with any money. And when she died, we found out what she'd done in her will. What she did, she left Charlie three hundred thousand dollars.'

I whistled. 'Which he frittered away?'

He smiled. 'No, sir. Great Aunt Eleanor had it all worked out. After she died, Charlie had two weeks to join the army. If he didn't, no dough. Well, he joined the army. I was in the Corps of Engineers, so that's what Charlie joined. And she really screwed the lid down. Charlie had to get through a three-year enlistment. And when he came out, his discharge papers had to have the magic word on them: Exemplary.'

'She sounds,' I said, 'like an ingenious old lady.'

'She was all of that. The way she worked it out, if he was going down, he'd go slower in the army. If not, if he could keep his sights on that three-year target and not fall off, it could maybe straighten him out.'

'And it did, that's what you're saying?'

He said, 'Yeah. I guess so. Charlie was a whole lot different. He was even a good soldier. The army suited him. He was doing his third tour up here, and the old Charlie'd never have made it.'

'How long,' I asked, 'before he was due to get the money?'

Foster said, 'He'd made it. Five days before . . .' and left the sentence unfinished.

Chapter 8

We were supposed to leave immediately, but the Arctic had done its unpredictable worst. In the area of Siberia that's sometimes called the Weather Kitchen, a pinch of something fizzy had been added to the brew and conditions in Northern Greenland had deteriorated savagely. Even at Belvoir, at the foot of the icecap, winds were somewhere over sixty, gusting up to ninety miles an hour. On the cap a full-blown Arctic hurricane was raging, accompanied by temperatures dropped to sixty below. There was no question of setting off back; it wasn't even sensible to leave the hut, for the accommodation at Belvoir stands out in the open. Grimly we settled down to drink more coffee and talk the night away, but we were all too tired. Finally, we fought our way along hand-lines in a raging blizzard and screaming icy wind across twenty yards of deep snow to a dormitory hut and went to sleep. Twenty yards doesn't sound much, but I got an idea of how Charlie Foster had died.

When we woke next morning the weather was, if anything, worse, but we stumbled back to the mess hall to eat and do our waiting in a little more comfort than we'd have done in the dormitory. And we learned that, remarkably, radio contact with Camp Hundred was good. However, the news wasn't. The diesel generator that had broken down was severely damaged, it seemed, and one of the others was running rough. With the reactor still out of action, Camp Hundred's power resources were dangerously stretched. Accordingly the big decision had been made and a new well was being opened up. Herschel had a long radio talk with Smales about it and learned that a length of the neoprene from the old well was to be used, cleaned out as well as possible. The snag was that to get below the level of snow which had fallen since the first atom bomb went off in 1945, they'd have to cut through seventy feet. Above that, radiation contaminated the snow layers.

I asked Herschel how the pipe was to be cleaned. 'They're only using a hundred and ten feet,' he said. 'They're gonna thread a line down the pipe, then pull clean cloth through like cleaning a rifle barrel, then wash it out with water melted from snow.

'In weather like that?' I said.

'They'll cut snow blocks from the walls with chain saws and melt the blocks,' he said. 'That part shouldn't be bad. Take a while to sink the well, though, and pump the water away.' He was frowning.

I said, 'It's serious now, isn't it?'

He thought about it. 'Too near the margins. A whole lot too near. There's a generator out and another running rough. That leaves one serviceable generator and the whole place running off it. Anything happens to that . . .'

Foster said, 'Reckon it'd close the Camp, sir?'

'It might,' Herschel said. 'And it'd be mighty uncomfortable in there. They're protected from winds, right enough. But the water system would go out fast without heating. The research programme would be finished for the winter. Unless they can get that reactor going real soon. Somebody's going to be making a big decision. There's three hundred guys up there. Oh, sure, they got fuel and food. They can sit all day round carry-stoves melting snow, they won't die exactly, but there won't be much left of the Camp Hundred operation.'

All our conversations over the next thirty-six hours, while the storm raged on, remained on the same gloomy level, becoming less frequent and more desultory as time went on. Reports from Camp Hundred, when they came in, were not particularly re-assuring. The well was being sunk, but the needs of the Camp itself made the heat requirements of the pressure steam hose just one of many competing factors. If they switched off everything and concentrated on cutting the well, there wouldn't be enough heat to keep the water pipes from freezing. The steam, therefore, was being used in short bursts, and the progress on the new well was slow. There was a good deal of talk between Cohen and Herschel about the possibility of having a couple of small stand-by generators flown up from Thule Air Base and parachuted down to Camp Hundred, but it was just talk; the idea wasn't practical. In that hellish blizzard on the icecap, the aircraft's crew would never see Hundred, let alone hit it. And if by some miracle they did drop the generators somewhere near, it was unlikely that the people at Hundred would be able to see the drop, or recover them. They'd only be able to go out in tractors; visibility, minimal anyway, would be nil through glass; in any case, the blizzard would cover the machinery in snow in a few minutes.

I asked whether the tractor engines couldn't be harnessed for power generation, but the answer was no. 'They're pulling machines,' Herschel said. 'With the standard Caterpillar you can draw off power, but not these.' He forced a wry grin. 'We eliminated all that. We're so smart. We got a reactor!'

There was some talk, too, about flying an aircraft in when the weather dropped a little, but it was wild talk. All the weather prognostications were bad, though the lethal severity of the storm might ease a little in a few hours. There was a possibility that the winds on the cap might actually drop low enough to be on the Beaufort Scale within twenty-four hours but no possibility at all of flying weather. I learned that flying up to the cap has, in any case, its own particular additional dangers. A standard compass is all but useless, because when you're in Northern Greenland, magnetic North lies to the west and its influence on the needle is erratic. Then there's the little matter of altimeter readings, which are thoroughly inaccurate over deep snow, because the electronic impulses beamed at the ground penetrate the snow to indeterminate depths. In fact, it's pretty well impossible to judge altitude or distance with any accuracy. And on top of all that, sudden weather changes can blot out visibility entirely, or make sky and ground the same shade of grey or white, so that it's impossible to distinguish one from the other and there's no way to tell up from down.

'What it comes down to,' Cohen said wearily, 'is that flying's out, and I mean out, unless the pilot can see both the Trail and the horizon the whole damn way.'

'It also means,' Herschel said grimly, 'that the whole shebang could be finished for want of a two-thousand-pound payload.'

'Two thousand?' I said, as an idea struck me. From what I'd seen of those big generators up at Camp Hundred, they weighed a lot more than two thousand pounds.

Cohen nodded. 'Yeah. It's a smaller model, lower output, too – '

I said, 'That weight's okay in the TK4.'

They looked hard at me and I felt a little like a doorstep salesman. So I behaved like one and started on the facts and figures. 'Furthermore,' I added finally, 'forty-knot winds won't hold me back. Nor will snow.'

They looked at one another. Herschel said, 'Two and a half thousand total payload, right?'

'Yes. Two thousand for the generator. Two hundred more for me and all the heavy clothing. There's room,' I said, 'for just one more inside. Ting, ting.'

Cohen and Herschel looked at me in puzzlement. 'English joke,' I said. 'Not very good. But the TK4's not an English joke, and she's very good indeed.'

They weren't used to light, fast machinery up there. Herschel had told me that Barney Smales believed in masses of steel and lots of power and so, basically, did all of them, probably rightly. The principle of meeting powerful onslaughts with powerful resistance is obvious sense, and the theory that says if you put a flyweight in the ring with a heavyweight, he may run away successfully for a while, but sooner or later, he'll be flattened, is also correct, almost all the time. But I was confident in the TK4. The run down to Belvoir had been so efficient that I had very little doubt of her ability to cruise back again in the right conditions. All I needed was a weather slot, about three hours long, and finally we got it.

The decision to take the generator meant, of course, that other things must be left behind. Three, in fact: two human and one neoprene, and the final decision was not made by us, or by Cohen, but by Barney Smales on the radio from Hundred. The radio contact was a lot worse now. The signal quality seemed to bear no relation to weather conditions. During the worst of the storm, they'd come over sharp and clear, yet when the weather was easing, the contact was weak and loaded with mush. Still, it was enough for us to hear. At Hundred the short length of neoprene had been cleaned, more or less satisfactorily, and would suffice. But the diesel fitters, striving to cannibalize two unsatisfactory machines and assemble one good one, were having a very hard time. Barney wanted the generator. 'And George Herschel,' he said. 'Foster and Scott can wait at Belvoir.'

'Sorry,' I said. 'I'm bringing Scott.'

There was a pause. Then he said flatly, 'Bring Herschel, Mr Bowes. That's an order.'

'Which I'm disobeying,' I said. 'I want an experienced driver's eyes. I don't want to wander off the Trail. I'm bringing Scott or I'm not coming.'

He didn't like it. From that moment, I rather think he didn't like anything I did, but he was wrong and I, fortunately, wasn't in his army. Cohen and Herschel didn't like it very much, either, but they had the sense, and the grace, to accept my reasons. What they didn't like was my deliberate disobedience of direct orders.

Thule Air Base had done their best with the weather forecast. The weather observation aircraft patrolling the Eastern Greenland coast and the satellite weather survey both suggested there were a few hours ahead in which winds would slacken and the weight of snowfall lessen.

So off we went. The brief daylight was over, the night black and moonless, the wind getting stronger as TK4 made the long climb out of Belvoir, up to the edge of the icecap. I stuck the two front skis down to counter any awkward gusts, warmed up the motors, and we belted off into the brutal darkness. If I have sounded over-confident, even a little flip, about the TK4's performance to this point, it's not because I'm a wild optimist or full of blind faith; it's because the TK4 is a damn good machine, beautifully designed, well built and thoroughly tested and modified until she's as good as we can get her. In spite of all that, I faced the hundred-mile dash across the icecap in a very sober mood indeed. Having spent a lifetime working with machines, I know very well that mankind hasn't yet succeeded in building one that won't break down, whether it's an electric toothbrush or a Rolls-Royce car. A good watch is probably the most reliable thing there is, but for all the dustproof, waterproof casings, the jewelled movements, the technical refinement, every watch can stop, and sooner or later it does. So, sooner or later, would the TK4, but not, I prayed, within the next hundred miles, or on the icecap with me or anybody else aboard.

What happened was, I suppose, testimony to the power of prayer. We'd just passed the Mile Fifty marker, after about two hours on the Trail, when I found my vision disintegrating into a mass of little flickering lights, lightning-shaped, migraine-style. I told Scott about it and he made me stop and let the engines idle. When I'd done that, he had me lie back in my seat, head dangling over the seat back. 'Now,' he said, 'just close your eyes and concentrate on looking into your head. Try to see the inside of your skull.' I obeyed meekly. It didn't seem to be doing any good, though. Then I heard a lighter scrape beside me and smelt smoke, and a cigarette was placed between my lips. 'Smoke it,' Scott said. 'Don't let your eyes move till it's finished.'

So I smoked, and tried to imagine the inside of my head, and felt my eye muscles begin to ache. When I could feel the cigarette's heat on my fingers, Scott said, 'Okay. Now try opening your eyes.'

I did, and raised my head, and promptly felt dizzy. But when the dizziness cleared, after a couple of rather sickening minutes, my vision was clear, too.

'Thanks,' I said. 'Who thought that one up?'

'Folklore,' Scott said. 'Handed down driver to driver through the long, long generations. Sure works, though.'

'It sure does,' I said. And we were off again as soon as I'd retracted the TK4's feet. Five miles later we went past the Swing like a bee buzzing past a beetle, exchanging headlight greetings, but not stopping. The wind got up a bit more, and for the last twenty miles the TK4 took rather more holding straight. We veered a bit, but no more than we might driving on an exposed road in strong winds, and then the marker flags ceased to flow at us in a straight line, and guided us round the approach into Camp Hundred. The trip had taken three hours twenty minutes, including the stop for impromptu eye treatment, and I was feeling pleased with myself, the TK4 and the world in general.

But I was also tired after all the concentration, and not particularly anxious to meet Smales that night. As soon as the TK4 was safely parked in the traction shed, I left the unloading of the portable generator in Reilly's big and capable hands and went off

95

to bed where, despite the pall of weariness that hung over my mind, or perhaps because of it, I couldn't get to sleep and lay in the darkness, while the sheets gradually wrinkled themselves and imaginary corrugations developed in the mattress and I became progressively more uncomfortable. Finally, I switched on the light and lit a cigarette, and reached for the novel I'd started a few days earlier. I read for perhaps an hour, not taking in anything much, but forcing myself to keep going until, with my eyelids feeling like heavy steel shutters just waiting to clang down, I put out the last cigarette, stopped resisting gravity, let my eyes close and drifted off.

I must have been down very deep because, though I was coughing, it didn't waken me, at any rate not immediately. When I did click into consciousness I was really coughing hard, almost choking and feeling dizzy, and there was an acrid smell of fumes in the air. I reached for the light switch, turned it on, but there was no light. A glance at the luminous hands of my watch told me it was 3 a.m., but that luminosity was all I could see. Meanwhile there was fire somewhere, though I could see no flame, and since the hut was wooden, I'd better get out of it quick. I began to fumble round in the dark, between cough spasms, trying to find the clothes I'd thrown round when I went to bed, and found some, but not all; in particular, I couldn't find trousers, and the thought of going out into the icy tunnels without them, fire or no fire, smoke or no smoke, wasn't attractive. Then my hand struck my book of matches, knocking them, naturally, to the floor, where I had to get down on my hands and knees and feel across the shiny linoleum for them. If anything I was coughing even harder, gasping for breath and beginning to feel woozy, and I broke two of the three remaining matches before I got the third one lit. By its light I saw smoke hanging in the air, but I'd known that it was there and I wasted no time looking at it, and concentrated instead on finding my trousers, socks and boots. Then I dressed hurriedly and with increasing difficulty, not bothering overmuch with buttons, zips or snap fasteners, because my head felt light and seemed ready to float away from me and it was as much as I could do to dress at all. When I tried to walk I lurched and fell and was violently sick, gasping and retching as I lay on the floor. I knew I was close to passing out, and what was worse, I'd lost all sense of direction. There were four walls in the room and I didn't know which held the door. My arms and legs were like collapsing balloons, my head was hardly there at all, and where the willpower came from, I don't know, but somehow I forced myself up on to my knees, felt for the edge of the bed, got some idea of my bearings, and set off across a million miles of linoleum for the door. About half-way, I thought I was going to pass out in the middle of the floor and die, and I remember that I no longer even cared. But then my knee landed on something pointed, a nail head sticking up through the linoleum, and the sudden sharp pain refocused my senses long enough to get me to the door, to find the handle, to turn it . . .

The handle turned, but the door did not move. I remember the dim hopelessness of the moment, hearing a weird distorted voice mumble the word 'locked', then another racking cough spasm that doubled me over . . . and suddenly the door was open and I was tumbling forward, somersaulting from the two-step-high level of the hut floor to the granulated ice crystals in the trench. There was precious little breath in my body, but the fall knocked what there was out of me, and I may or may not have blacked out for a second or two. Then I was gasping and coughing, lying among all that crystalline ice, but feeling cold air flood into my aching lungs. With my mind clearing, I realized why the door had appeared to be locked. It was because the Americans made doors that opened outwards, not inwards in the British fashion. Gradually I began to feel better. Not much better, but a little. My head ached fiercely, my lungs and stomach felt like half-perished rubber and the same rubbery, chemical flavour lay thickly in my mouth.

Also I was still in darkness. I sat up and got a whiff of smoke that made me cough again. Since the smoke must be coming from inside the hut, I must close the door. Getting to my feet started another spasm of giddiness and I sat down heavily, waited a few moments, breathing cautiously, then tried again. This time there was less giddiness; I swayed, but remained upright. After a minute or so, I stretched my arms out in front of me and began trying to feel my way towards something that would give me a basis for orientation. The snow wall didn't, and it was the first thing I encountered. Damn! The next was the other snow wall. I stood in the black cold, trying to decide whether the hut lay to left or right. It could only be feet away, in any case. Then I found it, sniffed smoke, reached the door and swung it to. With the door at my back, I knew I faced the entrance to the trench and had set off carefully towards it when the thought came that there could be others asleep in other rooms in the hut, who perhaps had not awakened and were even now in process of being suffocated by smoke. But Herschel had the other room in my hut, and beyond that lay a little rest room cum office. With Herschel still at Belvoir, the hut was therefore empty. That was a relief. But what about the other hut, towards the far end of the trench? I vaguely remembered that was empty too. A fair amount of the sleeping accommodation was empty, this late in the year, when most of the summer visitors had returned south. In any case, it was clear enough that whatever was burning was in my hut, not the other, and that the best course of action was to get out of the trench and raise the alarm.

I stumbled over my unfastened bootlaces, swore, and moved slowly forward again. The stumble must have thrown me slightly off course, because instead of reaching the door directly, I came first to the corner of the ice wall and had to work my way by touch.

Why was I in darkness anyway?

Then an icy little thought struck me. The door wasn't normally closed. I should have been able to see the lights of Main Street outside! I shouldn't *be* in darkness at all! I remembered the generator trouble, and thought that perhaps the lights were off as a precaution, and it was the middle of the night, with nobody moving about.

All the same, when my fumbling fingers found the door, it was locked.

For long minutes, I attacked that damned door. I tried to pull it, to push it; I swung my weight against it, hauled on the handle as hard as I could. I shouted, screamed and kicked, with no result at all, except that I became hoarse with shouting and my fists grew sore with banging. Nobody heard me. There would *be* nobody to hear me, not at that hour when almost everybody at Camp Hundred would be soundly asleep and those who weren't, the men on duty, would be warm inside their various huts and staying there.

I looked at my watch, grateful for the little points of luminosity, and discovered it was three-twenty, twenty minutes since I had awakened, and with more than three hours to go before I could reasonably expect some passer-by to hear me. And by God, but it was cold. My clothes weren't properly fastened either, which didn't help; there were plenty of little places where the chill air was getting at my unprotected skin, and though in the tunnel that was scarcely dangerous, it was most certainly damned uncomfortable. I spent the next few minutes putting myself in some sort of order, straightening wrinkles and tucking myself in, while I thought about the smoke and where it had come from.

The obvious source was a fire somewhere in my part of the hut, but no fire had been visible. There was no red glow, no pinpoint of flickering light to suggest burning, and surely in twenty minutes a fire in a wooden hut would have spread? Or perhaps gone out? Yes, that was more likely. Certainly I was going to get very cold and uncomfortable standing where I was for three hours and more. I made my way back to the hut, more confident now in the dark, found the doorknob and opened it.

My nostrils told me instantly that the place was still full of fumes and the small whiff I got set me coughing again. My lungs felt bruised, as though somebody had stamped on them, and I closed the door quickly. I couldn't use the hut, that was certain. I'd had a faint, crazy idea that if I could see what was burning I could perhaps dash in and pull it out to the trench, but that was certainly impossible. I felt my way along the side of the hut to the second wooden building, deeper in the trench. That was also a dormitory hut and the two weren't connected so there should be no fumes, and there ought to be beds in there, even if there were no blankets.

But even before I reached it, I'd changed my mind. If I'd been thinking with reasonable clarity, the idea of going into the other hut for the night ought to have been rejected, because both sense and duty told me that any kind of fire in Camp Hundred, even one I couldn't see, was a matter of importance and potential danger. And, anyway, when I did find the door of the second hut, it was locked.

I'd been hiding away from the thought, but now there was no alternative. It was clear what I must do. All too clear. Clear and frightening. Because the only way out of that trench was through the escape hatch, up on to the icecap.

Chapter 9

It had to be done; I knew it, but still I hesitated. The last time, indeed the only time I had been out through an escape hatch on to the surface, there had been that bloodcurdling demonstration from Smales of how to deep-freeze a pork chop. This time, I could be the pork chop, as Lieutenant Foster's cousin had been. And Charlie Foster was still up there somewhere, frozen meat now, his body not recovered and by now probably so well entombed in snow it would never be found. While I hesitated, I tried to think. On the surface there would be a line of escape hatches, one at the end of most of the trenches, and the line would be parallel to Main Street. All right, but would I see them? Hours earlier, when I had piloted TK4 into Hundred, the weather break was already ending, the wind rising. Now there was no way of knowing what was happening up there.

I remember the sound my throat gave as I swallowed, standing at the foot of the spiral stair, holding on to the handrail. One part of my mind was still telling me to wait until morning, until I was found, and the other, which had made the decision and should have been prepared to implement it, was wavering in face of what lay ahead. Then, in some extraordinary way, my feet began to climb and I was committed; there was no deliberate order from brain to foot, it just happened, and I was climbing in the dark up that steel stair, feeling my way ahead, stopping when my upstretched hand had touched the hatch cover to fumble for the winding wheel.

A few turns and it was open and at least there was a little light. Not much, for any moon or star there may have been was totally obscured, but where the world consists entirely of white snow, it is never wholly dark. As I poked my head up through the hatch, that faint light was the only friendly thing. The Arctic wind scoured across the snowfield, whistling madly, driving hard snow crystals before it like a sand-blaster. And it was wickedly cold. I paused there to draw the parka close about my face, turning the back of my head to the wind, and once that was done, tried to find landmarks, or some way of guiding myself. I knew there were guide lines out there. Charlie Foster had died because he failed to keep hold of one. But no guide lines were visible; almost nothing was visible in the impenetrable screen of flying snow.

I made myself stand, pointed my right shoulder at where I believed Main Street to be, and took five careful paces, then glanced back. The open hatch was still visible, but my footmarks were already indistinct, blown away, or filling. I took five more, then another five. Now I could no longer see the hatch cover. Fifteen paces and already I was alone, without landmarks, with nothing to hang on to but a vague sense of direction. Five more paces, one foot placed carefully in front of the other, pause, and a glance back to see the snow flying off my footmarks. I swallowed again and forced myself to move. I had calculated that between thirty and forty yards should separate the hatches, but after fifty paces there was still no sign of one. Even that was proof of nothing. Not *every* trench had an escape hatch. Most had, but not all. So the distance between them might be sixty to eighty yards, even a hundred and twenty if I was bloody unlucky, and I was feeling bloody unlucky. I knew only one thing with certainty: that Main Street, far beneath the surface, lay somewhere to my right, and the knowledge was scant comfort because the ramp down to Main Street lay at least a quarter of a mile away and my chances of finding it were remote indeed. Long before I'd walked a quarter-mile, I'd have wandered, or been blown, far off course.

Anxiously, five paces at a time, I edged forward, trying to line up the new five with the last five. Every step I counted, and at seventy the relief of seeing something sticking out of the snow was enough to make my whole body tremble. It was an escape hatch, all right, but even the way I found it was frightening, for it was to my right and very faint and I'd almost missed it. And if I *had* missed it . . . well, then it would have been a long, despairing walk to death.

For a few moments I busied myself clearing snow from round it, then I levered up the protecting lid and began to turn the handle. As the hatch cover came up, I prayed for a friendly gleam of light. The prayers, this time, drew no response; I was looking down into darkness. All the same, it was the way back and I climbed through the open hatch and down the stair, leaving the hatch open to admit any faint gleam of light it could. By the time I stood on the trench floor it was apparent that no light penetrated and I had to feel my way forward again. I stayed close to the trench wall, placing my feet carefully, with no idea what lay ahead. This could be a storage tunnel, there could be huts or machinery, packing cases, anything. Then my foot, instead of coming down on snow, bumped into some obstruction. I bent and felt it, trying to decide whether I could step over it, or would have to find a way round. Whatever it was was wrapped in cloth of some kind and my hands, in their thick felt mittens, told me nothing, except that there was also a steel frame round it . . . and that it was about two yards long . . . *and two feet wide.* Jesus Christ, I was in with the corpses!

For a while it all happened, just the way people say it does: my scalp crawled, cold impulses fled over my back, my hair stood vertical, parka hood or no parka hood. And I trembled violently. The sudden panic may have been irrational, but it was there, great waves of it that went for my guts and my mind simultaneously, and set me blundering in the darkness just to get away, to get some distance between me and what lay on the trench floor. What lay there, inevitably, was another body, and I tripped and sprawled full-length on it, my grabbing hands gripping something hard as a drainpipe, and which was probably an arm. My senses didn't return to anything like normal, but fear induced a desire, if not a capacity to reason, and I sat there among all the hobgoblins and devils my imagination conjured into the air around me, frantically trying to think what to do.

Very little presented itself. I was completely disorientated and whichever way I moved I'd be falling over bodies, or crawling past them. How many were there? I couldn't even remember. Six, I thought. No, seven, because . . . because Doc Kirton, what was left of him, was in here, too. And then I remembered something else. This trench, too, was locked.

I looked wildly around me. Far back at the end of the trench was the pale oval of the open hatch, leading back to the surface, and I laughed, I know I laughed once, loudly and hysterically, at the choice before me. I could stay there in the dark with seven dead bodies, or go back up into the blizzard and the gale and the unnervingly strong chance of joining these seven in whatever frozen Valhalla they might have found. I've wondered since, sitting comfortably, drink in hand, why I didn't stay, It would, after all, only have been for a few hours. The corpses couldn't have harmed me. But it's different, believe me, when you're saying it to yourself in a black snow tunnel and they're lying all round you, frozen hard as planks.

Though one wasn't. When I started crawling on hands and knees towards that grey patch of dim light, somehow or other I contrived to put my knee into an indentation in the floor and roll sideways on to one of the bodies, and in recoiling, put my weight on it. Where the others were hard, this one gave sickeningly under pressure, and my stomach squirmed with the realization that this could only be Kirton, or what was left of him, carefully wrapped.

A few seconds later I was away from them and heading fast for the stair, and my feet were clanging as I stumbled upwards to look in sober, dry-mouthed fear out into the Arctic night. Even since I'd climbed down into the trench, conditions outside seemed to have worsened. What had been gale and blizzard and bad enough, for God's sake, was now turning into an Arctic storm, and the force of the wind that funnelled down through the open hatch had me hanging on grimly to the handrail.

But I did it, I made myself climb out, pointed my shoulder at Main Street, and forced myself forward. Now, far from seeing five paces behind me, I could scarcely distinguish two, and by the time I'd covered fifteen careful yards I was already filled with the suspicion that I was lost. Even through the wadding of my cap and parka, I heard the whiplash crack of thunder roll across the sky above and the wind force was nearly bowling me over, forcing me along with awkward, involuntary, uncontrolled steps. I stopped after thirty paces, if they could be called paces. I *was* lost. I no longer knew with any certainty even where Main Street lay. I would certainly have died then, there can be no doubt about that. I'd have continued blundering, driven by that fearful wind, until I became part for ever of the Greenland icecap. And death would have come quickly, too, for the storm was worsening by the second. It was the storm, of all things, that saved me, for with one great, deafening smash of thunder, lightning suddenly flickered and God knows how many volts of electricity turned into a single wild flash of illumination. And there, ten yards from where I stood, was another hatch! I'd never have seen it but for the lightning. With normal visibility no more than six feet, I was thirty feet from it. But I saw it, and flung myself towards its safety and shelter, swearing to myself that whatever lay beneath, from invading hungry bears to Dracula himself, and even if the tunnel was locked, I was going to spend the rest of the night down there.

I clawed open the lid, wound the escape hatch open and, slithering in like a rat down a rope, and with my feet safely on the steel rungs and my head ducked down away from the storm, I found I could see light. *Light!* Not a mirage, but real honest-to-God light. The bulk of two huts stood between me and the tunnel entrance, but the entrance was open, and beyond it lay the lights of Main Street. They were dim, running on a reduced voltage, I learned later, but to me at that moment they looked as bright as advertising signs.

I looked at my watch and discovered with surprise that it was still not four o'clock, less than an hour since the smoke had awakened me. But what a hell of an hour! Finding myself among corpses, and then wandering on the icecap, had made me forget my original purpose in escaping from my own sleeping trench: to let somebody know there was a fire in there. Main Street was deserted. Who would be in charge of fire fighting? Who'd be the duty officer? I hadn't the slightest idea, and in hopes of finding out, crossed to the mess hall. Coffee was available there all night, I knew, so somebody ought to be around. In fact there was a solitary cook, staring wearily at some tattered comic, who didn't as much as raise his eyes until I spoke.

The words shifted, him though. At the mention of fire his eyebrows went up. 'You sound the warning?'

'Who do I tell?'

'Nobody,' he said. 'There's an alarm right there on the wall in Main Street. Man, you hit it!'

'I don't think it's serious,' I said. If nobody else had noticed a fire, an hour after it had started burning, it could scarcely *be* serious. 'I don't want to waken the whole camp. Where do I find the duty officer?'

The cook said, 'I'm coming too,' and took me to the command trench, where a young lieutenant, probably just as bored but with slightly better literary taste, was yawning over Edgar Snow's *Red Star Over China*. His name was Westlake and he, too, was galvanized by the word 'fire', and his hand streaked out towards the wall Tannoy microphone.

'It was an hour ago,' I said. 'Don't you think we'd better have another look first?'

'Well . . .' He was doubtful, but he put on his parka and followed me; then, his four a.m. mind seizing on the nub of things after he'd had two minutes to digest it, said as we walked along Main Street, 'An *hour*! Why in hell didn't you – '

'Because,' I said, 'the trench door was closed and locked.'

He grabbed my arm. 'No buddy. Not locked.'

'Locked,' I said.

'In that case, I need the goddam keys, right?'

He went back, got them, and joined me a few seconds later. When we reached the trench, the door wasn't even closed, let alone locked, and Westlake fixed me with a hard stare. He said, 'So show me the fire.'

I stood there, looking along the trench. Its lights were on, the door to the hut stood open. There was no smoke anywhere.

'Come *on*, show me,' Westlake said impatiently. I walked forward to join him, and we went into the hut, Westlake first. The hut lights were on, too, and Westlake took one look round the room and said dryly, 'You sure were right about not sounding the alarm. Oh, brother!'

Beside my bed stood a chair, and on it I'd kept cigarettes and matches. It was the chair cushion that had been burning and had now gone out. But neatly in the middle of the charred plastic foam lay a cylinder of grey ash, the remains of a cigarette.

I felt myself colouring in embarrassment, standing there,

staring stupidly at a small, accidental burn in a seat cushion. Westlake said two things, one after the other. The first was that I ought to take more water with whatever I drank so much of, the second that if I undertook not to inform Major Smales in the morning, he damn sure wouldn't, no sir! He left me then to my embarrassment and presumably went back to Edgar Snow's account of Mao-Tse-tung in the Yenan caves. All things considered, it was, I thought, decent of him.

After a while I checked that the fire was, in fact, truly out, and went back to bed, hoping to sleep, but for the second time that night I found I couldn't. My mind kept going back over the whole bizarre business, and some of the time I was forced to unpalatable conclusions. I'd certainly panicked when the hut door wouldn't open at first, and only then realized I was trying to open it the wrong way. Was it possible the trench door hadn't been locked either, and that I had been so panicky I hadn't even tried properly? But no, that *wasn't* true. I'd spent a lot of time on that door, pulling, pushing, twisting and turning, and it was closed and locked. Of that I was sure. The other door, in the trench where the bodies lay, was certainly locked, I knew that, and was kept locked, too, on Barney Smales's firm orders.

And what about the burn? Thinking back, I could remember ... I was *sure* I could remember it ... leaning over on my elbow to stub out that final cigarette in the ashtray, and stubbing it out, moreover, the way I always did, bending the tip over the burning end and pressing down hard. I *had*, hadn't I? I always did it that way, so I must have! Admittedly, though, I'd been damned tired, my eyelids closing.

At that point they must have closed again, because I fell asleep with the lights on and didn't awaken until nine, and I only woke then because there was a tap on the door and Sergeant Vernon came in and said, 'Sorry, sir, but Major Smales would like to see you right now.'

In the cold light of morning, which is hardly a precise description of the low yellowish lighting in my hut, it was clear enough to me that Barney Smales must, by now, know that I'd been out on the surface, without permission, without telling anybody, and alone, during the night. Three of Smales's sacred and sensible rules lay in ruins and it was unreasonable to imagine that Lieutenant Westlake, despite what he'd said, had not entered it all in the log. He'd have had to enter it; not to do so would have been severe dereliction of duty. So I was prepared for a roasting as I hurried towards the command trench and went into Barney's hut. Master Sergeant Allen, in the outer office, gave me a brief 'Good morning' and pointed to the door.

I hesitated, knocked, and went in on the word 'Come'.

Then I waited for the blast. Barney sat behind his desk, smiling benignly. I looked at him warily; the last days had accustomed me to his psychological tricks. He looked up at me and said, 'Ah, the Englishman, ain't that right?'

'Morning, sir,' I said neutrally.

He snapped his fingers. 'Something I wanted to say to you.'

'Oh.' I watched his face, waiting for the swift change of expression, the sudden rasp of anger.

'Yeah.' There was a pause. He reached for a ballpoint pen on his desk and looked at it. 'Kind of a neat piece of design, you agree?'

'The pen?' I said. I could feel myself being drawn into some kind of trap. Any second now, the world would fall on me.

'Sure,' Smales said. 'Real functional.' After a second, he added: 'Pretty colour, too.'

'Very.'

'Yeah.' He blinked.

I said, 'You sent for me.'

'That I did.' He held up the pen. 'I like things functional, things that do the job. Like your machine.'

He was talking, I realized with relief, about the TK4. Metamorphosis into salesman. 'Fine machine,' I said quickly. 'And she can do a lot more than that. I'm looking forward to demonstrating – '

He nodded. 'Functional,' he said. He was still holding the pen, looking at it, not at me. I wondered suddenly if he were drunk, then rejected the idea. The pattern of his words, the genial lassitude, were reminiscent of mild drunkenness, but the words themselves were spoken with clarity; there wasn't even the suspicion of a slur.

108

He said, 'It's my duty to tell you a thing like that. I'll also tell you – ' he paused again and it was a long pause – 'that I don't want air-cushion vehicles up here.'

I felt my scalp click back. I knew perfectly well that Barney Smales didn't approve of the hovercraft as Arctic transport; I knew also that he was the last man to say so before the trials had taken place. There was something wrong here and I'd better disengage myself before it became worse.

I said, 'Well, thanks for telling me,' keeping my tone carefully cheerful, turning for the door.

He didn't stop me. 'You ought to be told,' he said, as the door opened and closed behind me.

I found myself looking into Master Sergeant Allen's eyes. He said, 'Okay, Mr Bowes?'

I hesitated. Allen looked calm, competent . . . was there an enquiring look somewhere behind the formality? I said, 'I'm not sure.'

He regarded me steadily. 'Not sure?'

I thought about it, and Allen sat there, still and intelligent, watching me think. If I said anything, however mild, however delicate the hint, the meaning would be the same; I'd be saying, 'Your boss is going weird.' The phrases ran through my mind: 'a little strange this morning; did you notice anything? He must be tired.' All meaning the same, and if spoken by this possibly paranoid stranger who'd been seeing spooks ever since he arrived, further proof of a perhaps dangerous instability.

I searched for some lame phrase. Finally, I said, 'I wouldn't want *his* job!'

Unhelpfully, Allen said, 'Why's that, sir?'

'Not at a time like this. The strain . . .' *Strain*! The word had slid out. *Your boss is going weird.*

Allen lit a cigarette. He said slowly, 'The responsibility is very great.'

I thought about that. Was I reading more into all this than could possibly be there? Or was Allen coming to meet me? I looked at his face. It was calm, the dark brown skin uncreased, smooth on the planes and curves of his face. Allen was the senior non-commissioned officer, very senior, high-quality, but . . . but non-commissioned. Experienced, though, and knowing the rule-book backwards. I realized suddenly that it was possible this conversation was even more difficult for him than for me. He was outranked by a lot of men at Camp Hundred and all of them would react with hostility at the merest suggestion . . . No, there had to be another approach, an oblique one. And it was up to me, the civilian, to make it.

But what if I were mistaken? What if Allen weren't moving to meet me, and all these supposed undertones were part of my paranoid imaginings? In *that* case, I thought, he'd merely think I was a little nuttier than he'd thought in the first place.

But how to start? The atmosphere in the little office felt electric, but perhaps only I felt it. Allen still looked totally un-ruffled, except that there seemed to be something in his eyes, some gleam of – of what?

I said, 'What's tonight's movie, Mr Allen?'

'No decision yet, sir.'

'What,' I asked, 'do you have in stock?'

He looked at me for a moment, then rose and went to a filing cabinet. 'I have a list. If you've got some kind of request, I'll do what I can.'

'I'm a Bogart fancier,' I said. 'Got any Bogey pictures?'

He looked at the list. '*African Queen, Casablanca.*'

'I've seen them both too many times,' I said. I hesitated, know-ing the hesitation would add emphais when I spoke, but unable for a moment to force out the words. Then I made myself say, 'There's one performance I liked best of all.'

'What was that, sir?'

'Captain Queeg,' I said. 'In *The Caine Mutiny.*'

Allen gave me a glance. 'Guess we don't have that picture, sir.'

'You've seen it, though?'

'No.'

I pushed on quickly. 'Oddly enough,' I said, 'it's about what we were talking about. The responsibilities of command in dangerous situations.'

Did Allen's dark face soften a little? He said, 'I didn't see the movie, sir, but I did read the novel. As I recall, it was more about the responsibilities of subordinates.'

110

'None of whom,' I said, 'showed up very well at the court martial.'

'Yeah, that's right.' He was non-committal again.

Well, I thought, it was early days. Barney was benign and it was perfectly possible nothing was wrong and that he was merely playing psychological games. We'd all know soon enough if anything was seriously wrong with him. And that would be time enough. I said, 'Breakfast time,' and left.

I walked out of the command trench and into Main Street on my way to the mess hall. The lighting along the huge principal trench was down, the snow walls were grey rather than white, and the few men who moved along it looked dulled and depressed. In the mess hall, too, the atmosphere was heavy and voices low. On the night of my arrival – the *only* night, come to think of it, when things had been fairly normal at Hundred – there had been a kind of boisterous noise, a defiant good humour. There was none of that now. I sat at a table with one of the scientific officers, a captain named Vale, to whom I'd been introduced one night in the officers' club. Like most of the other scientists at Hundred, he worked for CRREL, the Cold Regions Research and Engineering Laboratory of the United States Army Terrestrial Sciences Centre. Captain Vale was not pleased with me, he said.

'Why not?'

'You made it to Belvoir, so I hear?'

'In my little hovercraft,' I nodded.

'Wish I'd known you were going. I'd have hitched a ride out.'

'Your tour over?'

He smiled. 'No tour's ever over till you make it out. Don't worry, I'm used to it. I been stuck a few times before.'

'For long?'

'Six weeks up here, one time. But in the other place it can be longer.'

'What other place?'

'The Antarctic. I've done two tours on Deep Freeze down there. One time we were three months overdue.'

'Depressing,' I said.

'It's okay if you can work. If you can't, the Heebies get you.'

111

'The Heebies,' I said, 'seem to be very much present.'

He glanced round the mess hall. A scattering of men were sitting over coffee or breakfast, some talking quietly, most silent. He said, 'I've known worse.'

'Here?'

'Hell, no. In huts in the Antarctic.' He gave a rueful grin. 'These guys are too used to the good life. They're over-reacting.'

'I think,' I said, 'that I'm over-reacting too.'

'Sure you are. So am I, really. So's everybody. First time in the cold regions?'

'Yes.'

'You'll find it grows on you. Two, three years, you won't want to be anywhere else.'

'You do,' I pointed out. 'You want to be at Belvoir.'

'I want,' he said, 'to be in Virginia. But when I get there, I'll want to be right back here.'

'So all this doesn't worry you?'

'Nope. Can't say it does.'

'Morale's low,' I said.

'It'll lift.'

'A chapter of accidents.'

'It'll end.'

I laughed. 'You're an optimistic fatalist?'

'I'm a glaciologist,' Vale said. 'In my game you get to take the long view.'

It was a reassuring little conversation. Vale was a quiet, competent man who'd seen it all. If he wasn't worried, why should I be worried? But the memory of Barney Smales nagged at me. I said, 'The Heebies – how do they show?'

'I'm no psychologist.'

'Even so?'

'Well . . .' he hesitated. 'People start going flat. They get obsessive about little things and ignore the big ones. Then that stops and they sit and stare at their boots or something hours at a stretch. Like I say, I'm no psychologist, but I'd say it's close to classical depression.' He rose, slapped my shoulder, and added, 'Meantime, the coffee's hot, there's booze in the club, soft beds and movies. Don't worry about it. You'll live.'

112

I watched him go, conscious of my own confusion. Vale was so manifestly confident, his confidence based on long experience, that it was absurd to doubt him. Indeed I didn't doubt him. But along with all the reassurance, he'd handed me one disquieting thought. People, he'd said, became obsessive about little things. And a ballpoint pen was little enough.

Chapter 10

We all have our neuroses; everybody's a little nuts in some direction or another. But I've always liked to think of myself as reasonably sane. I don't feel uncontrollable urges to murder people who step in front of me in bus queues and I don't turn into Frankenstein's monster once I get behind a car wheel; by and large I sleep undisturbed by conscience. But after a few days at Hundred I was beginning to entertain some doubts about myself. Walking away from the mess hall after my talk with Captain Vale, I was feeling more or less reassured. I remember telling myself inside my head to stop trying to make patterns out of random events and concentrate on the TK4 and the urgent need to sell the damn thing to the American gentlemen. Little nod of determination for my own benefit; conscious setting of jaw. And then the conversation with Master Sergeant Allen came back, with all its doubts, hesitations and possible overtones, and I realized that my mental state was changing by the second like a well-shaken kaleidoscope. Every time I talked to anybody, damn it, I took on a new viewpoint. One man said, don't worry, and I told myself not to worry. Another was mildly enigmatic and I started looking for the puzzle inside the enigma. Barney Smales was polite but withdrawn and I imagined . . .

The hell with it, I decided. It was their business, not mine. If the United States Army was having its troubles, at least it was equipped to handle them; I had a job of my own to do and at the moment there seemed no likelihood of its getting done. The weather was lousy up top and apparently relentless. I'd been told before I left England that there should be a few days within the following four weeks when the TK4 could give performance demonstrations. Past experience and weather records said so. But apart from the fast runs to and from Camp Belvoir there'd been no opportunity at all for me to demonstrate what she could do. Agreed that she'd done all that had been asked of her; the trouble was that nobody had *seen* her in action, and performance demonstrations, by definition, need witnesses; more important, they need witnesses who are going to influence the great decision to buy or not to buy.

I'd set off intending to give the TK4 a swift once-over-lightly, but the weather office was on the way. I decided I might as well go there first.

The weather office was Sergeant Vernon's home ground and I smiled to myself as I went in. Like the sergeants' club, this was old-soldier territory; it smelled of floor polish and pine and on a wall was a window framing one of the big, blown-up colour pictures, this time of a picnic site beside a lake somewhere. An electric coffee percolater gurgled contentedly on a side bench and the ashtrays were many and wiped clean.

Vernon returned my smile. 'Something I can do for you, sir?'

'I take it,' I said, 'that you'll have all the records here.'

'We try to calculate it every which way. If it's not in the form you want, sir, we can work it out.'

'Fine. Look, I'm wondering whether there's going to be a break soon. I realize you can't forecast with any great accuracy, but maybe past records will give some kind of indication.'

'Be a pleasure,' Vernon said. He crossed to a filing cabinet and began hefting folders. 'We got anemometers going round and round. We got mercury and alcohol thermometers going up and down. We got barometric readings, snowfall records, you name it. But –' the corners of his mouth turned down sympathetically – 'it's gonna be a statistical answer you get.'

'I know,' I said. 'But I can cling on to a hope if you'll give me one.'

'So okay. Here's the plots for the last five years.' He unfolded the charts and spread them on the bench. 'Temperature right here. Wind velocity. This one's humidity. We plotted wind and temperature into a windchill factor on this one. Here's snowfall. Now . . .'

Twenty minutes poring over the charts gave the statistical answer. Some time within the next twenty-eight days it was reasonable to expect there'd be four when the wind was down to thirty miles an hour or less. Two more with wind under twenty.

I said, 'Well, it's encouraging.'

'Just so you don't get too encouraged,' Vernon said. 'A lot of that's gonna break down into short slots. Two, three, four hours maybe as a front goes through.'

'How much warning?'

'Do what I can, sir. When the radio's open, I can get the satellite picture up from Thule. That can tell us a little more.'

'And pressure?'

Vernon shook his head. 'Highs and lows, they fill and empty too damn fast. You just gotta make a personal judgment here; data won't do it.'

I said, 'Do me a favour, Mr Vernon. Exercise your best judgment for me? An hour's notice, if I can get it, of a two-hour break. I need that to give any kind of demonstration.'

'Minimum?'

I nodded. 'The problem is that your people have to *see* what she can do. We've got to have time for a bulldozer to roughen the snow surface and build a few steps for the TK4 to climb. Once everybody's sold on that, we can take a few rides in rougher conditions, but I can't get to stage two before stage one's over.'

'Sure,' Vernon said. 'Coffee?'

We drank coffee while I answered his questions about the TK4. It struck me that Vernon was more open-minded about the potential of air-cushion vehicles than Barney Smales, not that his approval was much use. All the same, it was a comfort, and his promise to give me as much warning as possible of any potential weather break could be valuable.

I left him then and went to tidy up the TK4. I'd simply left her at the end of the trip back from Belvoir and I wanted her cleaned out, ship-shape and shiny, for demonstration time. The sergeant syndrome isn't far below the surface in me; a coating of dirt on the outside of an engine casing doesn't make the engine any less efficient, but for me at least it removes some of the enjoyment.

I looked her over carefully and the TK4 was in pretty good nick. In the rear hold a few drops of oil had dripped off the generator, but a handful of waste and a couple of brisk rubs soon shifted that. Otherwise the hold was like a new pin. The cabin wasn't bad, either, though it smelled a little of sweat and old tobacco smoke. I got a hand brush and cleaned the cabin floor of cigarette ash and spent matches, emptied the ashtrays and put a discarded matchbook on the screen sill for future use. Then I leathered the windows. Forty minutes' mindless work, satisfying in its way, and the job was finished, except for a routine check on oil and fuel levels, both of which were fine.

Reilly, the maintenance chief, wandered over as I was admiring her. The inevitable unlit cigar was clamped in the side of his mouth and he spoke round it as he offered the equally inevitable coffee. I was awash with coffee, and had been so virtually since my arrival at Hundred, but the game has rules and one of them is that it pays to be nice to maintenance crews. Reilly was still reading the manuals and hadn't been round the TK4 on hands and knees yet, but he reckoned there weren't nothin' he couldn't handle. I sensed, too, that he was impressed by the hovercraft's swiftness and efficiency on the Belvoir trip.

'Tell you what,' I said. 'First chance I get, we'll take a spin in her.'

He nodded brusquely, but under that matter-of-fact manner an enthusiast lurked. 'If I'm a-goin' in that thing,' he said, 'I'd sure better look after her. That right?'

'Right,' I said, grinning.

'You psychin' me, mister?'

'I hope so.'

He walked away, then, tough and hard. But he patted the steel side of the TK4 as he passed.

It was the last good moment of that day.

On my bed, when I got back to my room, lay an envelope. Even before I opened it, I sensed somehow that it was ticking like a time bomb. Inside was a note from Master Sergeant Allen to the effect that Barney Smales wished to see me, and the word immediately was underlined. In the outer office Allen gave me a wry look that contained a trace of sympathy, and pointed to the door.

I knocked, entered as bidden, and found Barney's eyes directed at me like a pair of shotguns. He gave me two or three minutes of level, low-voiced, furious abuse. It was what I'd expected that morning and hadn't collected – my come-uppance for: a) smoking in bed and carelessly; b) blundering out alone on to the icecap; c) failing to tell anybody I was going; d) behaving in general like a goddam cross between Sherlock Holmes and Captain Oates. My degenerate parents, apart from not enjoying benefit of clergy, had also passed on to me various congenital mental conditions. About thirty seconds into the tirade, I found myself surprisingly unimpressed. After a minute, it would have become almost funny, if the whole TK4 deal hadn't rested in large measure on Barney Smales's assessment.

Finally, I said, with deliberate rudeness, 'Why wait? What was wrong with this morning?'

'What in hell do you mean?'

'All that jazz,' I said, 'about the beauties of bloody ballpoint pens.'

He blinked. 'Now listen, mister, I don't know – '

I said, 'It's got real functional beauty, that's what you told me.' I grabbed the pen off the desk-top and held it up. 'You liked the pretty colours, remember.'

He snatched it from my hand. 'Now listen – '

By now I was almost as angry as he was, but as our eyes met I saw something in his gaze that had no right to be there . . . Fear? Puzzlement? I said, 'You don't remember, do you?'

'You can forget this morning.'

I said, 'Why? Were you drunk?'

I really thought he'd go off pop. His face flushed with rage and his eyes seemed to bulge.

'*Drunk!*' he roared. Then he paused and there was one of those abrupt shifts so characteristic of him. 'I looked drunk, eh?' He spoke, for him, gently, interested in the answer.

'Something like it.'

He rubbed his temples. 'Woke up this morning with a goddam migraine. White lights, the whole deal. Sick as a dog. Used to have 'em as a kid, but I haven't had one in years.'

'Has it gone?'

'Almost.'

'I'm sorry. Sorry about last night, too. It won't happen again. But at the time, the logic seemed compelling.'

He stood up and bent his brows at me. 'This time, Englishman,

118

we'll forget about it.' His tone was deep and measured, the accent British, and some trick of memory dragged recognition out of the dusty attics of my brain.

'Say it again.'

He grinned. 'Remember this, Englishman . . .'

I said, 'Colonel Sapt. *The Prisoner of Zenda*. C. Aubrey Smith talking to Ronald Colman a long time ago.'

'Great movie.'

'I saw it,' I said, 'the third time round.' And then, since the opportunity was at hand, grabbed at it: 'Why do you object to hovercraft?'

He blinked. 'Who said I objected?'

'You did.'

'Was that this morning, too?'

'Two hours ago.'

'Jesus,' he said. 'I woke with this damn migraine. Head was in a vice. I went to the hospital and helped myself to pills. Wonder what in hell I took?'

'Obviously not aspirin,' I said. 'But it seems to have done the trick, if in a roundabout way. About the hovercraft . . . ?'

He shrugged. 'Not enough weight, that's what I feel.'

That was hardly news, but it was a salesman's opportunity. Flat statements often are.

I said, 'Who did you vote for in 1960?'

Barney Smales cocked an eye at me. 'Kennedy,' he said warily.

'You a Catholic?'

'No.'

'The first *Catholic* candidate?'

He laughed. 'Oh, you bastard! Listen, Kennedy had it all turned round. He was cunning, too. The way he set it out, you *didn't* vote for a Catholic, *you* were the bigot.'

'That's right. He had to make the breakthrough.'

'Okay, okay. You'll get your chance.' He paused and added, 'Englishman.'

As I closed the door of Barney's office, Allen gave me an interrogative look. Or perhaps I only thought he did, but in any case I answered the unasked question.

'Nasty thing, a migraine,' I said. 'But it seems to be improving.'

I was crossing to the hut door when the phone rang. Allen said, 'Hullo,' and listened. Then he said, 'Jesus Christ!' He put the phone down quietly.

I said, 'What's the bad news?'

Allen didn't answer me. But he wrenched open Barney Smales's door. 'Sir,' Allen said, 'we got bad trouble in the reactor trench. They just told me Mr Kelleher's gone berserk.'

We came to the reactor trench at a dead run. Carson, the engineer captain in charge, was waiting inside, face very pale and with an angry red mark on his cheek.

'Where is he?' Smales demanded.

'In the office.'

Smales strode in. Kelleher lay on the camp bed used by the duty man. He, too, was very pale, but sweat shone on his face as he wrestled with heavy strappings that bound him to the bed.

Smales dropped to his knees beside the bed. 'Can you talk, Kelleher?'

Kelleher's head moved. He looked at Barney, then away again, his face showing no recognition. His muscles strained more violently against the straps.

'What happened?' Smales rose and turned to Carson.

'I never saw anything like it,' Carson said. 'My God, the way he – '

'I said, "*What happened?*" '

'Sorry, sir. He'd been resting. Right here in this office. We have the lid off the reactor, sir, as you can see. Suddenly the door opened and he came out into the vault and . . . goddammit, he tried to climb into the reactor kettle!'

'To *climb* – ?'

'I grabbed at him, sir. So did two of the men. He tried to fight us off. He did, too, for a second, then we got him again. Jesus, he's strong!'

'He say anything?' Smales demanded.

'Not a word.'

I looked down at Kelleher, dumbly and desperately fighting to free himself; his eyes were wide open and he stared straight up at the ceiling as his body writhed.

Smales said crisply, 'Mr Allen, find me the medical orderly. Tell him Mr Kelleher's got to have a strong sedative injection.'

'Right, sir.'

As we waited, Barney again knelt beside Kelleher, talking gently, soothingly – and pointlessly, because it was clear not a word was getting through. The big nuclear engineer thrashed dementedly in the narrow bed, wrenching and straining at the webbing straps. I felt sick at the sight.

I turned away and looked at Carson, who was absently fingering his bruised cheekbone, then through the door at the reactor. Kelleher was a nuclear engineer. Nobody knew the dangers better. So what crazy malfunction of his excellent brain had driven him to try to climb inside? Behind me there was a sudden exclamation from Carson, a scuffle of sound, and I turned to see Smales reeling back and Kelleher's fist raised for another blow. Carson and I flung ourselves at him more or less simultaneously, trying to hold down the arm that Kelleher had somehow wrenched free. Quick as we'd been, Kelleher had been quicker. He'd already wrested the other arm free and the strength of the man was unbelievable. I'd got hold of his right arm and was struggling to force it downwards, but he succeeded in lifting me bodily for a moment, then pulling the arm away, and the next second he'd smashed his forearm against my mouth. I heard myself whimpering with pain, but some defensive reflex snapped my hands to his wrist and I heaved my whole weight across his shoulder, and levered his arm downwards into immobility. I could feel my lips swelling like balloons and blood running from cuts in my mouth.

And all the time not a sound from Kelleher beyond small grunts of exertion. I concentrated on gripping the arm I held; hoped like hell that Carson was holding on to the other one. If he wasn't . . . Kelleher's body heaved and pounded . . . where the devil was the medic? This couldn't go on. Kelleher would do himself serious injury. Or do the same for one of us. My hands were sweating, my grip consequently weakening. It seemed absurd to say it, but his one arm felt, and was in those long moments, far stronger than my two. I turned my head towards the door, waiting for the running footsteps – and in doing so, must have lowered my head. There was a sudden, fearful pain on my cheek and I felt his breath, and he'd got his teeth into my cheek and was tearing at my flesh like a terrier, a bloody powerful terrier! I shouted aloud at the pain and then somebody was rearing over us and I heard a thud behind me and the terrible grip was suddenly loosened. I jerked my head clear and hung on desperately, and moments later the medic rushed in and injected something into the back of Kelleher's outflung hand. Then he began to count. I could feel the tension going from Kelleher's arm by the time the count had reached ten. At twenty it was limp and I made to rise. 'Ten seconds more, sir,' the orderly said cautiously.

Then I was up and the orderly was dabbing at my cheek and stripping the backing from a big plaster.

Barney Smales watched him, then slapped my shoulder. 'A few more seconds, boy, and he'd have torn your cheek away.'

'I know. What stopped him?'

'A smack in the puss,' Barney said.

'You?'

'Me. Jesus, will you look at him!'

I looked. Carson was clambering awkwardly off the bed, sweating but apparently unhurt. Kelleher lay slumped, unconscious, a trickle of blood coming from one nostril.

The orderly said, 'Major Smales, sir?'

Barney turned to him. 'Okay, I know. The answer's yes. If we've got a straitjacket, he goes in it. We got one?'

'Yes, sir.'

'Goddam planners sure think of everything,' Barney said bitterly. 'What about his legs?'

'We're – er – sir, the hospital *is* fully equipped.'

'And that stuff you pumped in. How long will it hold him?'

'Eight hours or so. But we can continue sedation – '

Barney said, 'You're not a doctor, boy.'

'No, sir. But I've been trained – '

'Wait a minute, wait a minute.' He thought for a moment. 'Okay, now listen. You, Carson, you tell your boys this thing's private, right? And I mean it. Anybody talks, I'll have his skin.

122

We move Mr Kelleher to the hospital and we keep the poor bastard immobilized. You – ' he turned to the orderly – 'you get on the radio to Thule and talk to the doctors. I know diagnosis by radio is a bad substitute, but it's all we've got. And tell the radio room no talking. Okay, son? So get the jacket, then get busy.'

As the medic departed, Smales closed the door behind him. 'Now listen. There's no ducking this. We got real bad news here. We're under strain, and that goes for every man in the place. If the strain can get to Kelleher, it can get to any man here. So, as far as we can, we keep it real quiet. Sooner or later it will get out, a few hours maybe, it'll be right round Camp Hundred. But those hours could be important. The maintenance crews have two of the three generators stripped right down. The third's not gonna work at all. We're cannibalizing it now. And we're running this whole place on that one machine you, Mr Bowes, brought up from Belvoir. And that little piece of information is secret, too. Not totally secret, and not for long, just like Kelleher. But, with luck, we'll have the big generators back on line tonight, one if not two, and with both generators on line, we don't have to worry too much about the reactor. But those hours are important. So what I want is I want Kelleher in that hospital and two men with him, plus the medic. You, Bowes, and you, Allen. Right? If it's safe, the medic continues sedation. If Kelleher breaks loose again, three of you ought to be able to handle him. Okay?'

Half an hour later Master Sergeant Allen and I sat staring moodily at each other across the doctor's desk. Kelleher had been brought along from the reactor trench in a sled, his face hidden, and was now in the little hospital's ward, straitjacketed, canvas-covered from neck to feet, strapped to the steel cot. The anaesthetic held him deep under. I had been unhappily aware, as we moved him and fastened him down, of how corpse-like he was.

Allen lit a cigarette and rose. 'One of us better be in there.'

I said, 'Both.'

Allen shook his head. 'No. Better he's quiet. Two of us, we're gonna talk.'

'All right.'

'When the medic comes, send him right in.'

The medic didn't come for a long time, and when he did it was with bad news. There was no radio contact with either Belvoir or Thule. He looked in on Kelleher, then spent an hour searching through the little library of medical books Kirton had kept, his face growing longer and more puzzled. Unable to help, I was careful not to watch him and kept my head bent over a paperback novel I'd found.

Suddenly he swore aloud, and as I looked up he banged a book back on to the shelf. To my surprise, his eyes were wet.

He spread his arms, and let them fall weakly to his sides. 'Jesus, what do I *do*?'

'First,' I said, 'you have some coffee. And a cigarette, if you smoke.'

'I don't.'

'Coffee then. And sit down.'

As he poured the coffee, his hand shook.

I said quietly, 'It's not your fault. You're not a psychiatrist. So let's forget about what you don't know and concentrate on what you do. You said that injection would hold Mr Kelleher for eight hours. Can you repeat it then?'

He shook his head. 'Not that. I gave him a full operative shot of a general anaesthetic.'

'So what next. In – ' I glanced at my watch – 'in six hours or so.'

'A sedative,' he said.

'And after that?'

His eyes closed tightly and a drop of moisture shone on his cheek. He wiped it away angrily. 'For Christ's sake, sir, I don't know what's wrong with the guy! Could be he's physically ill, too. Maybe he's incubating pneumonia or something. Then what I'm doing is – '

I interrupted. 'What you're doing is your best. With luck we'll have radio contact long before you need to decide.'

'Yeah, with luck! But what do I say, sir? The guy just cracked, that's all. Something went inside his head. And me, I didn't even see it. Nobody can diagnose from that.'

124

'You can take his blood pressure, temperature, pulse rate. And the psychiatrist at Thule will prescribe the drugs – '

The medic looked at me. There was fear in his eyes, almost despair. Then he said, 'What happens when the next one goes?'

Chapter 11

We were not talking only about Kelleher any more.

I said, 'Are you guessing?'

He took a swig of coffee, swallowed, shook his head. Then he sighed and his shoulders sank.

'Yes, sir, I'm guessing. But – '

I waited, but he didn't go on. 'But what?'

'It's hard to describe. The men are low, sir. Low mentally, low physically. They're under pressure. Too many things have happened already. Now we have another.' He nodded towards the ward and Kelleher. 'Already one guy cracked.'

'He's been working day and night,' I said, 'under far greater strain than – '

'Sure he has, sir. And why? Because every goddam thing has broken down. The men know that. But *why* has everything gone crazy? They don't know *that*! And I don't know, and you don't know, and Major Smales, he don't know.'

I said, 'What are they saying?'

He hesitated. 'Jinx, maybe.'

'People always talk about jinxes when things go wrong,' I said. 'While we've been developing that hovercraft, there have been jinxes all along the line. When you get the right answer the jinx goes away.' As I listened to my own voice pouring out soothing syrup, I was vaguely ashamed of myself. He was articulating some of my own doubts, and I was treating him the way Barney Smales had treated me. I added lamely, conciliatorily, 'Most of the time, anyway.'

'And when they don't go away, sir?'

Bad trouble, I thought, but didn't say it. Instead I asked, 'What else are they saying, jinxes aside?'

The medic looked at me, blinking.

I said, 'Go on. What do they say?'

He hesitated. 'Well, sir. One of the guys had one of those James Bond books.'

I forced a grin. 'Well, *he*'s not here.'

'No, sir. Maybe I kinda wish he was.' He too forced a thin smile. 'Anyway, at the front there was this quote from Al Capone. What he said was , "Once is happenstance, second time coincidence. Third time it's enemy action."'

I nodded. It was precisely what any group of men would be saying in these circumstances; I'd thought the same thoughts myself. But there were holes in the theory you could drive a tractor through. Kelleher was one such hole. I said, 'But who's the enemy? And why the action?'

He shrugged. 'Who knows?'

'All right,' I said. I was thinking: the medic was the first to share my own earlier suspicions, or, at least, the first to put them into words. And he knew Camp Hundred and its occupants a great deal better than I did. 'Let's take these things one at once. Start with the enemy. Who could it be?'

Again the thin smile. 'It could be any man here.'

'Me, included?'

'Well, yes, sir!'

'Or you?'

'Sure.'

I said, 'The helicopter crash and the man who got lost on the surface were long before I got here. Does that let me out? And *you* were here.'

He said, 'Aw hell, it's not me.'

'Then who? Have the men been speculating?'

'Sure.'

'And?'

'There's three hundred men plus. Could be any one of them.'

'No favourites?'

'No, sir.'

'Has it been narrowed down? Ten men, five, two?'

'No, sir. Look – ' he exhaled noisily, in exasperation. 'A posting up here to Camp Hundred is . . . well, it's not always popular. Some guys like it, or maybe they just like the idea, right? But when you're here, a month or so and all you want is out.'

'So it's somebody who wants out? And to get out, he's ready to sabotage the whole installation?'

He nodded. 'Something like that. Who knows what happens in people's heads?'

'Aren't you forgetting,' I said, 'that this nut of yours, whoever he is, is placing himself in exactly the same danger he's forcing on everybody else? If the whole place becomes inoperable and they have to get everybody out, he could be the last man to leave, not the first. And if it were to reach the point where people began to die, his chance of dying is the same as everybody else's.'

'Sure I thought of it. But did *he*? Maybe we're talking about a psychotic. Maybe he just hates the place and everyone in it and he can't think beyond hitting at it.'

I said, 'I like that theory a lot less even than the bad luck theory. And if you think about the things that have happened, one by one, there are a lot that nobody could have manufactured.'

'Like?'

'Like Mr Kelleher. Like the polar bear that slashed the fuel tank. Like the helicopter crash.'

He gave that thin smile again. 'Okay, sir, I got me a persecution complex. But there's things some guy could have done. Sabotaging engines, killing Doc Kirton – and, sir, *that* sure hasn't been explained. Not to me, not so I'd believe it.'

'It hasn't been explained to anybody's satisfaction,' I said. 'But do you know something special?'

'Yes, *sir*! Since you ask me, I sure do.'

'Go on.'

'Put it this way. Captain Kirton's body was by the main tunnel entrance, right?'

I nodded.

'Okay. Well, the Doc never went near the tunnel entrances. He had a kind of a block about it. He commuted between the hospital, the mess hall and the officers' club, that's what he said. He'd never been on top and he wasn't going till the day he went back Stateside.'

I said, 'It's a very thin story.'

'He said it more than once.'

'Even so, I can puncture that argument myself. The day the bear got in, he was with me, right beside the entrance. He went

128

into the fuel storage tunnel to see what the bear had done.'

The medic shrugged helplessly and gave a little grimace. 'It's just a feeling, sir. But to my certain knowledge . . . Well, he told me one time he hadn't been past the officers' club trench one side, and the reactor trench the other, in all the time he was here. He *told* me, sir. So one night – *night*, remember that, because the Doc spent all his nights in the club, you ask anyone – one night he goes along there and he dies. And snow buries his body and then the 'dozer turns him into ground beef. Story is he has a thrombosis, or something, right? He walks down there, where he never goes, and he has this thrombosis, and he falls down dead right where the snowblow'll cover him and the 'dozer'll mash him up.'

The medic's voice had risen as he spoke; he was arguing his case intensely, and, to me at least, fairly convincingly.

But I couldn't take his side; I couldn't say, that's right, I see it all now – and then spend another hour rooting with him through Camp Hundred's assorted troubles, because to do so would be to apply fuel to hot places. The medic felt strongly, and sooner or later, back with his mates, he'd talk it all over, and anything I'd said would be tossed into the eddies of speculation. Also it seemed to me that at the moment, with Kirton dead, the medic was pretty important to everybody at Hundred and the best thing I could do was to make some attempt to restore his morale. So I egged him on to talk about himself, his home town, his army career, his girl-friends and so on. It wasn't a particularly easy conversation, and it ended when Allen came out of the ward and said it was my turn to watch over the patient.

I took my book with me into the ward and sat beside Kelleher's steel cot. His mouth hung agape and he breathed noisily and wetly under the imposed relaxation of the anaesthetic. But at least he seemed peaceful. Looking at him now, it was hard to imagine Kelleher as he'd been a few short hours earlier, mouth distorted in that rictus grin, grunting and snarling like an animal. My cheek still ached painfully from his bite and I remembered the astounding strength in the man as he flailed on the cot in the reactor hut's office. The hold of mind upon body, I reflected, was a thing one took entirely for granted; a thing most of us maintain throughout our lives. But Kelleher that morning had demonstrated how tenuous the grip is, and how a mental trip-switch, once released, triggers off things we cannot conceive of. I'm no psychologist. I'm not now and wasn't then, and even in the light of later events, I still find it hard to understand the suicidal compulsion that drove Kelleher when he actually tried to climb into the reactor kettle.

My first spell on watch in there was uneventful. So was Allen's second. But I'd only been sitting there for a few minutes of my own second spell, reading quietly, when Kelleher muttered something.

I looked at him, all at once tense and alert. His eyes were closed and he was frowning a little, but the big body lay still under its restraining heavy canvas. I reached for the telephone, unsure whether he was muttering in his sleep or awakening, but anxious for support if the latter were the case.

He spoke again, before I'd lifted the receiver, and this time the word was clear. 'Jesus,' he said.

Something – perhaps a feeling that a crowd would upset him – kept my hand off the phone.

I said gently, 'How do you feel?'

He repeated the word, still far away, surfacing very slowly. 'Feel?' he said. 'Feel?'

I waited. Perhaps a minute went by. Then, 'Oh, boy, those . . .'

He was quite calm, as yet barely conscious. I lit a cigarette, deliberately injecting an everyday sound into the stillness. The cigarette was finished before he spoke again, but by now there were small movements of his legs and arms. Quite suddenly, he opened his eyes wide, blinked at the light and turned his head towards me. He said, 'I can't move.'

'Don't worry. You're all right.'

He blinked several times more, fighting his way up to consciousness, and said at the end, 'I had an accident?'

'In a way.' I was watching him carefully for any signs of incipient violence.

'Radiation?' he said sharply. 'Did I get a blast of radiation?'

I shook my head. 'No.' I was thinking that at least his mind was clear. He was aware he'd been unconscious, aware of one possible

130

reason for it. I smiled and said, 'It was a kind of collapse. You've been working too hard.'

He looked suddenly worried. 'Heart? I had a coronary?'

'No.'

He relaxed. 'Thank God. I was warned once to get some of this weight off . . . Why can't I *move*?' He frowned again, fear in his face, and I cursed myself for allowing the delay. I reached for the phone, told Allen he was awake, and stood back while the medic came in and gave him a sedative injection. Kelleher watched, too, as the canvas flap of the straitjacket was peeled back and the hypodermic went into his arm. He said, in brief horror, 'Christ, I'm in a . . . in a . . . in . . .' and he was asleep again before the word could come out.

Allen looked at me. 'He seems lucid.'

'Yes,' I said, 'he was lucid all right.'

'Back to normal?'

I said, 'What's normal?' and phoned the command hut to let Barney know. He was properly relieved and said he'd be along later to inspect the patient, but he sounded worried and distracted.

After that, the vigil continued its silent way. I finished my two hours and Allen took over, then I was back at Kelleher's bedside, and so it went on except that Allen was relieved temporarily by Sergeant Vernon while he went off to handle some minor matter of administration.

It was around eleven that night when Barney Smales finally came along in response to a message I'd phoned through to the effect that Kelleher was stirring again. He looked drawn and weary as he stood looking down at the cot.

Kelleher was moving drowsily, in so far as the canvas jacket and leg restraints would let him move at all.

'How was he before?' Barney asked me.

'He wasn't awake long, and he was still half-way under,' I said, 'But within limits he was rational enough.'

Barney took off his parka and cap and sank sighing on to a chair. He said, 'Not enough, unfortunately. It's this way, and it's a bastard. The reactor we've got was a new design for operations up here. It's still experimental. It's not leased. We bought it. So it's the army's but under certain conditions. One of those conditions is that any major work on the reactor has to be done under the supervision of the civilian manufacturers. That means that when we shut down and refuel, and when we go critical, one of their guys is in complete control. Under the terms of the contract, we can't do it ourselves.'

'But surely,' I said, 'under circumstances like these – '

He cut me off. 'The contract says *under no circumstances*. It's absolutely clear and absolutely specific that in the event of sickness or incapacity of the supervising engineer, work will be discontinued until he can be given a clean bill of health *by a doctor*. Or until he can be replaced.'

'So even if Kelleher's okay . . .'

'Even if I think he's okay, even if every man at Camp Hundred thinks he's all jim-dandy, that's no damn good. He's got to be seen by a doctor and certified okay. Or we got to get somebody else flown in here.'

'And the weather?'

'Stinks,' Barney said flatly. 'We got a phase three up there and a radio blackout. We're still on that one diesel generator you hauled up here and, boy, we're on the knife edge.' He rubbed his eyes wearily, then looked moodily at Kelleher. 'Thought you said he was coming to.'

'He was. He was stirring, anyway.' I rose and poured some coffee and handed the cup to Barney. 'That contract,' I said, 'doesn't sound very sensible to me. Not unless the Army's engineers are incompetent.'

'They're okay. Carson and his assistant both have masters' degrees in nuclear engineering. But Kelleher actually led the design team on this baby. That's the real point. Remember it's all still experimental.'

I said, 'What if you overrode the contract terms. As commander on the spot? Difficult decision, I know, but taken in the interests of the whole establishment?'

Barney mustered a rueful grin. 'The only authority I have over the reactor operation is to order a shutdown. And then only on qualified advice. If I ordered those guys to heat her up to the critical phase, first of all they wouldn't do it, because they know

132

the rules, too. After that, well, maybe it's not the most important thing in the world, but they'd log the order and log their refusal, and when their log goes back, guess who gets the fast chop?'

Kelleher, after the first twitches, had lapsed again into deep sleep and Barney decided against waiting. He rose, finished his coffee, and left.

About midnight, Carson came along and peered at the still-sleeping patient. He and one of his technicians were to take over the watch for a few hours while Allen and I got some sleep.

Alone in my hut, I put on pyjamas and climbed into bed. I myself felt almost anaesthetized; bone weary and fuzzy-headed. But, as so often happens when sleep seems infinitely desirable, it becomes unattainable, and I lay in the dark, full of resentment, with my mind slowly gaining a clarity and energy I didn't damned well want. My need was for sleep, not for a quick mental canter round Camp Hundred and its assorted problems and mysteries. But whichever lobe of the brain controls inquisitiveness was now firmly in the saddle and digging in the spurs, and despite myself, I began to brood. I felt pretty sorry for myself, too; full of those wee-small-hours blues that can sometimes come close to despair. Lying there in the dark, I felt them crowding in, and to drive them back a bit, I put on the light and lit a cigarette, and that brought back thoughts of another cigarette I'd smoked in bed, twenty-four hours or so earlier; the one that had damn near been my last.

I got out of bed and looked at the badly-charred chair on which the ashtray had rested the previous night. It was a perfectly ordinary wooden chair, with the seat upholstered in foam-rubber or plastic foam and covered in some kind of charred plastic sheet, PVC or something. The hole in the sheeting was cigarette-shaped, a couple of inches long, and the cylinder of tobacco ash still lay along it. We've all seen dozens of similar burns, caused by careless handling of cigarette ends, and there was nothing unusual about this one. But still, it puzzled me. When you're a smoker, you tend to have a way of putting out a cigarette, and I always fold the butt over and press down hard, so that the lighted end is crushed out by the tip. That way there are no sparks. Ashtrays I've used tend to contain flattened, V-shaped butts. So why was this one straight? Because I hadn't put it out: that was the obvious answer. I must have left it burning in the ashtray and the damn thing had rolled out of it and on to the upholstery. Well, maybe. But I don't put cigarettes down and let them burn away. Never? Well . . . *no*, I thought defensively, I don't do that. It's a thing I'm careful *not* to do. And in any case, there was a memory, almost distinct in my mind, of stubbing that cigarette out before I went to sleep.

The one I was smoking now had burned low, and I was putting it out automatically, when I caught myself in the act and examined what I'd done. It was in the middle of the ashtray, as always; bent over, as always. Hmm . . .

I bent and blew away the ash so I could look more closely at the chair seat. Inside, beneath the two-inch hole, the plastic foam upholstery was badly charred. Pushing my finger through the hole I tried to guess at the size of the burned area. It wasn't big. The burn had cut through the PVC cover and smouldered steadily through quite a few cubic inches of the foam. As I pulled my fingers out again, they were covered in a dark, dusty smear. I tried to brush it off, and couldn't, because the ash was moist.

Moist?

I rubbed my fingers together, the moisture and fine ash turning into a thin black paste on thumb and forefinger. How in hell had it become moist? Half-digested bits of long-ago chemistry lessons came back as I looked for the answer. Did carbon absorb moisture from the atmosphere? I thought so, but couldn't quite remember. Probably it did. On the other hand, this hut was heated. What effect would that have? The truth was that I simply didn't know, ill-educated lout that I am. But one thing I did know: water puts out fires!

Okay, I thought. Look at it that way. When I'd stumbled out of the hut, there had been smoke and fumes. The thing was smouldering hard enough then. But when I'd returned later with the duty officer, Westlake, it had been out. And now it was moist.

Also . . . well, also the tunnel door had been locked, and wasn't when Westlake and I returned. Even allowing for my state of near-panic at the time, I was reasonably certain of that.

So . . . ?

I stepped away from the chair and deliberately tried to empty my mind of the conclusion that was swarming all over it; tried to forget the conversation with the medic; tried to be logical and reasonable as I thought it through. I tried it all ways, looking for every possible reason for the sequence of events. But at the end, after half an hour spent resisting it, I found myself accepting the conclusion that fitted. To accept any other, I'd have had to accept, too, the fact that the habits of a lifetime had been temporarily suspended: that I'd mistaken a closed door for a locked one; that I hadn't been able to think straight.

I dressed quickly and left the hut. The lights in Main Street were very dim, keeping the load on the generator low, and the whole length was deserted. I turned into the command trench and went into the hut. Westlake was sitting at Master Sergeant Allen's desk. He looked up from *Red Star Over China*, saw who it was, and said, 'Start another fire?'

I smiled. 'No.'

'So what can I do for you?'

'Is there,' I asked him, 'a fire manual? I'd like to do some reading.'

He grinned. 'More joy in heaven over one sinner that repenteth – '

'The manual,' I said.

'Sure.' He passed it over from a rack of heavy army-issue books on the wall behind his chair.

'Thanks.' I took the plastic-bound volume. 'Mind if I borrow it?'

'Not if it comes back.'

I returned to my hut, lay on the bed and began to try to find my way through about three pounds of assorted fire regulations. Finally I found what I wanted: a complete paper on the effect of fire on plastics. It laid heavy emphasis, as they always do, on the dangers of cigarettes, the need for ashtrays everywhere. Then it went on to describe the particular hazards. PVC, I learned, produced a wide variety of highly toxic gases during combustion, among them phosgene and benzene. But it wasn't PVC that really concerned me. The seat cover was PVC, but the foam inside wasn't. Then I found the bit about polyurethane foam, and read that. Having done so, I read it again. And I wonder, dear reader, as the Victorian novelists used to say, whether you quite realize what it is you're sitting on when you relax in your soft, squashy armchair?

Because polyurethane foam, when it burns, produces, if I may quote the manual 'extremely large volumes from small quantities' of a) carbon monoxide, and b) hydrogen cyanide.' Just to underline the point, carbon monoxide is lethal. All those people who commit suicide by running a hose pipe from the exhaust into the car are making use of carbon monoxide's handy properties. But compared with hydrocyanic gas, carbon monoxide is gentle. Hydrogen cyanide is the stuff they used in American gas chambers to execute murderers – literally the quickest of all gaseous killers.

And polyurethane foam had been smouldering quietly about a foot from my nose!

'Careless fellow,' they'd have said at the inquest, if there had *been* an inquest. 'He left a cigarette burning.'

What I was suddenly burning to know was the name of said careless fellow.

Because I was sure now that somebody had tried to kill me!

Chapter 12

The first shock of realization: the first crawling of the scalp, the first sharp chill around the heart, all wore off after a while. The fear-generated adrenalin coursed round and round and finally wore off too, and I was left with another conclusion: that my great discovery had got me precisely nowhere. To Barney and Westlake, all this would seem like a desperate, not to say crazy, rationalization of my own carelessness. Barney had already muttered, once in my hearing, and probably several times out of it, the word 'paranoid'. If I went to him now and said, 'Look, I've just realized somebody's trying to kill me,' he'd say, 'Prove it.' And I couldn't; my proof rested in the main on self-knowledge, on my own certainty about the way I handled cigarettes, about the way I'd wrestled with the trench door. But to Barney I'd still be the fool who left a cigarette burning. Furthermore, he'd know all the fire and safety regulations backwards – that was the nature of the man. He'd know all about the poisonous gases generated in the combustion of plastics and be merely surprised that I didn't. No, Barney wouldn't take my theories at all seriously. But there was one thing he would take very seriously indeed, and *that* was anything he regarded as spreading alarm and despondency.

All I could do, for the moment at least, was to keep my knowledge to myself. And bloody well watch my back! And then I knew that that wouldn't be enough, because whoever was trying to kill me was also chipping away very effectively indeed at the whole fabric of Camp Hundred. The more I thought about it, the more I became convinced that the medic was right, and that somebody was trying not only to kill me, but to render Hundred uninhabitable. So somehow I must try to find out who was doing it. Above all, why?

I lay back, trying, now that the decision was made, to evolve some method. But my mind must, by that time, have had enough. I drifted off into a confused, disturbed, jumpy kind of

137

shallow doze from which I finally woke with a start of surprise for no reason at all. I'd fallen asleep with the light on and now, forlornly alert, I looked round the little, windowless room, half expecting trouble. The room was empty. Reassured, I glanced at my watch. I'd promised to go back to duty with Kelleher at five and it was now almost half past. Once again I dressed quickly and hurried out.

My nerves jangled an alarm when I went into the hospital hut and discovered that Kirton's office was empty; but in the ward the medic was dozing on one of the spare beds and Carson's corporal sat patiently reading a magazine.

'All well?' I asked softly.

The corporal nodded towards the medic. 'He gave him another shot around one. All quiet since.'

'Fine,' I said. 'Sorry I'm late. Time you had a sleep.'

'Sure is.' He stretched and rose.

I said, 'Did Mr Kelleher waken?'

'Well, he kinda half-wakened.'

'And?'

'Didn't say much. Just was I positive he hadn't had a coronary.'

'He was rational, then?'

'Getting that way. Kinda dopey, you know?'

He left then, and I went to look at the patient. Kelleher seemed completely calm; he was breathing regularly, and so too was the medic. I wished I were as relaxed. I felt unwashed, unrested and unhappy. A cup of coffee helped a little, but not much. I couldn't settle. As soon as I sat in a chair, it developed lumps and bumps and I developed corns and had to move. The conundrum kept rattling round my head and gave me no peace. Somewhere in this place was a man, or men, intent upon sabotage to the point where Camp Hundred folded up. Who? I thought round and round it, but there seemed to be no pointer anywhere. All right, *why*? There was an answer, of sorts, to that, but it was a pretty feeble answer. Hundred was cold and not too comfortable; it was a long way from the civilized pleasures; it must seem, perhaps, a bloody awful posting to a lot of the men. But would anybody seriously embark on a campaign of deliberate and expensive sabotage, and, worse, actually *kill*, just to shorten a posting? Which brought me back to madmen, and I smiled wryly at the thought that the nearest available madman was now sleeping peacefully a few feet away.

The train of thought moved over some points then, as I stood looking at Kelleher. Really, I knew very little about the man, except that from the beginning, and until the previous day's extraordinary seizure, he had struck me as very stable and reliable. It also seemed likely that there was no history of mental illness; had there been, no organization in a field as sensitive as nuclear engineering would have touched him with a very long pole. Come to think of it, I'd be prepared to bet that his company would have any man in Kelleher's line of country examined very closely indeed for chinks in his psychological armour. Lots of American companies, these days, give psychological tests to a salesman's wife before they'll take him on the payroll, let alone a man who's going to design and work on experimental atomic power furnaces.

I lit a cigarette and rather self-consciously looked for an ashtray. Two hours or so drifted slowly by in which nothing happened except that the medic awoke to give Kelleher a little tidying-up. While it was going on, I stood by in case Kelleher woke and became violent again, but he slept peacefully while the canvas leg restraints were removed and he was washed. When the straitjacket was back in position and fastened to the bedposts again, such mild tension as there had been vanished.

About eight o'clock Barney came along to inspect Kelleher again. He looked very tired, his eyes deep in the sockets and the skin dark below them. But his step was brisk, his manner cheerful, and he gave my shoulder an amiable thump. 'How's the patient?'

I said, 'Having the sleep of a lifetime. Whatever else he feels when he wakes up, it won't be tired. What about the diesels?'

He grinned and turned into a German engineer. 'Ve now haff ze Number Two chenerator vorking, mein herr. Und viz luck and maybe a toch or two of chenious, ve skveeze somezing out from ze Number Vun before too many hours, nicht wahr?'

'Good for you.'

'Sure is,' he agreed cheerfully. 'And that's not all. They'll run the Swing in here tomorrow and we've radio contact right now. I talked to Cohen at Belvoir, and they got two new generators ready and crated at Thule to be flown up by Caribou at the first weather break. Can't be more than a few days now.'

I felt myself relax. 'Better and better,' I said, and thought that perhaps the odds were now readjusting themselves in Barney's favour.

He, meanwhile, was prodding the sleeping medic awake with a persistent finger. The medic, eyes closed, first said, 'Hey, knock it off!' in sleepy protest, and then, at the next prod, opened his eyes and shot off the bunk to rigid and embarrassed attention.

'Beg pardon, sir.'

'Blood pressure, pulse rate and whatever else you need,' Barney said, 'then move your goddam ass to the radio room and talk to the shrinks down at Thule. We got the channel open.'

'Yes, sir.'

He turned back to me. 'I'll have you relieved, Engländer, and you can come and have some breakfast. For once, I'm good and hungry.'

I was far from hungry, my appetite dulled by too many cigarettes, irregular hours, broken sleep and a generally morbid outlook, but I nodded and promised to join him. Barney, cheerful, was better company than my own and I was more than ready for an hour or so of gregariousness and good humour.

But the pleasant future didn't materialize. I don't know whether Barney had got as far as dipping a spoon into his cornflakes before the bad news came. As for me, I'd put on my out-of-doors clothing and was waiting, and when Sergeant Vernon came briskly in, I assumed he was there to relieve me, but one glance at his face told me there was more bad news in the offing.

He said urgently, 'Sir, when did you last see Captain Carson?'

I was covered in Arctic clothing, and beginning to sweat, but the warmth was wiped instantly away.

'Why?'

'When did you see him, sir? What *time*?'

I thought for a moment. 'About midnight. When he came to relieve me.' I asked again: 'Why?'

'He just – well, sir, he doesn't seem to be around. Major

Smales asked me – '

'You mean,' I said harshly, 'that Carson has vanished?'

Vernon said, 'Major Smales's compliments, sir, and will you remain right here.'

'Has he?'

He gave a little puzzled shake of the head. 'Captain Carson, sir, he isn't in his quarters, or the officers' club, or the mess hall, or the reactor trench. But it's too soon to say – '

I said, 'Tell Major Smales, please, that when I came back here, around half past five, Captain Carson wasn't here.'

'He should have been here, sir?'

'Yes,' I said bitterly. Why the hell had I ignored it at the time? 'He should have been here.'

Vernon nodded. 'I'll tell the major, sir. Did you report Captain Carson's absence to the duty officer?'

I said, 'No,' guiltily, adding feebly, 'I thought he'd just gone off to bed.'

'Yes, sir.' Vernon was looking at me bleakly. 'I'll tell the major, sir.' He walked out, rigid with disapproval. After the door closed behind him, I swore, angrily and aloud. A minute later I went to the door and turned the key. When Barney came, I'd open it and face the music, but for the moment I felt safer behind a locked door.

I paced up and down. Somehow I didn't doubt for a second that Carson *had* disappeared. But how, and *why*? What the hell was going on in the reactor trench? Yesterday it was Kelleher, solid as a rock, who'd gone stark raving mad. Now, less than twenty-four hours later, it was Carson, also a nuclear engineer and also a solid citizen, who'd . . .

For a few moments I wondered whether there'd possibly been some radiation leak; whether some unknown effect of exposure induced madness? But Carson hadn't gone mad, not, at any rate, so far as I knew. Vernon had said only that there was no sign of him. *Once was happenstance, twice coincidence, the third time . . .* My eyes went to Kelleher. First Kirton, then Kelleher, now Carson; doctor and two engineers. Without them, Hundred had no medical resources and no reactor. In one of the coldest and most dangerous places on the face of the earth, those three men were vital both to physical and mental comfort. So if Kirton *had* been killed, and Carson had . . . But no. Kelleher didn't fit. Kelleher hadn't been attacked. Kelleher had simply cracked under the strain of day and night work. His mind had gone, bent or broken by pressure.

I was hanging up my outdoor clothes when the phone rang.

It was Barney. Or rather, it was Major Barnet M. Smales, US Army, formally correct, his tone icy. 'A few questions, Mr Bowes. One, you arranged with Captain Carson that you would relieve him at five?'

'Yes?'

'And this you failed to do?'

'I was late.'

'Captain Carson was not there when you arrived?'

'No.'

'No message?'

'No.'

'And you did nothing about it?'

I said, 'It was five-thirty a.m. I made the reasonable assumption that he'd gone to bed. What about Carson's corporal? Didn't Carson say anything to him?'

He didn't answer. Instead, 'You will remain where you are, in the hospital, until further notice. Under no circumstances will you leave it except under my direct instructions, until you will leave Camp Hundred by the first available means.'

'That's ridic – '

He cut me off. 'Do you understand?'

'Yes.'

He hung up. So, after a moment, did I. I was in the wrong, certainly, but not *that* much in the wrong. I should have reported Carson's absence, no doubt about that. No doubt *now*, at any rate; no doubt even in retrospect. But at the time . . .? And now I'd wrecked my whole purpose in being there. The TK4 wouldn't get its demonstration, the US Army woudn't buy, the order was lost.

I wandered morosely back to the ward, cursing Barney, Camp Hundred, and myself, and as I went in through the door, Kelleher said, 'Get a guy a cup of coffee?'

142

I went over to the bed and looked down at him with something approaching suspicion. My cheek, where Kelleher's teeth had ripped at it the day before, still ached dully. The frantic strength he'd displayed as we struggled to pin him down was vivid in my memory, and I'd no way of knowing his state of mind. He'd been quiet enough; he'd slept peacefully; he'd spoken almost rationally. *Almost*. Also he was about three stones heavier and a great deal stronger than I.

'C'mon,' he croaked, 'I got a mouth like they been shovelling ashes around inside.'

I said, 'All right,' and went to get it. When I came back, I said, 'Raise your head.'

He blinked at me. 'I'm in a straitjacket, right, Harry?'

'You are. Raise your head.'

I held the coffee while he sipped, straining upwards to get his lips to the cup. He swilled the hot liquid round his mouth, swallowed, and lay back. 'Why?'

'Yesterday,' I said, 'you acted somewhat strangely.'

'I did, huh?'

'You did. More coffee?'

He nodded and drank again. He seemed strangely resigned. Looking down at him, I tried to imagine what it must be like to awaken in a straitjacket: the surprise, the sudden fear that would probably turn to panic. Kelleher showed none of that. 'No sugar in the coffee,' he said.

'How do you feel?'

'Feel? Relaxed, I think,'

'Good.'

He lay thinking for a moment. Then said suddenly, 'It was dust. I had to get the dust out.'

Out of what? I wondered. 'Out of the reactor?'

'Well, sure. It was like rocks in there. Big boulders of goddam dust. It got inside there while the lid was off.'

'Did it? Have some more coffee.'

After he'd drunk he lay still for a while, but his eyes were restless. I took the empty cup and rinsed it out and when I returned, Kelleher said, 'But it couldn't be. Not like boulders!'

'Probably not.'

'I can see 'em, you know, right here in my head.'

'Boulders of dust?'

'Sure.'

'What else can you see?'

He thought about it. 'You know steel's got pores? Pores like skin?'

'I didn't know.' His rationality was open to considerable question, I'd decided, and the passing minutes reinforced my decision: the jacket would stay on.

'Well, it sure has.'

'What for? It doesn't sweat.'

Kelleher considered that. 'No, that's right. It seemed like the dust was blocking the pores, though, and – '

'And?' I prompted, after a moment.

'Well, I had to clean it away.' His eyes swivelled up at me, wide, suddenly appalled. 'This straitjacket! I'm crazy?'

I tried to put it carefully. 'These ideas, the dust boulders, the pores, seem very strong.'

Panicky now, voice taut with fear. 'I've gone crazy!'

'You saw the fallacy,' I said, 'but afterwards.'

Muscles and tendons tightened in his neck and I was suddenly apprehensive of another seizure. I said hastily, 'Don't worry!'

'It's like it's in the front of my head. Dead wrong, but up there in front.' His eyes met mine head on. 'You afraid of me?'

I shook my head, but not quickly enough.

'Jesus!' he sagged back.

I reached for my cigarettes and was lighting one when he said, 'They wouldn't let me do it?'

'No,' I said, 'they wouldn't.'

Kelleher gave a harsh little laugh. 'For Christ's sake, why – ' Then he broke off, paused, and added quietly, 'I was fighting. Fighting to get . . . to get *inside*?'

I nodded. 'You tried.'

'Yeah, well, they wouldn't let me – !' He exhaled strongly through his nostrils. 'Maybe my life got saved. Who did it, you?'

'One or two people.' I added encouragingly, 'You're seeing the fallacies more quickly now.'

144

He was suddenly anxious. 'I hurt anybody?'

'A knock or two. Nothing much.'

'Well, they wouldn't let me . . . *Jesus, I can't think straight!*'

'Straighter all the time. What else is in the front of your head?'

His eyes closed. Behind the lids there was no movement. Then he opened them. 'Well, did you see that space movie?'

'Which one?'

'With the waltz. What was it? The Blue Danube?'

'*Two Thousand and One*, the film was called.'

'Yeah. Remember the end. Kinda weird. Just going straight ahead through all the planes and patterns. Just through space. No meaning, you know?'

'I remember.'

'Well, like that.'

I said, 'Where were you going?'

Kelleher thought about it, then shook his head. 'I just don't know. Away, maybe.'

'From what?'

'Who knows?' He gave a sudden grin. 'Camp Hundred, huh? Look, do me a favour.'

'If I can.'

'Ask me some questions. About myself. I want to know how crazy I am.'

He answered all the questions easily and quickly. He knew where he'd been born, educated, employed; all the personal details were tabulated neatly inside him and came out pat. He was clearly relieved to find he could do it. I took a sourer view. If he hadn't been able to remember, he'd certainly have been in worse condition; the fact that he could did nothing to relieve my anxieties about his thought processes.

When the quiz was over, he said, 'You're not gonna take off the jacket, right?'

'No. I'm sorry.'

'You're a bastard, you know that? I'm gonna be okay.' But he wasn't angry.

Anyway, I'd had enough for the time being and removed myself to the office to give both Kelleher and myself a little peace.

I felt low enough to limbo dance under a cellar door, depressed both by the futility of my whole trip to Greenland, and by the wreckage of a tough mind a couple of doors away. I didn't share his certainty that he'd recover. In my limited experience – I had an aunt once who had a nervous breakdown, and there was a bloke I worked with who'd turned all of a sudden into a manic depressive – damaged minds seemed to stay damaged. Brains go on working, keeping the lid on the stresses, but once the stresses do burst out, they stay out. Primitive reasoning. I sat smoking moodily, wondering what had triggered the break. In Kelleher's case it was probably simple overstrain, but even so it was dismal to think that a first-class man, solidly sane one moment, had his mind in pieces the next. Well, perhaps not smashed. Not even broken, but bent out of true. I remember thinking that it seemed a good analogy: an iron bar, bent to an angle, and no matter how carefully you tried to straighten it, there'd always be a weakness where the bend had been.

I began to think, with foreboding, then, of the journey back, of the long uncomfortable haul across the icecap on the Swing, of the long faces at Thomson-Keegan when the news of my foul-up came through, and of the way Jim Keegan would be careful to be forgiving. And then, quite suddenly, out of the lumber-room of random thoughts, a couple of words squirmed out on to the surface of my brain and interrupted the train of thought. The first word was mind. The second, already linked to it, was 'bent'. Mind-bending – wasn't *that* how people described the effects of drugs? Minds were 'bent' or 'blown', weren't they? Certainly in the newspapers. And there were other words: 'psychedelic' and 'trip' . . . all related to the drugs that bent minds. Mainly to LSD, which was . . . what? Some acid, wasn't it? The name escaped me, but there was another phrase: 'acid-heads'. I sat there trying to recall what I'd read and came up with nothing but a mish-mash of half-digested newspaper stories about people claiming they could hear tastes and smell sounds. And an inquest on somebody who, on an LSD trip, had walked out of a top-floor window in the belief he could . . .

I thought carefully about that. Kelleher hadn't walked out of any top-floor windows, but he'd certainly achieved a fair equivalent. If any person in his senses knew a long drop was fatal, any nuclear engineer in *his* senses knew the dangers of the reactor.

There was something else, too, that I recalled reading somewhere: that any competent sixth-form chemistry student could manufacture LSD in a school laboratory if he knew how and had the materials. I didn't know what the materials were, but Camp Hundred certainly had its laboratories! Then another thought: colour came into it, too, surely? I seemed to remember that vivid colours were part of the LSD hallucination.

Kelleher looked up at me gravely as I approached his bed. I said, 'How much do you remember about yesterday?'

'When was yesterday?'

'That's when it happened. Yesterday morning. Do you remember it?'

He pursed his lips. 'I itch like crazy and I can't scratch.'

'Do you remember?'

He considered it. 'Let me think. Yeah, I remember. We worked through the night, then I had a cup of coffee and crawled on to a cot for a half-hour. I do that sometimes. Take a little break. And then . . .' He frowned.

'Go on.'

'I'm not too sure. I think . . . yeah, I got the idea about dust, that's right. So I went out and there it was. And I went to clear it. And –'

I interrupted. 'The cup of coffee. Where did it come from?'

'We got an ever-hot machine in there.'

'And sugar? You take sugar?'

'In my desk. Why?'

'Just answer,' I said urgently.

'I got those paper sugar bags in a little box.'

'You just took the top one and poured it in?'

'Well, why not?'

'Think about it,' I said. 'You stir sugar into your coffee. Then you drink it and lie down. And shortly afterwards you start having bloody great hallucinations about boulders of dust and steel that looks like skin, and you see colours whirling about. What does that little lot suggest?'

Kelleher stared at me. 'Welcome to the crazy club.'

147

'Go on. Tell me what it sounds like.'

He told me. He told me I was nuts, that it was impossible, that nobody at Hundred would do a goddam crazy thing like that.

'Like what?'

'Like putting acid in my coffee.'

'In your sugar,' I said. 'I believe sugar's the classic medium.'

In the next few moments, a variety of expressions came and went on his face. The only one that stayed there was the last, and it was relief.

He said, 'I told you I'd be okay. Now we tell Barney.'

'Not yet,' I said.

'Why the hell not?'

'Because he'll choose not to believe it.'

'Barney? Sure he'll believe it. He'll believe me, I know that.'

I said, 'Look, Barney saw you. After you tried to climb into the reactor, while you were fighting everybody off, Barney was there. If your nose feels sore, it's because Barney thumped it.'

'Oh, c'mon. I've known Barney years.'

I shook my head. 'He told me yesterday about the reactor contract. He's already made up his mind not to let you near the thing again. Barney is *not* going to listen.'

'Talk all you want,' Kelleher said. 'I still want to see him, right?'

I conceded. 'I'll telephone the command office.'

Master Sergeant Allen told me Barney wasn't there; he was out checking and rechecking every hut, supervising the search for Carson. I asked Allen to pass on to Barney a message that Mr Kelleher was awake and anxious to talk to him.

We waited, talking desultorily. Out of plain self-defence I didn't mention my theory to Kelleher. If he could convince Barney of what must have been done to him, that was fine; but if Kelleher quoted me to Barney, his own story would be damned from that moment. Kelleher seemed content to think that the LSD had been fed to him, if indeed it had, out of personal spite or malice. Maybe he'd been driving people too hard.

He dozed off again after a while, and I tiptoed out to the office to avoid wakening him. If sleep could knit his ravelled mind, I was all for sleep.

The medic came back eventually, having spent a lot of time on a very poor radio line to some Air Force psychiatrist at Thule base. It hadn't, I gathered, been a very profitable consultation. The psychiatrist had approved what had been done, had prescribed specified sedation as necessary, and wanted Kelleher flown out to the base hospital as soon as possible.

I said, 'Well, there's no need for sedation at the moment. He's asleep.'

He nodded. He, too, was out of his depth. I glanced at my watch and said, 'Why don't you get something to eat?'

He brightened a little and went to lunch. There was no way I could have guessed it was already too late – for him and many more.

Chapter 13

Some time after the medic had left, a complaining stomach reminded me first that I'd had no food that day, secondly that Kelleher had eaten nothing for at least thirty hours, and thirdly that no arrangements had been made for meals to be sent to us in the hospital. Something would have to be done. I picked up the phone, dialled the cookhouse number, and waited while it rang and rang. Then I hung up and dialled again. Still no response. Next I tried the command office, on the grounds that Allen would fix it. No response there, either, and that was strange: the command office was manned day and night.

Then, just a few minutes later, the door opened and Allen himself stood in the doorway. He was swaying, half-doubled over, his black skin gone greasy grey, his arms folded tight and low across his stomach. He started to say something, but gagged deep in his throat, half-turned and vomited uncontrollably out of the door. It took me a couple of seconds to reach him and when I did I could only stand holding him as he continued retching. Then he seemed to have finished and tried to straighten, but another spasm gripped him and he retched again, groaning and shaking and clearly in considerable pain. When he spoke it was in a strangled croak, so punctuated by contractions of throat and stomach that it seemed the words would never come. At last he managed to get them out. 'Food poisoning.'

'Come in,' I said. 'Lie down and – '

'Not just me,' Allen gasped. 'The cookhouse . . . half the camp . . . for God's sake look . . . look . . . in the Doc's books!' Then he was retching again, sinking to his knees in the doorway.

The next few hours were horrific. Almost eighty men were affected and it seemed at times that the entire population of the camp was collapsing in the snow with acute stomach pains, vomiting and diarrhoea, and there was no help to be had from the medical staff at Thule because radio communication had again disintegrated into mush and static. We all did what we could, pouring saline solution into the sufferers, hustling them off to bed, wrapping blankets round them. The book said victims must be kept warm, and the hospital's stock of hot water bottles numbered four. Anything that would hold hot water was filled and distributed. We didn't know what we were dealing with, and since the medic, who might conceivably have known, was one of the worst victims, we didn't even know if the treatment was correct.

By late evening, three men were dead and many others in a state of almost total collapse, being nursed by their friends. But by then we had radio contact again and were able to raid the dispensary for botulinus antitoxin. It almost certainly saved several lives. Kirton, if he'd been alive, might well have saved more.

I don't know when I heard about Barney. It must have been some time during the long afternoon that someone said Major Smales, too, was a victim, but I was too busy to take much notice, and in any case, with so many affected, it was hardly surprising. Later, it was rumoured for a while that he'd died, and Westlake too, but I learned later still that, though both were badly affected, they seemed to be holding their own.

By that night, Camp Hundred was in a mess. Two Air Force doctors from Thule had volunteered to be parachuted in, but the offer had to be turned down. Weather conditions up above were very bad, with winds gusting near a hundred miles an hour and the temperature thirty below. Two brave men would have been jumping to their deaths.

At one point in the afternoon, I'd slipped Kelleher a couple of sleeping tablets, in the belief that, since I couldn't release him to help and he would only chafe angrily if he were to lie helpless through it all, he'd be better asleep. They worked, but not for long. By that time he'd slept so much that it would have needed a hammer to keep his eyes closed for long. So, though he'd slept for a couple of hours, he'd also lain awake, thinking. I was sitting beside his bed, which I'd dragged into the office to leave more space free in the ward, drinking coffee and eating a bar of chocolate, when he said, 'You reckon this whole thing could be deliberate?'

I turned and stared at him. I'd been so busy the thought hadn't even occurred to me. 'How could it be? It's on too big a scale.'

Kelleher said slowly, 'You got a freezer at home, Harry?'

I shook my head.

'We have,' he said. 'The instructions, the books, the deep freeze centres, they all warn you the same way. It's dangerous to thaw and freeze again.'

'So?'

'So up here it's all frozen. Well, most of the stuff is. Meat is, that's for damn sure. You got any idea what those guys ate?'

I said, 'As far as we can tell, it was the ham they had at breakfast. Some of them were feeling queasy before lunch. Nobody seems to think it was the lunch food. How do you feel, anyway?'

'Hungry as hell, but I can sure resist it now.'

'Otherwise?'

'Fine. No problems. Head's clear. Whatever it was, LSD or what, it's all worn off.' He gave me a lopsided grin. 'But either you let me out of this goddam thing or you make like a nurse with bottles and bedpans.'

I was too tired to argue. I bent over the bed and began to undo strappings. A few minutes later he was on his feet, stretching cramped muscles and I turned my back on him. If he was going to attack, I thought wearily, it might as well be now. I counted to ten slowly, then turned to face him. He was holding on to the bedrail slowly doing leg-bending exercises.

'Tell you how it could be done,' Kelleher said. 'You've seen the food trenches?'

I nodded.

'Food, meat in particular, comes up on the Swing, stays frozen clear across the cap. When it gets here it's hung in a trench, still frozen. Keeps forever, almost, courtesy of Mother Nature. Now, we got a bad outbreak of food poisoning, right? Okay, so somebody maybe got himself a coupla sides of ham.'

'Go on.'

'Anyway, they're frozen. He takes them, hangs 'em some place warm for a while, puts 'em back; maybe he even does it again. Then he puts 'em right at the front of the rack of ham, okay? Then along comes the guy from the cookhouse. Ham for breakfast again, there's ham for breakfast every day. He takes the first couple of sides, slices it into strips and there you got it!'

I didn't answer; I was thinking about the dreadful suffering of eighty men. And even though I'd no doubts in my own mind that somebody *was* sabotaging Camp Hundred, it was hard to believe anyone would set out deliberately to poison so many.

'It fits,' Kelleher said.

'Yes,' I said slowly. 'It fits. Do *you* believe it?'

'I'll believe anything of the man who'd slip acid to a guy working on a reactor!'

I went and washed my hands and face in cold water. I felt sluggish and sleepy and dared not give in to it. If Kelleher was right, and if the homicidal idiot at Camp Hundred was now prepared to go to any lengths to wreck the whole establishment, nobody could afford the luxury of rest.

The cold water made me feel a little fresher, but not much. I wasn't at even the fifty-per-cent efficiency promised for life at Hundred; five per cent was more like it.

Kelleher, however, was like an Airedale terrier with a newly-discovered bone. 'I thought about all this. I can see maybe how it's all happened. What I don't see is *why*?'

I shrugged. 'Somebody wants Camp Hundred out of action.'

'Okay. Why?'

'Difficult to see. Hates the army perhaps.'

'Everybody hates the army. A little or a lot, but everybody.'

I said, 'We're talking about a madman. Death and destruction in bloody great bucketsful.'

'He's a smart madman!'

'That's not uncommon. Look, perhaps he hates the army and this is a way of striking back. *Or*, perhaps he hates Camp Hundred, and ditto. *Or*, he hates Barney, or you, or me even. What it is doesn't matter. He's hitting as hard as he can at everything and everybody in the place.'

Kelleher considered it. 'I don't go for that blind hate.'

'Give me an alternative.'

'Guy's got something to hide.'

'Like what? If anybody wants to hide anything, this is probably the best place in the world. Seventeen feet of snow every winter.

It'll cover anything.'

'No. Not an object. Some offence or other. Something that's got to be kept quiet.'

'All right. In that case we have another theory, but it's no more than that. If Camp Hundred were a normal army camp, somebody might be organizing a fiddle, flogging rations or petrol or something. But not here.'

Kelleher looked up at me. 'So we got to find out.'

'Yes.'

'Question is how.'

'Yes.' I wasn't being unhelpful. I'd been over this ground so many times in my mind that I knew every bump and hollow. My own brain wasn't going to dig out bright new thoughts. Kelleher's might.

He said, 'Okay, we start somewhere.'

'Like?'

'I'll tell you – ' but he didn't. Not then, anyway, because we were interrupted. The door opened and a less-than-young lieutenant entered and announced that until his seniors were recovered, he was in temporary command. His name was Coveney and I'd met him, exchanged a word or two in the officers' club. He'd struck me as dull and a bit taciturn.

Kelleher said, 'How's Barney?' His tone was flat. I got the impression he didn't like Coveney.

'Major Smales is very sick,' Coveney said. 'Conscious only in patches. However, I managed to speak to him briefly and he agrees to my assumption of temporary command.' He looked from Kelleher to me and back again. 'I understood you, Mr Kelleher, were under restraint.'

'That's right.'

'Under whose orders were you released?'

I said. 'I released him. There's nothing wrong with him now.'

'You're a qualified psychiatrist, Mr er – ?'

'Bowes,' I said, 'and even a hovercraft pilot can see he's okay now.'

He looked at me along his narrow nose. 'The restraint was ordered by the commander and has not been rescinded. A man who only yesterday was totally unbalanced can hardly be – '

I said, 'So rescind it.'

'On the contrary, I insist that Major Smales's orders be carried out.'

Kelleher said incredulously, 'You want me back in the strait-jacket?'

'That was the prescribed restraint.'

I said, 'Don't be bloody stupid!'

Coveney said, 'If necessary, I will call for assistance. I have no wish to use force, but if it should prove necessary, it will be used.'

'One problem,' Kelleher said with heavy sarcasm. 'Those jackets aren't made like raincoats; the guy who's wearing it can't fasten it up.'

'Mr Bowes will fasten it. He will also be responsible for you until further notice. Furthermore, Major Smales's orders concerning Mr Bowes continue in force. He is not to leave this medical block without the permission of the commander.'

'You?'

'That's right, Mr Bowes. Until Major Smales is recovered you answer to me. Now please put the jacket on to Mr Kelleher.'

I was going to refuse, tell him to shove off, be as corrosively rude as I wanted to be. What stopped me was the realization that Coveney *had* the power. If I didn't truss Kelleher, somebody else would. If I indulged my splenetic instincts, Coveney could simply separate us, and lock me up somewhere. So I went back to the ward, got the straitjacket and buckled the visibly-fuming Kelleher into it. Nor was that the end. Coveney insisted that Kelleher's jacket be secured to the steel bed and he watched while I fastened the straps.

I'd felt it necessary to restrain my reactions. Kelleher obviously didn't. As I worked on the fastening, he said scathingly, 'They get like this after they've been passed over for promotion a few times.'

Coveney looked at him. 'In the current crisis situation here I feel it necessary to take every sensible precaution. I regret having to order this, naturally, and I will say so in my report. But in view of Mr Kelleher's recent mental history there is no option. Good night.'

155

Kelleher was shouting, 'I'll be making reports, too, and don't you forget it.' The door's closing click punctuated the sentence; no doubt Coveney heard the first relevant words, but it was beneath him either to return or reply.

I bent over Kelleher, unfastened all the strappings and asked, 'Why does he love you?'

He gave a little grin. 'Playing bad bridge keeps him poor. Maybe it keeps him a lieutenant, too.'

'You've taken a lot of his money?'

'Let's just say I don't earn all my bread making contracts. I just reckon I could. I was gonna tell you where we start, right?'

'Where?'

'Here. Medical records.'

I shook my head. 'I thought of it earlier. The filing cabinets are all locked.'

'Keys must be around some place.'

We searched for a while and failed to find any keys at all. I said, 'Doc Kirton must have carried them with him. Presumably all his personal effects would have been taken from his body. They'll be wherever things like that are kept.'

'Barney has a safe,' Kelleher said.

'Which will also require keys.'

'Yeah.' The corners of his mouth turned down, then he rose and went over to the steel cabinets. 'Time was,' he said, 'when you could just drill a little hole, right here above the lock, and push a paper clip in and work the lock-spring.' He examined the cabinet closely. 'Nope. Not any more. Uncle Sam only buys the best!'

'We could lever it open,' I said. 'Burst the lock.'

Kelleher jerked his head towards the ward. 'No need. Allen's in there.'

'Allen,' I said, 'is a very sick man.'

'Sure. But he'll know where the keys are. Allen knows everything.'

'Except who's doing all this.'

We went through into the ward. It stank of sweat and vomit, and two young soldiers who'd volunteered to act as nurses looked almost as ill as the patients. Kelleher said to one of them,

'Take a half-hour break, son. We'll watch out.'

The boy looked grateful, wasted no time in accepting, and took his partner with him. We crossed to Allen's bed. He looked bad; skin still grey and sickly, sweat shining on his face, and he was dozing. I didn't want to awaken him; Kelleher didn't hesitate; he put his big hand on Allen's shoulder and shook it gently.

After a moment, Allen's eyes opened. He blinked, then gave a little groan.

'You strong enough to talk?' Kelleher asked quietly.

Allen blinked again, swallowed in that awful way of the nauseated, when it's a toss-up whether the forced swallow will overcome the regurgitative reflex. He looked a little relieved, and nodded faintly. 'What is it?' His voice was weak, not quite a whisper.

Kelleher said, 'When Doc Kirton died, what happened to his possessions?'

Allen's eyes widened. 'What do you want?'

Kelleher glanced round the ward. Not all the men were asleep. He said very softly, 'Mr Bowes and I, we think all this, the food poisoning, Captain Carson's disappearance, the whole deal, we think it's all been done by one guy.'

Allen looked at him steadily. 'You – ' he swallowed again – 'you got reasons for that?'

Kelleher said, 'What happened to me was a bad acid trip. Somebody slipped me acid. There are too many accidents now. Too much to explain. It's got to be tracked down. We want to see the medical records but the files are locked.'

'A bad trip,' Allen repeated. He paused, then turned his head to look at me. 'You saw . . . yesterday.'

'Saw what?'

'Major Smales. Right early. He was – ' again that suspenseful swallow – 'real strange. You noticed.'

I stared at him, recalling the interview that had so puzzled me, and the oblique conversation with Allen in his office afterwards.

'Yes,' I said, 'I noticed. Barney told me he had a migraine.'

'Migraine, huh?' Kelleher said. 'Tell you something. I'm a migraine man myself. One effect is a kind of flashing light, it's like you've just been dazzled.'

157

'It seemed to wear off quickly.'

'Maybe he only got a real small shot.'

'Maybe. How did he get it?'

Allen had struggled to sit up. Now, speech made difficult by the continuing stomach contractions, he managed to explain that Barney slept badly and always woke early and kept a flask of coffee at his bedside. He could have woken in the middle of the night, taken coffee, and slept again.

'Which means,' Kelleher said, 'that the stuff could already have been wearing off?'

'Right.' Allen turned, put his feet on the floor.

'Stay where you are,' I said.

He shook his head weakly. 'I can go into the command office for the keys. You guys can't do that.'

'You'd never make it,' Kelleher said.

Allen swallowed again painfully. 'I'll make it.'

I glanced at Kelleher. We were both reluctant even to let Allen try. All the same, weak and shaky though he was, he'd forced himself to his feet and now he took two or three slow steps. 'I ain't gonna win no marathons,' Allen said, 'but I'll make it.'

He was determined and Kelleher and I conceded, feeling guilty about it. We helped Allen into his parka and boots, and went to the door with him. As he was about to go, I said, 'Doc Kirton's effects. Where will they be?'

He turned. 'They're still on his body. What's left of it. We figured we'd leave all that. He was kind of a mess.'

Kelleher patted his shoulder. 'Listen, take your time.'

'Sure.' Allen looked as though he was about to be sick again, but he fought it and won. Then he said, 'Reckon I'll try talking to Major Smales.'

'Don't,' I said.

'Maybe he'll listen to me.'

'Don't bank on it.'

He went down the two steps and slowly off along the trench. We watched through the open door until he reached Main Street and turned towards the command hut.

There was nothing we could do, except wait for Allen's return.

158

We talked desultorily, almost pointlessly, going over the ground again and again. Kelleher, who knew Camp Hundred and its personnel far better than I, found himself totally unable to pick out a suspect. All I got from him was a new light on Barney's character: new and rather revealing. Ten years earlier, it seemed, when Barney had been in Antarctica on Operation Deep Freeze, he and half a dozen men had spent a winter on a big ice-floe. There had been trouble of various kinds: one man had fallen into super-cooled water off the edge of the floe, and the shock had killed him; another had died of peritonitis following a ruptured appendix, and there had been a fire in one of the huts. Barney had sent out an SOS and Deep Freeze had mounted a massive, difficult and wildly expensive operation to lift off the five remaining men. It had been held at the time that the SOS had been unnecessary; that Captain Smales, as he then was, had not shown sufficient durability. He'd almost been thrown off Cold Regions Research and it had taken him a long time to work himself back into favour.

I said, 'He worked himself back, though. They'd never have given him Camp Hundred otherwise.'

'Oh sure. But it's in his record, and he knows it. So he won't be exactly keen to admit it if things start slipping beyond his control.'

The minutes ticked by. Twice I went to the door and looked along the trench, hoping to see Allen returning, but there was no sign of him. After half an hour, when the two soldiers returned to duty in the ward, Allen still had not shown up and, what made it worse, there was no message from him. By now both of us were worried. It seemed to us that there were three possibilities: that Allen had collapsed somewhere and was being looked after; that he'd collapsed and was *not* being looked after. *Or*, the possibility that loomed in the forefront of both our minds, that he had been attacked and disposed of in some way.

At length Kelleher rose, crossed to the wall speaker, moved the switch and spoke into the address system. 'Will Master Sergeant Allen please report at once to the medical block.' He repeated the message and switched off. 'He ought to hear that.'

'If he's in a position to hear it.'

'Yeah.' Kelleher sat down heavily, drumming his fingers on the arm of his chair. He was frowning, staring straight ahead. After a moment he said, 'There's one thing's bugged me from the start.'

'Go on.'

'The water. Impurities in the water. That's what stopped us on the reactor, and I just don't understand it. Look, normally we use distilled water because you can't afford any contamination in the reactor. But melted snow, in effect, *is* distilled. It's been sucked up from the ocean, turned to vapour and then precipitated. So up here there's no need for distillation. Nowadays there's maybe some smoke mixed up in new snow, some pollution. But the snow that fell a hundred, two hundred years ago, well, water from that's as pure as you can get, right?'

I nodded.

'So all of a sudden it's polluted.'

'How badly?'

'Bad enough. Looks to me now as though our friendly maniac must have dropped something down the well.'

I said, 'Sergeant Vernon went down. He didn't see anything.'

'Don't mean a thing. You could let go any of a hundred things down there. Chemical salts, cleaning fluids, metal dust – there's a whole lot of ways – and the stuff's either so dispersed or dissolved nobody'd see anything. You'd need a real good lab to isolate what it was.'

I said, 'The top of the well's open. It wouldn't be difficult. But how many people are likely to know that the reactor could be disabled as easily as that?'

He shrugged. 'Hell, anybody would know. All the reactor people anyway. There'd be plenty who'd know.'

'I didn't.'

He gave me a dismissive glance. 'You haven't read the manual.'

'Perhaps our friend has. Where is it?'

'Plenty around. There's copies here in the camp library.'

Still no word from Allen. As we talked, we read the worry in each other's faces. Kelleher's feelings matched my own: frustration at our confinement and consequent helplessness, a resentment that was the stronger because it was, in a way, voluntary;

160

we were confined only by orders, and they were orders neither of us much respected.

The Tannoy came on then, with a click, and Coveney's voice boomed out of it. 'This is the Acting Commander, Camp Hundred,' he began, in one of those sharp military voices that snap and crackle like Rice Krispies. He sounded a bit like Field Marshal Montgomery with an American accent. The instructions came pouring out. Hundred was a shambles and must be cleaned. The men were scruffy and had been letting themselves go in the last few days. Starting now, all empty huts were to be fumigated and thoroughly cleaned and then the sick were to be transferred into them. Starting next morning, there would be an inspection parade in Main Street and he expected everything and everybody to be clean, pressed and shiny. And so on and so on.

I said, 'There'll be a bloody mutiny!'

Kelleher cocked an eyebrow at me. 'Don't bet on it. But you can bet there's gonna be chaos.'

'Opportunities for the maniac.'

He nodded. 'Sure. For us, too.'

Chapter 14

'Coveney will be back,' I said.

Kelleher gave me a tight little smile. 'I got a contract. It says a whole lot of things, and one of them is that I'm in no way attached to the Corps of Engineers for discipline, right?'

'I'm not talking about afterwards. At the moment he's in a mood to mount guards.'

'Don't worry. I got it figured.' His voice took on urgency. 'First thing is to find Allen. Get going.'

'What about you?'

'I got a little ole trick to set up here. Then I'll go to the reactor trench, okay? See you there in twenty minutes.'

I nodded, wondering about the little ole trick, then decided not to wonder any more. As I began to slip on my parka, Kelleher said: 'Take one of the others. Those guys in the ward sure won't be needing parkas.'

So I borrowed one that belonged to a sleeping victim called Douglas – the name was on a strip of tape above the breast pocket – put the hood up and pulled the drawstring tighter to conceal as much of my face as was reasonable. To have drawn it really tight would have attracted, rather than diverted attention. It wasn't much of a protection, but I wasn't going far and if I kept my head down it ought to suffice.

As I stepped down into the tunnel, closing the door behind me, I looked carefully around, but the long, ice-walled trench was deserted. Walking briskly, I turned into Main Street, heading for the command hut. There was nobody about and I wondered cynically whether they were already busy with razors and furniture polish. The command trench was two along and I made directly for it, but stopped as I passed the entrance to the ablution block. Could it be that Allen, struck by a further bout of nausea, had gone in there and perhaps collapsed?

But he hadn't. Or if he had, he'd left. The ablution block was deserted, the shower stalls and baths empty, the long line of unscreened lavatory pans unoccupied – probably for the first time in hours. As I left, three men came hurrying in, too preoccupied with speed and discomfort even to glance at me.

The command hut was manned through the whole twenty-four hours: by Smales and Allen during the day and then by the duty officers. But it wasn't manned now. There was no sign of Allen and no duty officer, but the lights were on. It occurred to me that Coveney, having moved in, must now be making a tour of inspection. Probably a thorough one. And a time-wasting one, too: his own time and everybody else's. In that case, I might not be disturbed for a few minutes. I went into Barney's office, just to be sure. Allen wasn't in there, and the room was empty. So where the hell *was* Allen? There was a kind of certainty and assurance about the man, and I'd been fairly sure I'd find him here. My stomach tightened suddenly. Allen had left the medical block to come here, intending to get the keys and come straight back. But I hadn't passed him and he wasn't here. So . . .

There was one of those flat key cupboards on the wall. I opened it quickly and began inspecting the labels. Beneath the blue and white plastic strip that said 'Medical Block Duplicates' was an empty hook. I gave a little sigh of relief. At least Allen had been here. Then I corrected myself. It didn't mean that, at all. He *might* have been here, that's all it meant. And if he had, if he'd taken the keys and left, why hadn't he come back to the medical block?

I closed the cupboard doors, turned to leave and swore softly to myself as a foot sounded suddenly on the wooden step outside. The door swung open and Sergeant Vernon came in. A ridiculous impulse made me turn my back on him to hide my face. I must have looked as guilty as a dog caught with the Sunday joint in his mouth.

'Okay, who is it?' Vernon said.

I turned, reddening.

'Mr Bowes? What are you – ?'

I said quickly, 'Have you seen Master Sergeant Allen?'

He was looking at me levelly. Did he know about Coveney's orders?

He knew all right. 'Sir, you are under orders to remain in the medical block.'

'Allen,' I insisted. 'Have you see him?'

'Sure I've seen him. He's in the medical block.'

'No,' I said. 'He left, half an hour or so ago, to come here. He hasn't come back. I came to look for him.'

Vernon nodded. 'I heard the Tannoy. What did he want?'

'I don't know. Didn't ask.'

Vernon said, 'You shouldn't have let him go. Allen's sick.'

'Also determined. And I lack authority. But he's got to be found. He might have collapsed somewhere.'

'Okay, Mr Bowes.' Vernon nodded. 'I'll handle it. I'll get some guys out looking. Now I have to ask you to return to the medical block.'

'I'll go,' I said. There was nothing else I could say. 'But Allen's ill. It's important to – '

Vernon's sterness relaxed a trifle. 'Joe Allen's a friend of mine,' he said. 'I'll comb the whole goddam camp. Don't worry.'

'Right.' I moved past him towards the door.

'How are those guys in there?'

'Smelly,' I said. 'A bit more peaceful now. But Mr Coveney hasn't exactly made a friend of Kelleher.'

He gave a little shrug, expressive for all its economy. It reflected wry patience, long experience of the curious ways of officers. 'We got a slipping situation. He's got to hold it tight. Better get back there, Mr Bowes. I'll get things moving here.'

'One more thing. How's Major Smales?'

'He'll pull through.'

'Where is he?'

'Hut fourteen. Right where he collapsed. Why?'

'I wondered.'

'Give you some advice, Mr Bowes. Stay away. You aren't too popular, right?'

I nodded wearily. As I left he was picking up the telephone.

Moving into Main Street, I thought about Barney Smales and hut fourteen. 'He'll pull through,' Vernon had said. *But* meanwhile he'd delegated his command to Coveney, and done it voluntarily, which must mean that Barney was not only feeling foul, but expecting to feel foul for quite a while. On the other hand, since it had been Barney's decision, he must have been conscious to make it. I could imagine that Allen's thoughts would have run along the same lines; that Allen, having first got the keys, had then decided to approach Barney himself. He'd been fairly sure, earlier, that Barney would listen to him. A small hope now flickered in my mind. If Allen had gone to see Barney, it explained why I hadn't met him, and why he hadn't returned to the medical block.

Hut fourteen wasn't difficult to find, since there were notices at the entrance to each trench. But having found it, I hesitated. It hadn't needed Vernon's warning to tell me what Barney thought of me. If Barney was conscious and I went into the hut, he'd simply order me back to the medical block. How, then, could I discover whether Allen was in there? The huts had no windows and their wooden walls were so well insulated as to make them pretty well soundproof. I was contemplating the doubtful possibility of opening the door and simply calling Allen's name in a phoney American accent, when I was saved both the trouble and the likely humiliation. The door opened and a soldier came out.

I said, 'Is Master Sergeant Allen in there?'

'No, sir.'

'Thanks. I thought he'd be with Major Smales.'

'No, sir. Lieutenant Coveney's the only one with the major, sir.'

'He's there now?'

'Yes, *sir*.' The soldier's face was red and resentful, I noticed. Coveney must have been exercising his charm.

'Well, thanks anyway.' I left the soldier to his misery and set off for the reactor trench and Kelleher. As I passed the entrance to the trench housing the diesels, two soldiers were coming out.

One said sharply, 'Hey, you.'

I stopped and turned.

'You seen Captain Carson?'

'No,' I said, 'I haven't.'

'Beg pardon, sir. I didn't recognize you.'

'You're still searching?'

He shrugged. 'Captain Carson, he's gone. Whole camp's been

searched twice. He just ain't here.'

I said, 'What's the theory?'

He shrugged again. 'Who knows? He's gone topside, something like that. No place down here we haven't looked. It's kinda spooky, you know, sir. Guy just vanishes.'

Since they'd been searching the camp, I asked 'Have you seen Master Sergeant Allen?'

'He disappeared too, sir?' It was a weary joke.

I dodged the question. 'Just looking for him.'

'No, sir. Haven't seen him.'

As I walked away, a thought struck me, and then another, and I didn't like either. The first was that only I knew Allen was missing. Kelleher was concerned, but didn't know as I now knew. And I was doing exactly what I'd done about Carson: failing to report the fact. No, not quite true; Vernon knew too and Vernon had promised a search. Damn it, I couldn't even think straight! I tried harder with the other idea that had stamped into my head and was more deeply worrying. I thought about it until I was sure my mental processes hadn't got this one scrambled, too. The fact was that everybody who'd had anything to do with the medical records was now gone or out of action. Doc Kirton was dead; the orderly was severely disabled by food poisoning, and Allen, who'd gone to get the keys, had vanished! Quick conclusion: there was something important in those damned records. But it was quicker and more facile than I liked. The medical orderly had been caught in the wide swathe of mass food poisoning; Allen wasn't known, except by Kelleher and by me, to be remotely interested in the medical files. Unless . . . *unless* somebody had seen him collecting the keys in the command hut!

But it was getting me nowhere; it was all maybes and possibilities, all ifs and buts and nothing hard anywhere – nothing to point to a man or a group of men; nothing to indicate purpose. The truth was that somebody, somewhere, had a motive. Whoever he was was sociopathic, too: a man able to appear normal while carrying on a mad murderous campaign against the whole installation and everybody in it.

The door to the reactor complex was locked. I hesitated, then

166

banged on it, and after a moment a key turned and the door swung open and one of the engineer sergeants looked out at me enquiringly.

'Mr Kelleher here?'

'Nope. He's in the hospital, sir.' The sergeant held a hefty stick.

I pointed to it. 'What's that for?'

He gave a tight smile. 'From here on in, we repel all boarders.'

I thanked him and turned away, sick now with concern, not to mention a growing fear for the safety of my own hide. Now Kelleher was missing! Well, this time I was going to do the right thing, immediately and without debate. The first job was to report it. With two men disappearing inside an hour, and three in a day, the sheer weight of statistics must now overwhelm both Smales's belief in runs of simple bad luck and Coveney's obsession with military order. I'd march down to the command hut, see Vernon and get the place turned upside down. I also thought mirthlessly that Coveney's hunt for Kelleher wouldn't lack determination.

Approaching the entrance to the medical block trench, though, I hesitated. It was just possible Kelleher was still there; that his 'little ole trick' had taken longer than he expected. Better check.

Turning into the tunnel, I felt suddenly colder, and halted. Cold air blew through Camp Hundred the whole time, but here the current was stronger, prickling icily at the hair in my nostrils. I stepped to the wall and looked along the trench, past the sides of the huts, then moved forward again. There was nothing to be seen. The snow walls and the arched roof looked as they always looked: the packed snow was greyish in the dim light that came in from Main Street. But as I moved forward, still close to the ice wall, I knew I wasn't mistaken. There was a sharp current of icy air blowing along the trench. I came level with the first hut and entered the narrow passage between the hut's side and the trench wall, and the air current strengthened, flowing round me like very cold river water. I broke into a clumsy run, felt my boots skidding on the crystalline ice and stumbled towards the far end of the trench, already knowing what I'd find.

167

Even before I got there, I could hear it despite the parka hood. As I came closer, the jet of air battering down at me carried with it the roar of the brutal weather above us. I stopped then and looked upwards, watching the flying white of snow across the open hatch cover twenty feet above my head.

I raced up the spiral steel stairs. Loose snowflakes were falling fast around me and already the treads were treacherous, each with its inch or so of fresh white snow, indented with a footprint. Somebody was out there!

At the top I shoved my head and shoulders out through the hatch, and promptly ducked down again as the sheer force of the wind threatened to knock me from the steps. Huddling down, I drew the parka hood tighter until there was no more than a two-inch aperture. Kicking the loose snow from the stair treads, I took a firm grip on the steel handrail before I raised my head again, like a cautious tortoise.

Peering through the narrow opening of my hood at the hell outside, I saw nothing. Visibility was no more than two or three feet and the hard snow was flung against me by a shrieking, banging gale of frightening malevolence. To try to see footprints outside was absurd. Whoever had gone out into *that* must already be beyond hope and help. Nor was there a lifeline tied, as per regulations, to the hatch cover. Thankful to hide myself from the storm's anger, I withdrew my head, pulled the hatch cover down and began to fasten it. Then I stopped. Better leave the catch undone. If somebody had gone out, was struggling to get back and by some miracle succeeded, a locked hatch cover was a death sentence.

Slowly, almost despairingly, I climbed down the steel stairs, my head still ringing with the violence of the Arctic wind. With the hatch closed, all was still and silent and even the cold walls, seen by the dim light visible from Main Street, seemed somehow almost indecently safe and secure. I was trying hard to think what reason any man could have to venture out through the hatch into the deadly and implacable world of the empty, intolerant icecap. Only a madman would . . . *But the madman was below and secure.*

Backing down the stair was awkward. I turned to face the way

168

I was going and my foot slipped on snow-coated steel and I stumbled, tried frantically to recover my balance, failed, and fell eight or ten feet to the tunnel floor below. It was a painful, bruising fall, but the heavy padding of my Arctic clothing must have absorbed some of the worst of it. I lay grunting and cursing for a few moments, then began to haul myself to my feet. As I did so, my hand touched something beneath a pile of loose, dry snow that had drifted through the open hatch. I brushed the snow rapidly aside. Allen lay beneath it.

Pulling off my mittens, I touched his face and it was icy cold. I bent painfully, took hold of his arm, hoisted him in a rough fireman's lift and staggered back along the trench to the hospital block. I knew there wasn't an empty bed, so I took him straight into the little operating theatre and dumped him on the table and stood beside him for a moment, looking helplessly at the lifeless grey colour that had invaded his fine dark features. I was sure he was dead. His arm hung limply down, his mouth gaped, and as I bent to put my ear to his mouth, I could neither hear nor feel any trace of respiration. Ripping his clothes open, baring his chest, I bent again to listen. Nothing. I calculated the time since he'd left the block and then went to rummage in Doc Kirton's desk for the stethoscope. Finding it, I fumbled the earpieces into place and tried to listen for Allen's heartbeat. My total inexperience didn't help. I seemed to hear only the movement of the instrument in my own ears. But then, very briefly, I heard something – a faint flickering sound like a few drops of water gurgling out of some faraway wash basin. Seconds passed. There it was again! Whipping off the stethoscope, I bent, placing my mouth against his icy lips, and forced my own warm breath into him. Another breath: pressure on his rib cage to force it out, then another breath; a minute passed, then two. And suddenly, joyfully, I watched his ribs lift a fraction and then lower. It happened again, and then, after an agonizingly long pause, a third time. I stood back drenched in sweat and relief, watching him breathe, very slowly and shallowly at first, then more steadily, and there were odd, low but audible sighs to confirm to my ears what my eyes could see.

It was once considered unwise to warm too quickly a body

which might have been attacked by frostbite. The practice then was to rub the victim with snow in the hope of minimizing the murderous pain as circulation returned to frozen flesh. Nowadays a different view is taken. Warmth should be applied as soon as possible. In the next few minutes I had stripped off Allen's boots and trousers and draped towels soaked in warm water over feet and legs. A few moments fiddling with the anaesthetic apparatus and I'd got oxygen flowing into the face mask and with that clamped to his face, Allen's breathing strengthened and steadied. About ten minutes after I'd carried him inside, I was wringing out a new towel when I heard his voice, muffled, through the mask.

As I turned to him and lifted the mask away, he lifted his arm weakly, and said, 'Gee, my head.'

'Can you hear me?'

'My head. God, my head!'

Moving behind him, I drew my fingers gently through his hair. His breath hissed and he winced suddenly as I touched a lump like a small mountain at the back where his hair was thinning. He hadn't got *that* collapsing in the snow!

I said, 'Who did it?'

Allen's head moved weakly from side to side.

'Who?'

He blinked up at me; real consciousness was returning now.

'Somebody *did* hit you?'

'Sure he did.' Allen's eyes closed tightly.

'Who?'

'Didn't see who. Had his . . . his parka hood tight. That's all I saw. Then – *Bam!*'

'You've no idea? No clue at all?'

'No.'

'Where did it happen? Before or after you got the keys?'

Allen looked puzzled for a moment, then said slowly: 'Oh yeah, the keys. Never got that far.'

All the same, the keys had gone from the rack.

'Coffee?' His eyes had closed. He didn't open them as he nodded.

Walking out of the theatre to the coffee machine in Kirton's office, I felt chillingly alone. Allen was in no condition to help; there was no sign of Kelleher; and inside me lurked an uncomfortable certainty that I was next on the list of targets.

I still had no idea why.

My hand shook a little as I filled the coffee-cup. My brain pounded with that question: *Why?* Why the long chapter of destruction, the skilled sabotage, the readiness to kill men, singly like Kirton or indiscriminately with the blunt sweep of poisoned food? Why, why, why? But I had only questions. No answers. And even if the answers had been there to reason out, my brain now seemed incapable of hard thought; Hundred had deadened it and there was just dull reaction to events, followed by weary frustration at a deadly riddle which grew hourly less answerable.

I took the coffee in to Allen and watched morosely as he sipped. The acute discomfort in his guts and the brutal bang on the head combined to make him almost helplessly weak. He needed to be warm in bed, not lying awkwardly on this damned operating table. If only there were a bed . . . Then I groaned at my own stupidity. Of course there was a bed; there was the one Kelleher had occupied.

I went through to check and stared in astonishment. Kelleher was in it, his eyes glaring up at me!

'What the – !' But the sight told its own story. Kelleher was back in the straitjacket, the straitjacket was fastened to the bed, and there was a wide strip of surgical tape across his mouth!

171

Chapter 15

I bent to strip the plaster from Kelleher's mouth, thought better of it, and instead unfastened the strappings of the jacket. Once his hands were free, he took off the plaster himself with a mixture of impatience and extreme care. He massaged stiff, sore skin carefully as he told me what had happened.

'Door opened and I heard Coveney's voice, just minutes after you'd gone. I climbed back in here just to avoid trouble, and turned away, pretending to be sleeping, damn it, so I didn't get the chance to see who did it.'

'Did what?'

'Listen. I'll tell you. Coveney looked at me; I know it – I could sense his septic aura – then he went out. When he'd gone, I started to sit up and somebody tried to bust my head. When I woke up, I was strapped in.'

'Somebody from the ward?'

Kelleher shrugged. 'Who knows? There were some guys with Coveney; it could have been one of them. Stayed behind a moment and – splat!' He shook his head and muttered at the pain.

'Can you stand?'

'Sure I can stand.'

'Good. We need the bed.' I told him about Allen, and together we carried the master sergeant in, stripped him down to his underwear and tucked him up. As I up-ended his trousers to fold them and preserve the still immaculate creases, a bunch of keys fell out of one of the pockets, and as I bent to pick them up, a thought struck me. The camp had been searched for Carson, but had *all* of it been searched?

I said to Allen: 'Is there anywhere in this place that's out of bounds?'

'Sure,' he said. 'There's – ' I let him finish, but had the answer already. Why the hell hadn't I thought of it, or anybody else for that matter: Coveney, Smales, Allen himself, anybody?

172

'There's that trench where the bodies are,' Allen said.

'Who can get in?'

'Two keys to the door. One on that ring. Major Smales has the other.'

'Did you look inside?'

He shook his head.

Kelleher said, 'But Barney would, surely.'

'Why should he? It's been locked for days. There are only two keys and – '

'Locked it myself,' Allen said, 'right after we put Doc Kirton's body in there.'

I held up the key-ring. 'Which one?'

Allen pointed with a weary hand. 'Okay.' I turned to Kelleher. 'Let's go have a look.'

'We're gonna be spotted,' Kelleher said. 'Leastways I am.'

'We've got to risk it. Do what I did. Pinch a parka with somebody else's name on it. And carry something. Nobody looks twice at a beast of burden . . . take some sheets, you'll look like part of Coveney's clean-up.'

We grabbed another of the parkas the sick men wouldn't be needing and gathered some soiled sheets from the laundry baskets and left the medical block cautiously, ready to duck back if we encountered anybody. But Main Street was deserted. We hurried to the trench. A notice on the locked door read: 'No admittance under any circumstances' and we glanced at one another grimly. I turned the key, the lock slid smoothly back, and in a moment we were inside and locking the door.

I had brought a handlamp from the hospital, but we didn't need it. The light switch clicked and the overhead strip lights flickered on.

There was no sign of Carson, but we went the length of the trench to make sure, sidestepping bodies as we walked. At the bottom of the escape hatch stair, Kelleher looked at me and gave a little shudder. 'C'mon, let's get out of here.'

I shared his keenness to leave, and we turned and walked back briskly towards the door. But something only half-remembered began to prickle in my mind and I stopped, looking down at the bodies.

'Just a minute.' Each of the bodies, blanket-shrouded, lay fastened to a steel-framed stretcher sled.

'You spotted something?'

'Hang on. Let me think.' I tried to remember the time I'd been in here before, in the darkness, when I'd blundered in a panic among these hard frozen remnants that had once been men. And there had been something odd about one of them. I'd assumed it had been Kirton, but . . .

I said, 'How many men should be here?'

'Seven, I guess. Six from the helo crash, plus Doc Kirton. Why? And what in hell are you doing?'

I was on my knees, swallowing my revulsion and making myself run my hands over the shrouded forms. The fourth was the one that had lingered in my mind. I glanced at the identifying label tied to the sled, and said, 'Not much left of Private First Class Marvin K. Harrer.'

'He was in a helo crash!' Kelleher said impatiently. 'What do you expect? Leave the poor guy alone!'

Ignoring him, I began to unfasten the ties that held the shrouding blanket: as I pulled the material back from where the head should have been, I found myself looking down at a chunk of kapok wearing an Arctic-issue hat. 'I think,' I said, 'that we'd better see the rest of him.'

Kelleher said, 'Be your age. There's got to be something to bury. The army sometimes has to return the body to the family with the lid screwed tight.' But the convicion was going out of his voice, and by the time I'd peeled the blanket right back to reveal lengths of wood positioned where the arms and legs would have been, he had no protests left. 'Six bodies,' he said.

'And there should be seven. So where's the other one?'

We stared at one another and both of us shuddered.

'Wait. Wait a second,' Kelleher said. 'Let's just be damn sure this is right. We got – '

'It's right!' I said, and my voice sounded harsh in my own ears. 'Somebody has *used* a body for something, and faked this up to make it look as though they're all here.'

'What about the others?'

I examined them quickly, squeamishness suppressed. There

174

was a corpse on each of the remaining sleds. I didn't linger; one glance at each of the pale, waxy, dead faces was more than enough, and when I came to the pulverized remnants of Kirton, my stomach threatened revolt. As I moved from sled to sled, Kelleher followed behind, in silence, replacing each cover. When we'd done, I rose and said, 'Why would he steal a corpse?'

'Because of what it would show?' Kelleher hazarded. 'Because the pathologist could prove something from it?'

I nodded. It seemed the likeliest explanation.

Then Kelleher said slowly, 'But it would have to be something obvious, that's for damn sure. Look, they fly these poor guys out to Thule first chance, okay? They unwrap the corpses, dress 'em up to ship 'em Stateside. But they know *how* they died. A helicopter crashed. So nobody's looking for anything suspicious.' He paused a moment. 'Listen. Thule's got the whole works, pathologists, morgues, even a mortician, for God's sake. The whole deal. It's a big place and people die, right? So . . . this guy who steals a corpse, what's his reasoning? I'll tell you. There's something about that corpse, about Pfc Harrer, that's gonna attract attention and fast! When the bodies arrive, the pathologist takes a quick look because the book says look, then he gives the okay to the mortician for the screwed-down lid. Only he doesn't, not with Harrer, because that quick look's gonna ring alarm bells. So the body has to be stolen and got rid of.'

'Wrong,' I said.

'Why?'

'Because alarm bells ring anyway. Instead of a body there's a bundle of wood and kapok.'

Kelleher sighed. 'True enough. Maybe I did go nuts back there!'

'The minute that little bundle arrives,' I said, 'all sorts of things happen, and the first is a bloody great investigation of what's going on up here. Shipping this out *draws* attention.'

'Maybe the other thing was worse.'

'Perhaps.' But it didn't ring true. We stared at one another for a moment, bafflement complete. I said, 'Let's try Allen.'

As we slipped cautiously out of the trench, Coveney and a couple of others were moving purposefully along Main Street about fifty yards off, fortunately heading away from us. A glance would have been enough, but nobody seemed to turn and look. Kelleher carried his bundle of sheets at face level as we hurried back to the medical block.

Allen was sleeping, but Kelleher didn't hesitate. His forefinger was prodding the master sergeant awake as I closed the door into the ward. Rapidly we told him what had happened. He was physically very low, blinking with the need for sleep, but he listened with determined attention. Our account finished, we stood still, watching him try to think.

Finally he said, 'Nope. Can't see any reason.' He was sick and bone weary; it was an effort to stay awake and after a few moments his eyelids closed.

I was exasperatedly lighting a cigarette when he said, suddenly and clearly, 'What did you say the name was?'

'Harrer,' I said, 'Pfc Harrer.'

Allen pursed his lips. 'We had this show a coupla months back. Stage show. Camp concert. Funny sketches and comic songs, you know the kind of thing.'

I thought for a second he'd begun to ramble. 'What about Harrer?'

'Harrer did a comedy routine about Doc Kirton. Best number in the show.'

I didn't see the point, but Kelleher suddenly snapped his fingers. 'You mean he *looked* like Doc Kirton?'

Allen gave a little nod. 'Enough for that kind of show. Big build. Dark hair. He wasn't a double, it wasn't even close, but on that stage with make-up and a stethoscope and a white coat . . .'

Kelleher interrupted him. 'So if that's not Kirton in there . . .'

We talked, we thrashed at it, we speculated, we postulated, and at the end of it all, we still had only questions. Not an answer in sight. There was still *somebody*, malevolent, cunning, ruthless and inevitably insane, who was responsible for everything that had happened at Camp Hundred, but there was no clue to his identity or even to his thinking. There were plenty of insoluble mysteries, with a new one added: what possible use might have been made of Harrer's body and his resemblance to Kirton?

176

It was Allen who finally said, 'Got to know whose body it is.'

The state of the body was still vivid in my mind. I said, 'It'll be very difficult to do. Whoever it is, he's in a terrible state. He was flattened by the tractor.'

'Fingerprints?' Kelleher said, impractically.

Nobody bothered to reply. Then Allen said, 'Boots.'

'What about them?'

Allen smiled faintly. 'Boot size is stamped into the leather binding inside the top of the boot.'

Kelleher opened the clothing locker. Inside were Kirton's various overalls, some sealed in sterile packs. On the floor of the locker were operating theatre footwear of green rubber. He picked one up and examined it. 'Eleven.'

I said, 'That's no use unless we know Harrer's size.'

'Well, we know Kirton's an eleven, regular fitting,' Kelleher said. He turned to Allen. 'How many fittings are there?'

'Three. Narrow, regular, wide.'

'Odds are two to one, then. And eleven's a big size.'

'Harrer was a big guy, too,' Allen muttered.

'We'll go look at the boots,' Kelleher said.

I grimaced, but it was obvious we had to return to the trench. Kelleher picked up his bundle of sheets and I collected a knife and some scissors, knowing we'd need them.

There wasn't a soul moving in the whole length of Main Street. We hurried to the death trench, slipped inside and got to work. It was macabre and grisly and horrible. The felt boot was frozen to the crushed foot and I had to cut it away as best I could. The size was ten and a half, wide fitting.

'A difference,' I said, 'But it's not much to go on.'

Kelleher thought for a moment. 'Dog tags. They should be round his neck, on a string.'

But they weren't.

Kelleher said, 'Rule is, they wear them the whole time. Maybe our friend took them off, before he . . .'

'Perhaps. But it's not enough, is it?'

'Rings? Watches?'

Together, sickened, we managed to get at a pocket, we prodded and probed, but it was empty. This had been a man; now it was like a tangle of meat from a freezer. We found his left hand, badly mangled, and cut the glove away with difficulty. There was no ring, nor was there a watch on the wrist.

Then, quite suddenly, I was staring at that broken hand, noting broad, practical fingers and nails which, though clean, were thickened and grainy. The third finger, the only one undamaged, had a ragged cuticle. I crouched there, thinking back, remembering Kirton as I'd sat drinking his coffee and listening to his music and how I'd noticed his precise, surgeon's hands. These weren't the fingers whose dexterity I'd envied.

As I lifted my head, my eyes met Kelleher's. 'That's not Kirton's hand!' I said.

He nodded. 'Not in a million years.'

It led to a lot more talk, which I won't go over. We went back to the medical block for the benefit of Allen's advice, but by now he was sleeping deeply and this time even Kelleher hadn't the heart to awaken him. We stood beside his bed, talking softly, tracing and retracing the ground, trying to make sense of a situation that seemed to have no sense in it. It was unlikely and probably impossible that Kirton could still be alive, and we could see no reason why Harrer's body should have been dressed in Kirton's clothes and dumped where the tractor would run over it and thereby render it unidentifiable. There seemed no point in making one of the sleds look as though there was a body in it, when the deception would be discovered, and investigated with real determination, as soon as the bodies reached Thule.

So?

So nothing.

So two men, Kirton and Carson, were now missing for totally unexplained reasons. And, presumably, were dead.

At last I said, a little wearily, 'Look, it's not your business and it's not mine. We have facts now. It's criminal not to tell Coveney. At least he can take action out in the open.'

Kelleher said 'No,' with sudden vehemence.

'Why not?'

'Because whoever the hell it is who's doing all this, he doesn't know what we got now. The minute we tell Coveney, the whole place finds out.'

'And maybe he gets caught?'

'Sure. More likely he doesn't. There's still no solid information.'

I stared at him in sudden anger. 'So we do nothing?'

Kelleher stretched. 'No. There's one little thing I'd like to try.'

'What?'

He hesitated, then bent to pick up the bundle of sheets. 'Leave it with me, Harry. I'll be in the reactor trench.'

'You're not going to tell me?'

He was already moving to the door. 'Sure I'll tell you. But later, okay? Give me a little time. And cover for me if Coveney comes in.'

I watched the door close behind him, annoyed at what I saw as wholly unnecessary secrecy. Allen slept peacefully in the bed Kelleher had occupied and I thought with irritation that if Coveney did arrive and saw a black face where he'd expected a white one, covering-up would be rather less easy than Kelleher had made it sound. Not that that there was much to be done about it; there were no spare beds.

For a while, I sat smoking in Kirton's comfortable chair, recovering my temper. The place was quiet now and I realized I was tired, and pulled out a desk drawer, put my feet up and let my eyes close. I'd no intention of sleeping, and didn't, because my brain, active if ineffectual, insisted on carrying out a review of events. Pointlessly, as ever, and destructive, too, because in my experience physical comfort demands mental comfort as a precondition and my futilely busy brain kept me shifting in the chair, so that the cycle of irritation and frustration completed itself and I couldn't relax at all.

A couple of times I went over to look at Allen merely for the sake of something to do, and the third time I succeeded in barking my right shin on the open desk drawer and hopped about on one leg for a few seconds, swearing. As I slammed the drawer shut, it occurred to me that a search of Kirton's desk, if it achieved nothing else, would help to pass the time.

The loose-leaf notebook wasn't exactly hidden, but there were papers and folders on top of it. What struck me was the handwritten title on the front: Studies in Discomfort. When I opened

it and began to read, I realized after a while that Kirton had
begun it with the intention of producing a paper for some medical
journal or other on the way men behaved within the difficult
parameters of Camp Hundred. Then the content seemed to
change style, becoming mildly humorous rather than gravely
academic. Clearly he'd abandoned the serious project and was
merely amusing himself. Later came another change. There were
half a dozen small character sketches, none more than a single
handwritten page in length. No names or ranks were mentioned,
nor even specific jobs. All the same, the first one was inevitably
and unmistakably Barney Smales, and though a note of Kirton's at the beginning of the notebook said he would avoid
psychological jargon, a marginal note on Smales's profile said
'manic?' I continued reading, recognizing nobody else, until I'd
finished the notes. But I didn't close the notebook; instead I
turned back to profile four: Mr Chameleon Constant.

'It took me a long time,' Kirton had written, 'to realize that the
man I encountered was not the man others saw. Most of us, in
early life, make some kind of decision about the front we want
to present to the world, and then simply go on developing it.
Chameleon Constant goes one better, or perhaps six better. His
game, and I'm certain it is a war game for him, lies in presenting
marginally different pictures of himself to everybody he meets.
He's Jekyll and Hyde and a few more, including traces of Einstein
and Svengali, and there are times when I have to restrain myself
from going to watch him at work. I believe he knows I know
about him because very occasionally he'll give me a glance that's
almost conspiratorial. Other people's opinions of him vary
ludicrously, from "the worst bastard I ever met in my life", to
"as near total decency as any man is likely to get". What's so
strange is that he seems to get away with it all. In some extraordinary way he doesn't get talked about. He came to see me
the first time about another man who seemed to be worried and
depressed. Would I have a look at him? When I saw the man, he
was certainly worried and depressed and said the reason was that
Mr C.C. was on his back. Specifically how? Impossible to pin
down. C.C. just radiated hatred and threat. I gave him some anti-
depressants and when I saw C.C. again, told him what I'd done,

but not the reason and that was the first time I saw the conspiratorial glance. I made a note to investigate. After that I mentioned his name to a few individuals, but never to groups, and the puzzling picture began to emerge. Everybody said something different. What it all comes down to, I suppose, is some notion he's got of total superiority. Trouble is, I suspect it's not unfounded. And I sometimes think that, given different circumstances, West Point or Harvard, C.C. might by now be either General of the Army or President of the United States. One of these days I'm going to get him interviewed, one at a time, by some high-grade psychiatrists, because he'll not only baffle the be-Jesus out of them; he'll have them fighting in groups when they try to agree on what he is. Meanwhile, I keep quiet about it because I want to go on observing.'

I read it a third time, fascinated and wondering, and looking now for clues. Could this be a portrait of the killer? Certainly it could, but the damn thing was so worded it didn't even hint at Chameleon Constant's identity, or even his rank or age. And then there was that curious reference to Einstein. I had an impulse to awaken Allen and ask whether there were any mathematical geniuses around the place, but if Kirton had been right, Allen's impression of the man might well be something very different.

Still, I could try it on Kelleher. I glanced at my watch. It was two o'clock in the morning and, with luck, few people would be about; so I ought to be able to get to the reactor trench unchallenged. There was a possibility – no, more than that, a probability – that Coveney would still be awake, and perhaps prowling, but I'd simply have to take a chance on that; the combination of my general itchiness, Kelleher's secrecy and Kirton's character sketch was too much to keep to myself.

Since I'd last been in Main Street, the power voltage had obviously been reduced, and some of the lights were out. I walked steadily along, grateful for the lower lighting. Even if I walked smack into Coveney, he'd be hard put to recognize me unless we were both directly beneath one of the roof lights.

But I didn't walk into Coveney. What I walked into, with astonishing suddenness, was total darkness. Without warning, without even a preliminary flicker, all the lights went out. I stopped in mid-stride, thought about it, and moved to the snow wall, calculating that the fourth trench on the right housed the reactor and that I could feel my way along until I reached it. I'd gone about twenty yards and passed the first trench-opening, my mind full of what might have gone wrong with the diesel generators, when I heard the soft crunch of footsteps. I stood, listening. They were coming towards me, moving fast, and I could hear a man breathing, too, with the effort of running.

I made a decision quickly – and wrongly – and didn't move out to tackle him, reasoning that it was somebody from the diesel shed on his way to get help. A few seconds later he was well beyond me and I knew how wrong the decision had been, because all of a sudden there was light again: but this time, it was the flickering glow of firelight, and it came from the diesel trench!

Briefly I contemplated turning and giving chase, but by then it was hopeless. Instead I ran towards the trench entrance, turned in, and stopped, appalled. The whole side of the hut was ablaze. I grabbed the fire axe and extinguisher from the trench wall and raced for the hut door, my feet splashing, for some strange reason, through *water*!

Chapter 16

I flung open the wooden door and heat blasted at me. Already the fire had too strong a grip for any hope of saving the diesel shed and the air was full of choking wood smoke that stung water into my eyes and threatened my lungs. My eyes ran swiftly round the flame-lit scene; soon the smoke would be too dense to see anything. The three big permanent diesels, bolted to the steel-plated floor, were obviously immovable. I stepped quickly towards the portable generator I'd brought up in the TK4 from Camp Belvoir and glanced at the switch panel. Off and the connections broken. But it was on wheels. I grabbed the tow handle and pulled, but the thing weighed two thousand pounds and my strength wasn't enough to move it. The axe handle then; as a lever. The fire was already eating fast at the far wall as I pushed the oak haft beneath the mounting and heaved upwards. I could feel the fire's heat through my parka. But at least the generator moved a few inches. Another heave and it moved again, but the heat was increasing rapidly and I could scarcely see through the tears forced from my eyes. A third heave – I was gaining no more than six inches at a time – and behind me the heat was becoming intolerable. I snatched a second to grab the extinguisher, knock down the plunger, and stand it where the spurting foam could offer its limited protection to my back, and heaved and heaved again, frantically propelling the killing weight across the floor. Three walls were burning now and the roof had caught, but for the moment the floor remained sound, protected by its steel coating. But there was ten feet and more to go and the sheer effort involved was draining strength from already aching muscles in my arms and shoulders, my back and legs. And the heat was now intense. My chest burned from in-haled smoke. Another frantic lift at the lever, another small, slow forward movement, a few more inches gained. Again. And again. And each desperate heave was more panicky and less strong than the one before. Above me the roof rafters crackled and burned, now showering sparks down on me. The fire was spreading with astonishing speed. But now I'd manœuvred the generator closer to the door. Only two or three feet remained. A burst of uncontrollable coughing halted me for long seconds, and grew worse as the spasms drew more choking smoke deep into my lungs. I wrenched at the handle, repositioned it and wrenched again, and then, behind me, part of the wooden wall crashed outwards and the roof lurched downwards. Two more heaves and the end of the generator was poised in the doorway. Three more and the wheels slumped down over the threshold . . . and jammed the mounting hard against the woodwork! Another . . . Oh God, it refused to move! With sweat pouring over me and my parka hood smouldering, I struggled to shift it the few extra inches that would tip the generator past the centre of balance and let it fall on to the saving snow of the trench floor.

But the effort was beyond me now. I swore in fury and frustration, knowing that the generator's survival was Camp Hundred's survival; without the one, the other could not exist. As the flames roared nearer I wrestled despairingly to try to make those last inches of movement, but the heavy steel was anchored, its weight crunching down on the wooden threshold.

I knew I'd have to leave it; that or be burned to death, burned or suffocated. I staggered towards the door, and realized that in jamming the generator in the opening, I had almost blocked my own way out. But no, I could squeeze past. As I began to do so a head appeared dimly in the billowing smoke. I glanced behind me at the fast-encroaching flames, stepped back and beckoned, and the man hesitated, then forced himself past the generator into the hut.

There was no need to explain. I positioned the axe handle and together we grasped it and heaved upwards. The generator lifted briefly, then settled back.

I yelled, 'Again!' waited, nodded, and heaved upwards with all my remaining strength. Slowly it lifted, and all down my back and thighs the muscles strained and then trembled as the strength went out of me. Grunting under the strain, I struggled to hold it, to continue the lift . . . forcing every ounce of energy I could muster into one last upward burst. Slowly the monster began to tilt, to lean forward, to begin to balance itself, to move through the point of balance . . . and suddenly with a crash the axe handle rose free and weightless and the generator crashed out into the tunnel on its side.

As I staggered after it, the far end of the hut began to disintegrate. I knew from the direct heat on my body that my parka was burning and hurled myself full length to the trench floor, rolling over and over so that the snow could douse the fire. It took only seconds, because the trench floor was water-covered. I'd forgotten that in the panic. Now, instantly, it soaked me, the water ice-chilled, and in no time at all I was shivering, my teeth chattering.

'You okay?' the other man shouted.

I nodded, coughing.

'I'm gonna get some help.'

I nodded again and heard him splashing away. Then my thought processes resumed some kind of function. Help meant, ultimately, the arrival of Coveney, and I'd better make myself scarce. I lurched to my feet and staggered off down the smoke-filled tunnel towards the darkness of Main Street, still coughing hard. I turned gratefully into the cold clean air that blew along that vast trench between the two entrances, and headed for the reactor trench, feeling better as the ache in my lungs began to subside a little, but shivering in the icy grip of my soaking clothes.

A couple of minutes later I was telling Kelleher what had happened. An emergency lantern burned on his desk. He listened, rummaging round for some clothing for me, and I stripped as I talked. When I told him about the water, he nodded grimly.

'Simple. He cut through the water lines. They'd just drain themselves into the tunnel. But, boy oh boy, we're in bad shape now. The water line'll have to be fixed before the power can come into use. And new electrical connections'll have to be improvised. Time margin's gonna be narrow.'

'Four hours, Barney told me, the first time the lights went.'

'Maybe a little less. Everything's been low-power. What heat there is will dissipate faster.'

'And he's free to strike again. And it's dark.' I bent to lace the dry boots.

'Right. But maybe at last I got something now.'

My head jerked round. 'What?'

'A fluke. Christ knows what the odds were in parts per million! I came back here and got going on the water samples again. Never did figure that contamination.'

'Go on.'

'Got nowhere in the beginning. Then there was a real flash on the spectrometer. Couldn't figure it at first. Not one hundred per cent sure even now. But when I got it isolated on a slide and used the microscope I reckoned I knew.'

'What was it?'

'Tissue.'

I blinked at him. 'Human tissue?'

'Christ, I'm no pathologist.' He watched me, waiting for me to come to the conclusion he'd reached.

Nor was it difficult. 'Kirton,' I said.

His mouth tightened. 'Maybe Carson, too.'

'No,' I said. 'The well was out of use before Carson disappeared.'

'Sure, but it's a hell of a handy place to dispose of a body.'

'Doesn't tell us who he is, though,' I said bitterly. 'Nothing ever does that. He burns down the bloody diesel shed and actually goes by me in the dark and still we've no idea.' I reached for my soaking jacket top and felt in the pocket for the sheet I'd taken from Kirton's folder. 'Read this. It doesn't tell us anything either. But I've got a feeling in my water that this is him.'

Kelleher unfolded the wet paper carefully. The note had been written with a ball-pen and fortunately remained legible. He read it slowly. 'Where'd it come from?'

I told him. Then I said, 'Kirton knew who it was. Must have known. That has to be the reason he was killed.'

'Well, he sure can't tell us.' Kelleher gave a long sigh of irritation, a sigh that suddenly caught in his throat. 'Wait a minute,' he said slowly. 'Maybe he can at that.'

'Spirit writing or table-tapping?' I said sarcastically. 'Or maybe you're a medium?'

186

'Uh-uh,' Kelleher said. 'But Kirton kept a diary.'

'If he did, it'll be in his quarters. Or it will *if* our friend hasn't stolen it.'

'He kept it on him.'

'How do you know?'

'I do it, too. Have since I was a kid. We talked about it once.'

I stared at him in silence, not wanting to contemplate the consequences of this piece of information about Kirton and looking for sensible objections. I said, 'Diaries are paper. If it *is* Kirton down there, it'll be illegible by now. He's been down there for – '

Kelleher handed me the sheet of paper I'd given him. 'Look at it. It's wet, sure, but you can read it. The diary's in a pocket, held together. It'll be soaked, but it'll be readable.'

'Even so, there's no guarantee.'

He took the sheet from me. 'What's it say here? Listen: "I made a note at the time." That's what it says, and the diary's got to be where he made the note. I *know*, believe me. I know all the crazy mechanics of writing up a diary. And there's another little thing you've forgotten.'

'No,' I said. 'I haven't forgotten. But if Kirton was already down there *then* – '

He didn't wait for me to finish. 'If! Okay, but *if* he was dumped later, our friend has fingered his pigeon in the unlikely event that Kirton's found. Don't forget – a new well had to be started immediately.' He looked at me steadily.

I said defensively, 'It's not on! In any case, there's no power.'

Kelleher glanced round. 'You can feel it. It's a mite cooler already. It'll get a whole lot colder real fast. One more little accident and Hundred's finished. Maybe it's finished right now. But if the guy can be identified positively, at least there'll be no more sabotage, right?'

'There's no power for the motor!'

'Wrong,' Kelleher said. 'There's power, muscle power on the winding handle.'

I opened my mouth to speak, but the words didn't come quickly enough and Kelleher went on grimly: 'We need one more guy and him I can get. Only question is, who goes down: you or me?'

The protesting words came, then, but they were only words, and they rolled off Kelleher's answers. Coveney, he said, wouldn't go for this theorizing. Coveney's hands were full and his antagonism plain; he wouldn't even listen. But the attempted cover-up in the death trench and a body in the well were proof enough of murder, and the diary, if it was there, might well be proof of guilt, powerful if not totally conclusive. Enough to force action. But I knew, and Kelleher knew too, why I was arguing so desperately: it was a matter of relative weight and strength. Kelleher was more than fifteen stone and strong as a horse whereas I, wet through, weighed less than eleven.

But he was determined to play out the farce of random choice and pulled a quarter from his pocket. 'Call.'

Whatever I called, the answer would have to be the same, but I went along. As it happened, the forces of chance for once recognized the force of logic, and pointed to me. Suddenly the temperature seemed to drop violently, and I began to tremble.

Reaching the well trench was not difficult. As we slipped along Main Street there was no one to see us, though the glow of rigged emergency lights from the diesel tunnel cast a pool of light further along. Once inside, we closed and locked the door, and as I turned, the beam from my handlamp illuminated the circle of corrugated iron protecting the old well-head and the metal hoisting frame above. Kelleher fitted the handle quickly. I walked unsteadily towards the well and shone the handlamp down into the unimaginable depths and immediately began to shiver again. Not far below, giant icicles hung into the void like the waiting teeth of some implacably hostile giant, their tips pointing like signposts of death to the black, narrow neck which led through into the second chamber, and more icicles which I couldn't see but knew to be there. And below *them* . . . Bile climbed abruptly into my throat. I turned away quickly, and said, 'No'.

Kelleher's 'other guy', a sergeant from the reactor staff named Mulham, said, 'Can't say I blame you.'

There was a moment's heavy silence. Then Kelleher spoke. 'Okay, then, I'll do it. You turn the handle.' He reached for the bosun's chair, swung it up and out. 'Let's have some light here,' he said, as he began to strap himself in.

'I'm sorry.'

'Christ, you're a limey, you're not even involved here! I sure don't blame you, brother. This is an American problem.' He bent his legs, letting the bosun's chair take the weight. 'Okay, let's have the 'hard hat and the rest of that gear.'

Numbly, guiltily, I took off the hard hat. It had been picked to fit me and on him it was ludicrously small, wobbling and liable to fall off. I thought about the extra four stones of Kelleher's weight, the other things to be carried, the back-breaking physical labour involved in the long lowering and raising, and suddenly heard myself say, 'I'll go.' To this day I don't know how I came to speak. It was some involuntary, impromptu impulse beyond either my control or understanding.

Kelleher's hands stopped moving and he turned to me.

'You sure?'

I nodded, committed now and resentful of it. 'Yes,' I said, and my voice caught on a rusty nail. I cleared my throat and said yes again.

'Think about it for a minute. Be sure.' He was all consideration and sympathy and somehow that enmeshed me further.

'I'll do it.'

He grunted and began to unfasten himself from the seat. Two minutes later I was poised over the well opening, swaying gently, with my heart in my mouth. I glanced back over my shoulder at the two of them, waiting at the handle. Kelleher reached across, stopped the swinging motion. 'Okay?'

I nodded and swallowed. 'Lower away.'

'Good luck.'

Looking upwards a few seconds later, I couldn't even see them, and the metallic click of the ratchet on the lowering mechanism was growing fainter. As I lowered my eyes, I realized that even the action of looking up had imparted a little swing to the cable, and concentrated on sitting very still and holding the equipment close to my body to minimize the possibility of contact with those fearful icicles that were now sliding slowly past me. We'd discussed and abandoned the idea of knocking them down before making the descent. The trip would have been safer, but the great

189

falling masses of ice, ripping more off as they crashed down through three chambers, might well make it impossible to see what lay in the bottom.

My left leg felt briefly uncomfortable. As I moved it I must have touched the chain saw, where it hung beneath the seat, because suddenly I was swinging again, and Kelleher's voice came sharply out of the little battery-powered walkie-talkie slung around my neck. 'Keep still, Harry, for Chrissake!'

My breath hissed out as I came within inches of a ton or more of sharp-pointed ice, and swung away again. I sat rigid, paralysed with fear, feeling the chill of the thing. Slowly the pendulum swing eased.

'You okay?'

'Okay.' Stiffening muscles would bloody well have to stiffen. The longer the length of cable above me, the wider the arc of swing and the greater the danger of tapping one of these monsters and tripping it from from its seating.

The ticking of the ratchet grew fainter and vanished as I dropped deeper into the first chamber. The beam of my lamp, endlessly reflected from the ice surface all around me, miraculously gave illumination to the whole, immense, onion-shaped cavern. It was difficult now even to know if I were moving; the lowering was so slow, the distance so great and the time so endless that I seemed suspended immobile in the middle of that huge, cold space. But slowly the curving bottom came up to meet me, and every few feet Kelleher's voice asked softly if I was all right. When he wasn't speaking, I ached for the reassuring sound of his voice; as soon as he spoke I was terrified that some trick of reverberating sound would precipitate one of the vast ice-spears from high above to smash me down for ever into the depths of the icecap.

Below me, very slowly, the dark hole widened as I slid soundlessly down towards it. I whispered into the walkie-talkie, 'Entering the neck soon.'

'How far?'

'Four feet.'

'Try communication soon as you're through.'

'Right.'

190

The lowering continued, and soon I was no longer in an immense space, but in a tight, white bottleneck that inspired sudden, panicky claustrophobia. If an icicle had fallen earlier, it just *might* have gone by, giving me only a glancing blow as it passed; but here, the whole shape of the structure would guide any falling weight directly on to me.

Slowly the neck widened, the walls of the second chamber beginning to slope down and away from where I hung. 'Through the neck now,' I muttered softly.

'You okay?'

'Yes. Keep lowering.'

I tried to envisage the two of them up there. This, for them, was the easy part, with the ratchet taking the strain. Coming up would be another matter, with muscles wearying through the long haul and the pressure of time always goading them to further effort.

All round me another crop of immense icicles hung like an inverted and petrified forest, gleaming and winking in the light of my lamp. They were, I thought soberly, even worse than those at the entrance to the upper chamber: longer, thinner, some distorted in shape like twisted fangs. Here the rising vapour from the steam hose would have been denser and warmer, its action stronger on the snow of centuries and adding drop by frozen drop to the tip of each rod of ice. I held my breath as the bosun's chair slipped past, concentrating on stillness. The need to tear my eyes away from their hypnotic menace was almost irresistible, but to look up or down seemed now to be to risk setting off a pendulum swing. If the icicles had been anchored to something solid, as the normal small icicle clings to a gutter, the danger would have been small. But they clung only to compacted snow.

Minutes passed and I moved beyond their threatening points, slowly down into the centre of the onion-shaped bulb, and again there came the feeling that I had ceased to move, that the world had stopped and that I would remain for ever strapped to my tiny seat in a bubble in the immensity of the icecap.

'You okay?'

'Yes.'

'How far?'

I glanced carefully downwards. Below me the walls were beginning to close a little towards the black eye of the third chamber. 'Forty feet.'

As I sat helplessly, inching downwards, anger welled up in me: anger at myself for embarking on this crazy descent; anger at the lunatic somewhere above me whose brilliant and implacable malevolence made it necessary; most of all, though, at Smales, who should long ago have closed off this death trap, and hadn't. It was a natural enough anger, born of danger and fear, but its intensity frightened me, constricting my throat, tensing my muscles, tripping a pulse in my temple that thumped in my head like a drum. Shutting my eyes tight, I tried to force the anger from me, but it had its effect. On a head full of blood the hard hat felt uncomfortably tight. I raised a hand to ease the pressure, took too deep a breath of icy air, and coughed. The hat tilted, slid quickly over my scalp, and fell. I made a grab for it, missed and began to swing a little as it fell.

I sat rigid, waiting for disaster. The hat bounced and bounced again, skittering round the sloping ice before it fell into the hole, and then a silence followed until, seconds later, it hit the bottom of the third bulb. I'd have expected a splash, but it bounced repeatedly. The water at the bottom of the well must have frozen again! The clattering could only have lasted a few seconds, but it seemed to go on and on as the steel hat ricocheted from one ice surface to another and the ice-bulb below me magnified the sound and funnelled it upwards through the neck. Sweating, even in the icy cold, I waited for it to end, but when it did, another sound remained . . . a high-pitched hum that seemed to have no source, but vibrated like a tuning-fork . . . and then an icy breath swirled round me and I knew and cowered as, with a soft whoosh, a huge icicle fell past. A tiny movement of my hand would have let me touch it as the white, shining projectile dropped slowly past, its forty-foot length seeming to fall in slow motion, to go on for ever. Miraculously it didn't touch me, but I watched it continue its fall, down into the neck, and through it like an arrow, not even touching the sides, then disappearing into blackness until it landed with an immense crash in the icy base of the bulb.

Again noise crashed below me, reverberating upwards, and

192

again the singing, tuning-fork sound began. I wrapped my arms around my unprotected head in an instinctive but futile gesture, and waited for death. For the next icicle wouldn't miss, and if the fall of the hat had been enough to unseat one of them, the monstrous impact of the ice-spear crashing down must surely loosen the others.

The ringing tone seemed to last so long as to be a permanent part of the atmosphere, then slowly, it began to fade. And nothing had happened! The forest of ice above had rung to the music of death, and yet had stilled! Slowly, disbelievingly, scarcely daring to move, I lowered my arms. The light of the lamp shone back at me from the great, shining walls; the silence was total. I let out a great, shuddering breath and cringed at the sound of it.

'Harry, Harry!' Kelleher's voice crackled urgently from the walkie-talkie on my chest.

I said, 'I'm okay.'

'What happened?'

'Icicle,' I whispered.

'We'll bring you up.'

I heard the words with a vast sense of relief. More than anything in the world I wanted to be lifted out of that ghastly place, to stand once more on something firm, to be free of the interminable menace of that battery of deadly, pointed, hanging spears above me. I knew that, even though they had not fallen, they must have been loosened by the long vibration; that the chance of a fall had immeasurably increased. I sat trembling in the chair, my mind whirling with both fear and a resurgence of fury.

Fury.

Fury that directed itself suddenly at the man who had done all this to me. The man who wanted Camp Hundred closed, and was on the edge of succeeding.

Damn him!

I gritted my teeth. 'Continue lowering.'

Chapter 17

'Harry?'

'Continue, damn it!'

A tiny jerk and I was off again, a little bundle of rage and revenge dangling at the end of a long, long cable, helpless in the space and cold, yet feeling suddenly like a hunter. I would reach the bottom, and if the answer lay there, I'd damn well find it.

I was going to get that bastard!

Into the neck, through it, and the light picked out another thick clump of icicles, slung like so many giant stilettos from beside the opening.

'Kelleher?'

'Yeah?' His voice was faint. 'Still okay?'

'I'm into the bottom chamber. Keep lowering.'

The chair slid slowly past the hanging ice fingers. Here, where the rising steam from the hose had been densest, there were more of them; they were larger, and thicker too, reaching more than half-way down the entire height of the chamber. They were almost more than I could bear, and I closed my eyes and counted slowly to two hundred before I opened them again. Then I sighed with relief. I was past, dropping steadily towards the base of the great cavern.

The speaker crackled. 'Repeat?' I turned up the volume to maximum.

'How far?' The words were almost indistinguishable.

'Thirty feet,' I said, and turned the lamp beam downwards to study the base of the ice chamber.

As the beam played across the surface of the frozen pool, it glittered back at me from ten thousand facets of shattered ice. The huge icicle, as it fell, had done several things: its initial impact had penetrated the ice layer and starred the smoothness of the whole sheet. New cracks radiated from its crash-point out towards the edges. It had also exploded into thousands of tiny, diamond-bright fragments that littered the entire surface, in an

194

opaque, reflecting layer.

'Hold it!' I said urgently, and the downward movement stopped. An indecipherable mutter came from the speaker.

I ignored it, and began to examine the surface yard by yard. I could see precious little even from where I sat; lower down it would be impossible to see anything through the ice.

Looking for shapes, I saw only shadows as the ice played tricks with the light. The hard hat, though, was visible, a bright orange blob, apparently undamaged, lying to one side of the almost perfectly circular ice sheet.

Minutes ticked by as my eyes swept slowly across every inch of the ice, searching for a dark shape that could be the body of a man. Nothing. I began again, aware that the cracks, white streaks down into the ice sheet, prevented my seeing large portions of the pool, and that the angle of sight reduced my chances. What was needed was what I dared not do: to set the bosun's chair swinging, to take me directly above other areas and to change the line of sight.

Nothing. I stared down, angry and frustrated. Directly below me lay the ten-foot white star where the icicle had crashed down, where the thick ice had crazed like a car's windscreen when a stone hits it. I reasoned that anything falling through the neck must crash on to the ice where the icicle had crashed. However it fell through the chamber neck, gravity would see to that.

'Lower me again,' I said into the handset. 'Stop when I tell you. Can you hear me?'

The sounds that came back were not distinguishable as words any more, but the sequence and pattern told me my instructions were being repeated.

I swung lower, down towards the centre of the star, trying not to think of it as it was: as the central spot of a target, where any crashing ice would fall directly on to me.

'Stop.' I said it with careful clarity, but had to repeat it before movement ceased. I thought for a moment, and said slowly, '*One* tap like this' – I rapped the microphone sharply, 'means lower. *Two* means *stop*. *Three*, start hauling me *up*. Understood?'

A vague crackle.

'Tap if you understand.'

195

One tap.

I tapped twice, waited, repeated it, and after a moment began to move downward. With my boots three feet from the ice, I tapped sharply twice, and stopped. Nice to know it worked!

The chain saw touched the ice first. I'd forgotten about it for the moment and it would in any case be useless. There was too great a risk of the sound of a petrol engine bringing down hanging ice.

As my toes were about to touch, I rapped sharply twice, and the chair stopped. Cautiously, I pressed down. The ice seemed to hold, but it was damaged more than my earlier survey had indicated. Chunks of it had in fact been broken and turned like floating boulders. Little bright lines of water shone in the interstices, making it impossible for me to rest my weight on the ice chunks, big though they were. Unless I swung. Was it possible? I looked upward, shining the lamp along the taut length of cable to where the massed icicles pointed wickedly down at me, and nowhere was the cable more than four feet from them.

One tap. Two taps. I moved down another foot, and slid the ice-axe from my belt. My legs were bent now, feet resting flat on a large piece of ice. Leaning forward a little, careful to keep the balance as it was, I shone the light downwards.

The irregular surfaces were white, blue, yet yellowed from the lamp's light, deeply shaded in places, almost bright in others. I searched among them for a glimpse of green or brown, for something to indicate that Kirton's body *was* here. With the haft of the ice-axe, I began to push at the lumps of ice, turning them, examining each with care as it moved. But there was nothing. I'd have to go up again. I wanted nothing more than to leave this dreadful place, but the thought of doing so with the mystery still as puzzling as ever after the ordeal of the descent, of facing the worse one of the ascent with nothing to show, that prospect repelled me. I sat prodding with a kind of hopeless determination, turned the blocks, searching the cracks. And suddenly, as a chunk tilted, I saw red; not the red of anger, but perhaps the red of blood. Not much: just a small discoloured patch on a flat piece of ice that must have been part of the surface before the impact.

I prodded again and again, but without success, widening the circle in my anxiety, taking risks I shouldn't take. Then suddenly it happened: a block turned and an arm appeared, the hand dead white, the dark green of the sleeve blackened by the water.

Quickly I reversed the ice-axe and extended the metal head towards it. At the first try, it slid limply away. The second time, the curved end caught briefly and a shoulder and head rose slowly to the surface between two ice blocks. Dark hair swam lank in the water, but the body remained face down. But at last I anchored the steel head in the neck of the parka and lifted, and Kirton's face, swollen and white, but unmistakeable, rolled slowly upwards.

What followed took a long time. In the water, the body could be moved, if clumsily. The moment I tried to lift it clear, sheer weight defeated me. I struggled, tiring now and chilled, without any success at all, until I sat still and thought about it as an engineering problem.

Finally I managed to pass a loop of line round his shoulders and knot it to the hook beneath the seat of the bosun's chair. It meant jettisoning the saw, but the saw was useless. Also, I remember thinking wryly as I let it go, it wasn't *mine*. Then, with the ice-axe head, I fished for his legs and hauled them to the surface. At last, leaning precariously over, I reached for the zip of the parka, slid it down and began to search the pockets of his tunic. Why didn't I just give the three taps, have Kelleher haul the two of us up, and search him at leisure on the surface? Two reasons, both equally strong: first, I wasn't bloody well going to move now until I *knew*; secondly, I was reasonably certain two men would not be strong enough to haul a combined weight of twenty-five stones and more through four hundred feet.

I found a small squarish leather object in a breast pocket, but it was a wallet, not a diary. Stuffing it into my own parka, I fumbled on, my ungloved hand bitterly cold. The diary was in an inside pocket and I knew what it was as soon as I touched it, numbed fingers or no numbed fingers.

The diary was sodden, its papers held together by water. I took off my gloves, letting them dangle from the sleeve strap, then opened the diary carefully and began to peel pages apart, at

197

random. The paper, thin but strong, stood up to it. Kelleher was right about one thing: Kirton had been a committed diarist; every page seemed to have its entry, variable as to length, but written-úp religiously. I turned towards the back of the little leather-bound book, where the paper was blank, and began to work backwards towards the final entries. The last one said, 'Polar Bear entered Hundred overnight. Entry point clear, but no exit tracks? Maybe shambled out via tractor shed? Life puzzling and dismal. Shouldn't have played Mozart C Maj. last night. Prescribed A Maj. for mental balance, but not wholly successful.'

My hands were getting clumsier as they grew colder. I peeled that page away, then the next, scanning the entries quickly, with the lamp held awkwardly under my arm. Kirton was no Pepys. He simply mentioned each day's events, the music he'd played on his hi-fi, the books he'd read. He'd told me he found Camp Hundred dull, and the tedium showed.

As page followed page, with the entries varying little apart from the titles of the music and books, disappointment crept over me. It began to seem as though I'd made this hellish drop into the well for nothing. But then: 'Bold glance from the Chameleon. Tell Smales? But what? – A glance and a feeling that young F. was frightened. But events justified fear.'

My scalp prickled. Who was F? And who in hell *was* the Chameleon?

There was nothing else. In the loose-leaf notebook there'd been that tantalizing reference: 'I made a note to investigate,' but there was no sign of it here in the diary. Perhaps it had been only a mental note. I put the diary in a pocket in my parka and took one last look round the base of the chamber, my eyes resting longingly on the hard hat. It would make not the slightest difference if one of the icicles crashed down, but that didn't stop me from trying to work out some desperate way of reaching it. The knowledge that I'd have to leave without it made a little shudder pass across my shoulders.

'Pull me up,' I said into the walkie-talkie. There was no response. Instantly my heart began to hammer in my chest. I tried to control it and tapped three times on the microphone. There was a pause that seemed like hours but could only have lasted a few seconds, and then three faint responding taps sounded from the speaker. A moment later my feet lifted off the ice. The long upward haul had begun. Twenty feet up, I realized I had stopped moving and tapped again. Almost immediately I began to move, but after a few more feet the movement stopped. Sitting rigidly still in the bosun's chair, I began to ask myself panicky questions: Was I too heavy? Would the effort of lifting me through four hundred feet be too great for them? Then a tiny jerk told me I was on my way again and I thought I understood the pattern. They were resting at frequent intervals and I'd just have to live with it. I only looked up once and the sight of the big icicles, all seemingly pointed directly at me, made me determined not to do so again. I sat there, patiently paying out the thin nylon line attached to Kirton's body and trying not to think about anything except the need to restrict movement. The journey would end, one way or another, within some finite time. Either I'd be killed by an ice fall, or I'd reach the top, and the only thing I could do to influence the outcome was to come as close as possible to doing absolutely nothing. Gradually I became accustomed, or as near it as was attainable in the circumstances, to the repeated sudden realization that I was hanging motionless in the void. Then there'd come the reassuring little movement of the chair as Kelleher and his sergeant took up the strain again. I thought of them sweating with the effort and wished I could change places, because now the cold was working its way into me. Hands and feet were chilled through, damped with the contact with the ice, with Kirton's body and the diary. Any danger of frostbite was remote, but the discomfort was increasing steadily.

Coming up into the neck of the bulb, and with the first icicles now below me, I tried again with the walkie-talkie during one of the breaks, and heard Kelleher's faint voice with relief.

'Find anything?'

'Nothing conclusive. I got the diary.'

'Hold on. We'll get you up.' He was breathing heavily as he spoke and I didn't prolong the conversation.

The minutes went by. As I emerged from the neck, once more the chair stopped moving. My feet were almost exactly level with the base of the bulb. I heard a tap then: but just one. A moment later there was another. Neither seemed quite to come from the handset, though they could have come from nowhere else and it must be some trick of acoustics.

All the same, I spoke into the mike: 'Kelleher?'

No answer.

'Kelleher!' I said sharply, a few seconds later, anxiety breaking through.

Still no response. I tapped then, and called him, and tapped again, fear mushrooming inside me. The loudspeaker remained silent. For a little while, hanging on to the remnants of control, I tried to reason that it must be some malfunction of the walkie-talkie, that the tapping noise had meant Kelleher had dropped and damaged his handset. Soon they'd start again and I'd be on my way.

But they didn't start again, and I stayed where I was. By now I was looking at my watch every few seconds and a cold block seemed to have formed in my chest. By the time ten leaden minutes had dragged by, I knew all too well there would be no more winding. Something had happened up there; something that had stopped them; something that would leave me suspended there, three hundred feet down in the icecap!

Air seemed to flow, for some reason, slowly between the two bulbs and to draw warmth from me as it passed. My whole body was chilled now, as my mind was chilled with the fearful knowledge that I would almost certainly hang here until I died. Another glance at my watch showed that it was fifteen minutes since I'd moved; fifteen minutes of no contact, no hope, no company except icy speculation that this, for me, was the end. The meaning of those two, spaced-out taps still baffled me. One tap had meant 'lower'. Two had meant 'stop'. Could it be that what Kelleher had meant was that they'd have to stop? But if so, why? There was only one answer that made any sense, and that one was pushing me steadily towards the edge of panic: the killer up there had found two men working at the well hoist! But if he'd done that, if he'd attacked them, surely he'd have cut the cable, too, to ensure that whoever was down the well stayed down. But the cable was steel, and in any case there was no need; he disposed of me just as effectively by marooning me.

I began to think half-seriously about suicide. It might be better to unfasten the straps and die quickly than to dangle here as life slipped agonizingly away. There were no other possibilities. No man alive could hope to climb either the ice walls of the bulb or the thin steel cable that rose through several hundred feet to the ice trench above. And now, at last, even the light from my lamp was fading as the battery's power drained away. Soon I would be waiting for death in the freezing dark.

It became increasingly difficult even to flex my hands inside my gloves as my blood circulation slowed. How pathetic, I thought once, in a sudden spurt of anger, to go like this, not knowing; how pathetic to die *failing*! How pathetic not to know who the Chameleon was, who F. was. 'Young F.' who could –

I blinked. The seat had moved! I shone the now-dim lamp towards the top of the neck, but the top of the neck wasn't there! It was below, ten feet, even twelve . . . now fifteen. I was moving upwards fast, far faster than Kelleher and the sergeant had been able to wind in the cable. Which must . . . could *only* mean the winch!

The nylon line jerked in my hands and I hastily paid out more, and kept on doing so as the chair rose steadily upwards. In no time I was passing the icicles, moving into the neck, passing through into the topmost chamber. Again and again I tried the walkie-talkie, but without getting any reply. I'd been right, then – the thing *was* broken. It had to be broken, because somebody must be up there, in the trench, working the winch.

Somebody working the winch! Somebody who didn't reply! Somebody who – I heard the click of my nervous swallow – might be waiting for me to appear at the well-head, strapped helplessly in the bosun's chair.

Tilting my head back, I looked upwards to where the dark thread of the cable ran up into the well-head. There was a circle of dim, yellow light from the trench, a complete, uninterrupted circle, with no head leaning over to watch me. Frantically now, I paid out the remainder of the nylon line, letting it hang loose, and tying the end to the seat. Then I pulled the ice-axe free. There was no more than thirty feet to go now, and I fumbled with numb fingers to unfasten the straps that held me in the chair. It began to rock slightly, swinging me within inches of a huge icicle, and I froze into stillness as I swung back, breathtakingly close to another. Was I going to touch? The chair moved back again and I was safe, at least from the icicles. The strap parted and I clung grimly with one hand to the chair frame, the other hand gripping the ice-axe, my eyes measuring the distance as the yellow circle moved down towards me.

It was then, at the precise moment that the chair entered the narrow tube to the well-head, that my brain gave a little click and spilled an answer into my mind. For days I'd been thinking about it, trying to force out conclusions, and there had been none. Now, when all my awareness was concentrated elsewhere, the mental print-out chattered!

But there was no time to think about it, no time for even the smallest flicker of satisfaction. The cable ran smoothly over the pulley and I could hear the steady whirr of the electric motor, the soft clicking of the ratchet. Raising the axe in my hand, I waited for the switch-off, the watching face. There'd be a fraction of a second for identification, then I must strike, instantly and accurately.

Ten feet. I called Kelleher's name once, twice, a third time, and my words vanished into unresponding silence.

Tensely I waited for the upward movement to stop. The top of the frame loomed nearer; my eyes came level with the bottom of the corrugated steel ring and therefore the floor of the trench . . . and then I realized suddenly that it wasn't going to stop, that the chair was to be dragged right up to the frame, where the power of the motor would drag me and the seat against the pulley. I dropped the ice-axe, grabbed desperately for the corrugated iron and hurled myself sideways, out of the bosun's chair, but the swaying seat robbed me of any accuracy of movement and only my left hand reached the metal. My right hand clawed at empty air as I hung there over the well and the bosun's chair crunched into the ironwork above and was destroyed!

Chapter 18

Two frantic lunges with my right arm missed the rim of the iron-work and I could feel my left hand beginning to slip. Numbed, cold fingers lacked the strength to hold me and I knew with total clarity that I had only a second or two left before the tenuous grip broke and I plunged into the depths of the well. Once more . . . and my last chance. If this final grab failed, it was over for me. I swung my right arm back, and touched something with the back of my glove. The nylon line! I grabbed it despairingly and took a turn round my wrist as the fingers of my left hand began to slip inexorably over the metal. Would the nylon hold? It cut viciously into my wrist as my weight swung on to it, and I waited for the long fall . . . then the agony on my wrist told me it was holding and I lunged again, desperately with my left hand, and got a grip, a better one this time, and made myself swing twice on the line until I could make a grab with my right. And this time I got it. A minute later, heart beating wildly, I was clambering over the iron surround on to the floor of the trench, relief and fearful anticipation whirling together in my head. If he was there, why hadn't he simply knocked my hand away from the well-head?

I stared wildly round me. The trench seemed empty. But no – it wasn't! Kelleher lay on the trench floor beside the well-head, and the sergeant lay against the wall, beneath the winch control box. The electric motor whirred on. Quickly I bent to look at Kelleher. As I turned him on to his back, his arms moved limply, lifelessly And then I saw the little hole in his parka, over his heart. Kelleher was dead!

The sergeant was dead, too, lying in a puddle, already congealing, of his own blood. As I looked at him, I saw the red smudge of blood that ran across from the well-head to where he lay, and the little channel his body had made in the crystalline floor as he'd dragged himself towards the motor. There was more blood on the wall, where he'd somehow forced himself upright. It was so plain what had happened: the two of them at the handle, the trench door opening and closing, the two shots: Kelleher killed instantly and the sergeant, mortally wounded, using the last moments of his own life to reach the switch in a last desperate attempt to save mine. He'd known that when electric power was restored, the winch would come on automatically, hoisting me out of the depths of the icecap.

Now I knew the two single taps had been gunshots, probably from a distance since the sound had not been loud. They must have been fired from close to the door. A glance at my watch showed that about eighteen minutes had passed since the shooting. How had those minutes been used? And who had used them?

And then, quite suddenly, I knew! In seconds the mystery of days had been resolved. I knew now who 'young F.' was, and who the killer must be, and where he must have gone now.

Bending over Kelleher's body, I rapidly searched his pockets for the keys, then raced along the trench to the door, turned the lock and stepped out into Main Street. I pulled my parka hood tight and kept my head down as I hurried in the direction of the tractor shed. As I opened the doors and stepped inside, cold air rushed over me. The big outer doors now gaped inwards! A light burned in the office and I tore over to it. Inside, the duty mechanic was slumped over the desk, an open paperback beneath his head. I shook his shoulder, but he wasn't sleeping; he was unconscious. Leaving the office, I went to the main doors. Heavy snow was falling. I looked at the tracks imprinted in the fresh snow and already being filled, their sharp outlines blurring. And the snow was falling vertically because the wind had dropped. It all fitted now. The weather-change had precipitated things, providing one last chance for the killer to maintain the mystery, a chance he'd had to take.

My TK4 stood, silent and shiny, to one side of the huge shed. I began to cross to it, then stopped. I'd need a weapon. A drum of petrol, probably used for engine cleaning, stood on a wooden packing case. I found a bottle, filled it and stuffed cotton waste in the neck.

The TK4, icy cold as she was after being immobile for days in low temperatures, didn't start first bang. Bad advertisement, I thought with professional sourness, relieved no one had been present to see it. But she started at the second time of asking and gave a few pleased puffs as the rubber skirt ballooned and lifted her and the engines roared cheerfully. I eased her forward, nosing out through the doors into the blackness, then stopping briefly to give my eyes some chance to adjust. I didn't want to use the lights.

The snow was very thick, cutting visibility back, and clouds blanketed the moon, but I dared wait no longer. The heavy tractor was slow, but the distance was small. He'd be there already, and searching. I turned the hovercraft eastwards and moved slowly over the snowfield, trying to remember all the details of the layout of Camp Hundred.

I knew that the camp perimeter was marked at a range of four hundred yards by triangular flags on high, flexible, steel poles mounted on barrels and sunk into the snow at five-yard intervals. He'd have followed them, and so must I. Visibility through the heavy snowfall was less than twenty yards and, tense with frustration, I kept the speed down.

I swore suddenly. The tracks! All I had to do was follow his tracks! Fifty-per-cent thinking again! I eased the TK4 back towards the dim yellow square of light from the tractor shed, opened the side window and leaned out, searching the smooth white surface for the wide track-trail of the big diesel tractor.

There! As I moved her forward, creating a wind, bitter cold flooded in through the open window, chilling my face. I pulled the drawstring of my hood tighter and ghosted across the snow-field, through the thick curtain of silently-falling snow, in the wake of the big diesel tractor. Within a few yards I was suffering one of the hazards of a hovercraft running slowly over powder snow: the downward pressure of air blown out from beneath the skirt blasted dry crystals upwards into a fine fog all around me. They whirled higher than the cab, like an impenetrable fog, and enough blew in through the narrowed aperture of my parka hood to start chilling nose, cheekbones and chin. At speed the problem diminishes; the blow-up snow spray is left behind before it can cause a problem. But I couldn't go at speed. The need to follow the tracks without light dictated my rate of progress. I was also uncomfortably aware that the small snowstorm the TK4 was creating would serve to blank out the tracks behind me.

There was also the possible hazard of running into the tractor. With visibility so short, it was likely that by the time I saw it, it would be too late to slow. I had to catch up with the tractor and its murderous occupant, but preferably not that way!

Then the hut loomed suddenly, only yards away. I had to cut the engine power and fling the steering round frantically to miss it, and that set me another problem. The tractor was not yet in sight but the hut was my starting point and if I went past it there would be trouble and delay in locating it again. I came to a decision quickly, backed off to set the TK4 down on low pressure a dozen yards or so from the hut, climbed out and walked towards it, my feet sinking inches deep into the soft, dry snow of the icecap.

Reaching the hut, I turned to look round at the TK4, now little more than a vague shape that hummed quietly, its outline blurred and its engine noise muffled by the sheer weight of the snowfall.

At first I thought the line had disappeared, blown away by the hurricane winds of the last days, but then I realized that snow reached a third the way up the side of the hut and that the line, instead of being waist level, would be at ankle height. As I hunted for it, I looked over my shoulder every few seconds, puzzled and menaced by the absence of the tractor, expecting an attack at any second. But nothing moved within my small circle of visibility and I kept telling myself that the harsh beat of its massive diesel would be clearly audible.

Then my foot brushed against the line and I bent to pick it up, slipped it into the dog's lead clip of my parka belt. Another cautious look all round me: no sign of man or tractor. I took the line in both hands and pulled, lifting it clear of the snow, and began to move along it. After ten yards I reached the first of the flag-topped anchor posts, unfastened and refastened the clip, and moved on again, examining the surface carefully at each step. A lot of precipitation had occurred since the last time anybody at Hundred had been able to venture out on to the cap, and what I was looking for would by now be thoroughly buried.

I had reached the third anchor post and was re-clipping my belt when I remembered with sudden horror that I was still wearing the same boots in which I'd gone down the well. *And that they were damp!* Instantaneously, my feet felt cold. Was it psychological or actual? It couldn't have been more than a couple of minutes since I'd left the cab of the TK4, but two minutes in damp boots is a long time on the icecap. Thank God the wind had died!

I trudged on, worried and frightened. It was crazy to have tried to give chase alone, yet the pressure of time had allowed me no other choice and I'd been aware of the risk; I'd also been close enough to death in the last hours and days for this pursuit to be only an extension of that peril. Irrationally the prospect of frozen feet was far more deeply horrifying; the thought that if I survived, it might be to hobble for the rest of my days on stumps, dried my mouth and prickled the back of my neck.

Longing to turn back, I still marched on. The snow surface was marked only by windwhip, not by boots or mechanical tracks. As 1 pulled up each yard of buried line, it cut smoothly through the recent, loose-packed snow, to stretch ahead to the next anchor post.

I was at the tenth now, and hurrying, flexing my toes inside my boots to reassure myself that feeling and movement were still there. But heels cannot be flexed, and it was at the heel that cold was likely to strike first. Eleven. Four more would be about half-way. Re-fixing the clip I pulled the line, and this time only a yard or two came up. Ahead of me it ran taut and at an angle, to a point well down beneath the surface. I knelt then, and began to dig rapidly in the snow with my mittened hands, flinging it aside in a spray of dry particles. Why hadn't I brought the spade from the hovercraft? The usual reasons: lack of thinking power, lack of foresight, lack of concentration! If the snow had been even lightly compacted, it would have been impossible to dig like that, but it wasn't compacted and I was swiftly two feet down, then three, scrabbling like a dog with his forepaws until . . . my hands touched something hard in the snow, something that became dark in the surrounding white as I swept the powdery flakes from it. I knelt for a moment then, sickened by yet another death. But I was sure now. Sure except that one small yet critical point remained to be confirmed. I grabbed the line again, ran my hand along it until it touched not only the body but the hard, metal shape of a dog clip. The line ran through the clip and away, and when I reached beyond and pulled, it cut upwards through the snow to run tight and straight to the next anchor post.

I stood then, knowing it was true. The innocent cause of all Camp Hundred's problems lay here in the snow at my feet . . . feet that were becoming colder inside my dampened felt boots.

Quickly I bent and pushed back into the hole the snow I had dug away, then smoothed it as well as I could. Even when I'd finished, it stood out a mile, rough and disturbed among the surrounding smoothness. But as I looked, I realized it was already being covered; ten minutes more and it would begin to blend into the endless snowscape. I thought of trying to uproot the anchor posts to make the killer's search more difficult, but realized it couldn't work. Only by severing the line could the body be hidden, and in severing the line, I'd be destroying the evidence. I turned and began to work my way back the way I had come, along the line, knowing he was out there somewhere – probably waiting to see if he'd been followed – and that somehow I must stop him before he could reach the spot and at last conceal the continuing proof of his guilt.

The hut lay only a little more than a hundred yards ahead, but I was slowed by the need to clip and re-clip my belt. With nine anchor posts behind me the hut was still not in sight, but I thought I could hear faintly the idling note of the TK4's engine. The temptation to run towards it was almost irresistible; once inside there would be the safety of the metal structure, the warmth of the heater, the speed of the machine itself. Inside I'd be safe. But the knowledge that I was not alone out there dictated caution. He might have – probably *had* – the rifle, unless he'd taken the risk of returning it to Barney's office so that its absence would go unremarked. Time was one of *his* problems, too; he dared not be absent long enough for the absence to be noticed. If he could destroy the evidence and get back quickly, it might be difficult, even impossible to pin on him his long sequence of crimes. And if he could get rid of me, it would almost certainly be impossible. If my body, too, were lost beneath the snow, the diary would be lost with it, and the sheet from Kirton's notebook!

I went down full length in the snow and began to kitten-crawl forward, parallel with the hand line but no longer fastened to it, and pushing before me with my hands a tiny wall of snow no more than six inches high.

I saw the hut at the same second that the idling engine note became a roar and the huge diesel tractor swung into view, lights blazing, from behind the hut. I shut my eyes tight, but not quickly enough, and the powerful white beams assaulted my widened pupils, blinding me completely. Shakily I rose to my feet, sightless and disorientated by dazzle patterns, and tried desperately to gauge direction by sound alone. The roar was from my right, though it seemed now to fill the night air all round me. He must be twenty-five or thirty yards away and his maximum speed six miles an hour or so. I swung left and tried to run, but my foot caught in the slack hand line and I pitched full length. As I struggled to rise, my foot remained hooked in the line, briefly but enough to delay me, and already the massive roar of the big diesel engine seemed to be on top of me. I turned my head, squinting my eyes against the glare, and thought I discerned, among the redness in my eyes, a wide dark shape with the glare of the lights above it, and I knew then that this was not just a tractor but a bulldozer, blade down, that was hammering down on me. I made two or three lumbering strides away from it, but my foot slipped on the loose snow and I spun off balance, and by the time I'd steadied myself again, it was almost on top of me. Terrified, I turned to face it, knowing there was no way now that I could avoid that eighteen-foot blade: it would be on me before I could move aside. The half-seen black rectangle with those blinding white lights mounted high above it roared down on me, only a few feet away, and knowing suddenly there was no other way, I dived towards it, seizing desperate handholds on the top edge and lifting my feet clear of the surface and hanging there as the blade drove onwards.

He must have seen me clearly, because a second later the blade began to rise in the air as he brought in the hydraulics. I clung on grimly as it lifted, guessing what would happen next, but shaken by the suddenness as the hydraulics were cut and the blade crashed down, seeking to dislodge me. An appalling drag on my arms and shoulders signalled that it was lifting again and I knew I'd never survive another drop. Already my hands were beginning to lose their hold and the blade had only swung half up. I'll never know what made me let go then deliberately, rather than be shaken off a second or two later. I slid down the blade's curve, on to the snow, and rolled frantically beneath its leading edge, praying I'd make it before the blade crashed down again.

Swivelling round, I lay flat, and along the whole length of my body felt the *whump* as the blade was released. I was trapped now in the ten-foot gap between the two huge tracks, still almost sightless, but crawling fast towards the rear. If he pivoted now, it was all over. Free now of these murderous lights, blinking rapidly, I discerned dimly the rectangle of snow behind the moving bulldozer and drove myself, almost swimming in the loose snow, towards it. The huge steel body of the machine was only inches above my head, the tracks hideously close to my moving hands. And then above me, the roar of sound changed subtly as the power was adjusted on the tracks and he began to turn the machine.

I crawled with it in an overwhelming panic, swinging my body round with the machine, and somehow making forward ground in that moving, lethal tunnel of machinery. One of the tracks actually buffeted my boot as I crawled clear. But I *was* clear, and now I could take up a position behind the tractor, where he couldn't see me. And I stayed behind it, holding on to the rear of it and stepping carefully sideways as it swung, pivoting through a full circle, the headlights sweeping the ice while he searched for me.

If only I'd had that home-made petrol bomb! But I hadn't; it was in the cab of the hovercraft and I didn't even know where the hovercraft was! I tried to put myself in his place, at the controls of the bulldozer. He'd be wondering, surely, whether he'd got me. With luck he'd be half-convinced, *more* than half-convinced, that he had. He'd be hoping that nobody could vanish beneath blade and tractor and survive. But he'd need to be sure, to go on looking, to prove to himself that nobody but himself was now moving on that bleak snow surface.

Now, at last, my sight was recovering from that dreadful glare and suddenly, past the slowly turning bulldozer, I saw the hover-craft caught clearly by its knifing lights through the heavy curtain of snow. And I thought I saw something else. Not with certainty; it could have been an optical illusion; but watching carefully, I became increasingly sure. A wind was starting to blow. I turned my face into it briefly and felt its cold breath, and suddenly the snow was no longer falling vertically: caught by the air move-ment its downward path tilted. And now I *was* sure: the hover-craft itself, with only the touch of its skirts to provide friction on the loose surface, was beginning to drift on the wind. It was like a boat in so many ways, and this was one!

Still keeping to the rear of the tractor, I backed rapidly away. Now the tracks had stopped swivelling as the driver wrestled with the levers to reverse them and to bring round the lights to bear on the TK4. The drift was carrying it at an angle across the front of the tractor and he'd have to turn back a good deal further to bring it into focus. Knowing he'd be concentrating on the controls, I turned and ran towards the TK4, which was now sliding slowly away from the swinging lights and almost, yet not quite, towards me. Our paths converged, but with an awkward obliqueness, and I'd be caught in the beams before I reached it.

With every ounce of energy I could summon, I plunged on, the icy air driving into my lungs, and the dry snow crystalline beneath my feet. A swift glance to my right showed the beams turning as the big bulldozer swung round on its tracks, and the sideways glow of the light gave me a clear sight now of the slowly gliding hovercraft. Seconds later the first of the beams had caught me, but I was less than five yards from the TK4 now, cutting across in front to let its bulk shield me. It seemed to be picking up speed, too, with every passing second. Then abruptly I was there, grasping the handrail, my foot scrabbling for the mounting step, and missing, and my heart high in my throat as I was dragged along. I tried to jump, to thrust myself up, away from the clogging snow, and got my toe just on to the step. Arching my back, straining, I forced myself up, got a better grip . . . in seconds now I was inside the cab, giving her throttle and wrench-ing at the controls to let air flow down and give me lift.

Then came a curious little flick-smack sound and one panel of the glass screen crazed. So now I knew: he *had* the rifle!

But I had the speed, if there was time to use it. As the propellers chewed the air, I slipped off into the darkness and concealment of the snowblow. It was impossible to be sure, but I thought then that I half-heard, half-felt the impact of another bullet, somewhere behind me. I was trying to decide how many rounds he had left. He'd used two in the well trench, perhaps two more now. And Smales had talked, hadn't he, of an old rifle, with the mag locked in his desk. One left, then, two at the outside. Perhaps they'd all gone? But I squashed that optimistic thought. He'd keep one.

Behind me the already dimming lights from the big tractor vanished suddenly. Yes, I thought grimly, he's kept one. And now the hide-and-seek game was reversed. *I* had to go and get *him*! I slowed, tripping the heater switch and adjusting the airflow to direct warmth at my feet. They were bitterly cold, but I drew what comfort I could from the fact that I could still feel them, though my toes, as I tried to move them, seemed strangely lethargic.

Now I had to find him! Somewhere there in the cold dark of the icecap, he was waiting for me, waiting with a rifle, himself protected by tons of heavy steel. Keeping an eye on the compass, treacherous though a compass was in these latitudes, I swung the TK4 through a hundred and eighty degrees and began to creep forward. There was no means of measuring distance; no means, that is, beyond my own judgment of eye and speed; and there was the wind to allow for, too.

A touch of the rudder moved my heading a little to the left. I'd calculated three hundred yards to the hut and I wanted to approach it from wider out, to use, if I could, its scant shelter to hide my approach. Outside the open side window the snowfield flowed by, its smoothness almost impossible to measure, and I tried to calculate distance additionally on the basis of my own forward speed. The doubt began to grow until it was a certainty that I'd missed the hut; it had passed, unseen, somewhere to my right. But where? Not far, surely.

Then, looking down, I thought I saw a depression in the snow surface; yes – filling rapidly, already beginning to lose definition beneath the new layer, but it was a tractor track, with the faint oblongs and ridges still vaguely to be seen.

Again I turned the TK4, taking care not to lose sight of those precious marks. I thought grimly that he had two tasks now: to fend me off, *and* to do the job he'd come out here to do – to destroy the evidence that must convict him. And time was pressing. Dare he wait for me, perhaps in the lee of the hut, with the rifle, or would he be moving the tractor along that hand line? I let the TK4 creep forward. A single flick of the headlights might tell me whether my direction was right, but their glow would also pinpoint my location and I daren't try it. I sank low in my seat, to give myself the maximum protection of the hull plating, knowing that a rifle bullet fired at close range would go through both it, and me, without being even briefly delayed.

Suddenly, carelessly, I'd let my eyes stray from the tracks. *Damn!* Halting, I reversed a little, and failed to find them! I stopped, then, and slid across the seat to the other side window – and there it was, five or six yards away, mantled in snow: the hut!

But which way to go round it? Did it matter? On no basis of judgment at all, I went to the right, because it was the easier way and required no steering, and beyond it I picked up tracks again, fresher tracks that bit clean and revealing into the snow. Now I could be only a few yards from him, a hundred at the most. I tried to listen, but the sound of my own engine killed the roar of his and, in any case, the wind was behind me now: behind and rising, and snow blew almost horizontally past me.

As the TK4 crept forward, I searched my pockets clumsily for matches and sagged in disappointment when there were none. Without them even my single crude weapon was useless. Matches, *matches!* Damn it, I hadn't been caught without matches in years! Then some trick of memory sent my hand to the fascia. When I'd cleaned out the TK4, there'd been a book of matches; where had I put them? If they'd slipped . . . I couldn't feel them, but I knew they were there somewhere. I stopped the hovercraft and stared ahead. No sign of the tractor. I'd have to risk the TK4's cabin light. I felt for the solenoid switch and turned it low so that

213

my own lights wouldn't blind me this time, then I pushed and turned.

Got them! A small rectangle of cardboard, compliments of British Airways, with four matches remaining. I clicked the light off quickly and edged forward.

Ten yards, twenty, thirty . . . and suddenly there he was: a dark, slow, shape looming out of the snow, moving slowly forward beside the hand line and the flag-topped anchor posts, and as the distance lessened slowly I could see that the back window of his cab wore a coating of snow. With luck, then, he wouldn't see me until too late. I inched the hovercraft outwards, parallel to him and a little behind, gripped the steering with my knees and bent low to open the match-book. Four matches. The first two broke. I lifted my head to glance forward. The tractor's door was swinging open. I bent and scratched the third across the worn striking pad – and snapped the head of the flimsy cardboard matchstick. Oh, *Christ*! One left. That one bent, too, as I struck it, and fell out of my awkward fingers on to the floor, its tiny flame beginning to die even as it fell. I grabbed the petrol bottle and stabbed the cotton wick towards the flame. Had it been anything but petrol vapour, my clumsiness would have killed it, but the tip of the wick was instantly aglow and smoke broke thickly from it. I knew I'd only seconds now; if the petrol bomb didn't get him, it would get me. Five or six feet more and the TK4's cabin would be level with the tractor's. Damn it, had I left it too late for the lights? I switched on the big main beams; they'd shine past him now, but *perhaps* the sideways glare would give me a ghost of a chance. I no longer dared risk raising my head. With one bullet left, he'd shoot only when he could see me.

But the whole wick was aflame now, lighting the inside of the cabin. I squeezed myself flat, cowering down beside the open window and watching as the tractor cab slid slowly into view: first the rear pillar, then the first glass pane. Another pillar and then it would be the doorway – and the rifle. So the time was *now!*

Backhanded, I flicked the bottle out, across towards the open door, and in that instant I was flung across the cab as the heavy bullet smashed my right arm. For what seemed an eternity, I lay collapsed, bruised and in pain and dazed with the shock of impact, and with one thought drumming in my brain: he'd won. And I had lost! I was helpless now, and weaponless, and he could finish me off as he chose. I turned my head, only half-seeing, and only half-comprehending what I did see. And even then I was hoping that I was wrong, that by some miracle the killer could still be someone else, someone I hadn't liked and trusted. But then I saw his face. It was lit a ghastly yellow-red by the burning petrol that had splashed his parka, and his mouth gaped as the flames blew up at his exposed skin. And, as I knew it must be, it was the face of Sergeant Vernon, and Vernon's eyes that glanced murderously across at me. He'd only to jump down and roll over in the snow for the flames to be doused. I saw him take a step forward to jump, knowing that soon he'd come up to finish me off.

And when he was gone from my sight, I tried to haul myself into a sitting position, but it was beyond me. The bulldozer was moving very slowly. He'd be able to jump back, when the flames were out, and use the blade to flatten both me and the TK4.

I sagged back, and then began to struggle again, and this time I did manage to force myself up a little and lean wearily across. The pain from my shattered arm made me want to scream, and I could feel the blood pumping from it. I forced myself to look out, and now the hovercraft had moved just ahead of the bull-dozer. Sick and dizzy, I got my left hand to the throttle and began to turn the TK4 around. Had he left it too late? Was it possible I could still escape? But even if I could, he'd be out there, un-injured, unclipping the line he'd forgotten to unfasten when he'd murdered the Foster boy, that day weeks before, as they'd returned from the weather hut. If the line were unfastened now, and he moved young Foster's body even a few yards, the charge of murder would be difficult to establish. Slowly the headlights turned as I pivoted the TK4, and I waited for the beams to catch him. But maybe they wouldn't; maybe he was beside me now, climbing aboard to kill me, as he so easily could with his hands alone.

No sign. And the use even of my left hand seemed to be going. My fingers moved like great weights towards the throttle control and, when they reached it, seemed to be moving in slow motion. Dimly I heard the engine revs increasing. And then, as the hovercraft began to move, I glimpsed him. Vernon lay flat in the snow, the dark of his parka level with the snow surface. And dimly I understood, for the track of the huge bulldozer patterned the snow on both sides of him. He must have stepped on to the moving track and been carried forward – and under! As the TK4 slid past, I looked down at him stupidly, still waiting for some trick, half-expecting him to rise and come for me. But he still lay there, as, with my vision unexpectedly dimming, I turned the hovercraft painfully to my left and headed for where I hoped the ramp led down into Hundred.

Chapter 19

I hadn't been aware of it, but while I'd been out on the icecap, the Cold Regions Research fliers from Thule had been taking a chance in the same brief wind break to parachute two Air Force doctors in. They jumped for the lights of the Swing and were lucky, and a bulldozer went ahead with them to Hundred. But for that, it seems, I'd have died in that bleak early morning. I remember nothing of it, of course, but somehow I must have stayed conscious just long enough to set the TK4 to the ramp. After that, the loss of blood was too great, and I must have lain unconscious as the hovercraft glided down the slope by force of gravity, and then careered like a great, slow, dodgem car, half-way along Main Street, until it burst through a snow wall into one of the trenches and hanging ice stripped the propellers.

Even after it was clear I wouldn't die, that the transfusion had been quick enough and the shock from loss of blood just a fraction short of lethal, they thought I'd lose my arm. But then, after all the foul weather, the disasters, the lousy breaks, Herschel arrived on the Swing and some good luck piggy-backed in on his shoulder.

For fourteen hours there was flying weather. Generators and pipes arrived, and sick and injured and dead were flown out. There must have been frantic activity all round me, but I have no recollection of any of it. I woke in a bed at Thule's big, modern hospital with a nasty post-operative hangover, my arm repaired and an army surgeon telling me with a smile that I was lucky. Not too long after that, I was flown first to McGuire Air Force Base hospital in New Jersey, then home to England.

I'd been home a few days and had reached the point where I'd almost mastered the art of dressing one-handed, when the telephone rang one morning.

'Mr Bowes?' An American voice.

'Yes.'

'One moment, sir. I have a call for you.'

I waited. Then an unmistakable voice said, 'You are ze man viz ze flying fan?'

'Yes, Barney,' I said.

'I'm coming right over to see you. Give me two to three hours. You gonna be in?'

'Yes, Barney.'

The grey suit, creased from travel, somehow diminished him. Polar bears are for Polar regions. As he sat in my flat he was a grizzled, middle-aged man, weak after illness, the legend fallen away. There was also the fact that his whole personality, his quality of attack, was suited neither to a suburban flat nor to what he had to say. I gestured to the bottles on the sideboard and told him to help himself, and he assembled the constituents of a Martini into what was clearly going to be a slice of humble pie. He took a swallow and said, 'The enquiry's over. You'll get the official report. And I've been asked to tell you how helpful your own account was. We appreciated it.'

'Did they,' I asked, 'find out why?'

'Vernon?'

I nodded.

Barney looked at his glass. 'Maybe. The shrinks tried awful hard to put a picture together. They came up with some kind of amalgam of high ability and disappointment, tossed in middle-age, paranoia and opportunity. But Christ, who knows? I'd known Vernon ten years and more. He was a real solid, reliable guy.'

'Until something changed him.'

'Until he came across the kid with all the dough. I suppose it's got to be that simple. Maybe it all happened a long time before and he was just looking for his chance. Still, I'll tell you what's known and what's supposition. Fact: young Foster stood to inherit a hell of a lot of money when he finished his service. *If* his sheet was clean.'

'I know the story.'

'Okay. Supposition: Vernon knew that. How he found out...?' Barney shrugged. 'Kid must have told him some time, over a few beers maybe. Another fact: Vernon was in charge of the Hundred

218

office at Fort Belvoir when the personnel selections were made that time. He put Foster's name on the list for Hundred.'

I asked, 'Is that kind of thing left to sergeants?'

'You know how it is. Lists get made, then approved higher up. Finally by me. There was no reason Foster should *not* have gone to Hundred. Another fact: we found two cheques, for fifty thousand dollars each. One in Vernon's wallet, the other in his locker. Both signed by Foster, both made out to cash, both undated.'

'Were the signatures genuine?'

'Sure they were.'

I said, 'But that's crazy! The moment Foster died his account would be frozen. By killing Foster, he made the cheques worthless!'

'That's right.' Barney's hands gestured his own incomprehension. 'Still, here's some more. Supposition: and this one's not all that good. But remember they were stuck in the hut, just the two of them. So maybe Sergeant Vernon was getting round to chiselling even more dough out of Foster. Foster only inherited if he got his discharge with the word exemplary plastered all over it. One charge – indiscipline, insubordination, even failure to maintain personal cleanliness, goddammit – and that conduct sheet would have been wrecked. Vernon really had Foster by the shorts. So you could put together some kind of a scenario in which Foster attacked Vernon first, right? Vernon defends himself, knocks the kid unconscious, panics, and just leaves him out there to freeze. Well, it's possible! Then, when he's back inside Hundred . . . well, that's when he has to work out a story real quick, and he says Foster blundered away from the rope and got lost in the white-out.'

I nodded. 'Then later he realized that Foster's body must still have the line attached. And when it was found . . . but *would* it have been found?'

'Sure it would,' Barney said. 'Come the spring and a little daylight, the whole surface area's gone over. Markers and lines are lifted and repositioned, general tidying-up.'

'And the body tied to the line was positive evidence Vernon had lied.'

'Right. He had to get out and cut that line. But the weather stayed closed. Heavy snow, too, remember that. Soon the whole thing would have been buried deep and there'd be almost no chance for one man alone to find Foster. When he realized that, the shrinks reckon, *that's* when he started the attack on Hundred itself. It's kind of a classic pattern: the structure's a threat, so he sets out to attack the structure. With Hundred abandoned, Foster's body never would have been found. He'd have lost the money, okay, but he'd have been in the clear.'

We sat and looked at each other. I said, 'There's another thing I've never understood. Why on earth did he muck about with the bodies? Why take Harrer's body out of the trench and put it where the bulldozer would crush it? I mean, dammit, if he hadn't done that, we'd never have rumbled him.'

Barney shrugged. 'Who knows? He was crazy anyway, but a supposition was slung together. You told us in your evidence that Vernon probably saw Doc Kirton with the food wrappings after that business with the bear. Likely he heard you talking. He knew Kirton wasn't going to find any saliva to analyse, because it was Vernon himself who'd scratched open the oil tanks and the emergency rations. No saliva, no bacteria, so no bear. Therefore proof of sabotage. So Kirton had to go.'

'It's a hell of a supposition!'

'Less than you'd think. Vernon kept a paper he stole from Kirton's office.'

'What paper?'

'Kirton's report. He'd done the microscopic analysis, and written up the results. The report said no bacteria, no evidence of animal saliva or animal hair or animal mucus. Vernon took it, which may have made sense to him. But he didn't destroy it, which just shows how crazy he was.'

I said, 'It still doesn't explain – '

'I know it. Listen: he killed Kirton. Probably did it right there in the hospital. So he had a body to get rid of, right? He puts Kirton on a sled-stretcher and hides him under something, a few boxes, anything, then he hauls off to the well trench, which is off limits, anyway, and not far away, and he knows he won't be disturbed in there as he drops Kirton down the well.'

'I realize all that. But why bring out Harrer's body?'

'Because having dumped Kirton, he realizes Kirton's going to be missed. There'll be a big-scale search. Maybe he's left some clues somewhere, something that leads to him. He hasn't but he can't be sure. Then he remembers there are other bodies, and one of them is Harrer's. Now Harrer doesn't look like Kirton, except they're both big men, and dark. Nobody's going to mistake one for the other, not unless – '

'Now I understand.'

'Yeah. The body's unrecognizable, there's a man missing, two and two make four. Nobody wants to look too close.'

'And the nuclear engineer, Captain Carson?'

'Carson's body was outside the escape hatch of the trench where he lived. Head beaten in. Vernon must have carried him up the ladder and dumped him outside. He'd fixed Kelleher with drugs and killed Carson. The reactor was going to be out of action a long, long time.'

I said, 'He only missed by a whisker, didn't he? He almost *did* force Hundred to shut down.'

'He came closer than you think,' Barney said.

'What do you mean?'

'Hundred's closing in the spring.' As I looked at him he seemed infinitely sad.

'Why?'

'That's the Army for you. Research project completed. Shy away from a can of worms.' He shrugged, then gave an apologetic little grin. 'So you see, we won't be needing too many hovercraft.'

'Many! You mean *any*.'

'That's right, Harry. There'll be compensation, naturally, but – '

'But no sale,' I said.